Y0-BCR-221

DATE DUE

APR 2 5 2012		
MAY 0 8 2012		

LP   Lindsey, Johanna
Fic   Love only once
Lin

WITHDRAWN

STUTSMAN COUNTY LIBRARY
910 5th STREET SE
JAMESTOWN, ND 58401

Love Only Once

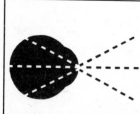

This Large Print Book carries the Seal of Approval of N.A.V.H.

A MALORY NOVEL

LOVE ONLY ONCE

JOHANNA LINDSEY

THORNDIKE PRESS
A part of Gale, Cengage Learning

WITHDRAWN

STUTS... C...LIBRARY
...5 ST SE
...OWN ND 58401

GALE
CENGAGE Learning™

Detroit • New York • San Francisco • New Haven, Conn • Waterville, Maine • London

GALE
CENGAGE Learning™

Copyright © 1985 by Johanna Lindsey.
Thorndike Press, a part of Gale, Cengage Learning.

ALL RIGHTS RESERVED
This is a work of fiction. Names, characters, places, and incidents are products of the author's imagination or are used fictitiously and are not to be construed as real. Any resemblance to actual events, locales, organizations, or persons, living or dead, is entirely coincidental.
Thorndike Press® Large Print Famous Authors.
The text of this Large Print edition is unabridged.
Other aspects of the book may vary from the original edition.
Set in 16 pt. Plantin.

LIBRARY OF CONGRESS CATALOGING-IN-PUBLICATION DATA

Lindsey, Johanna.
   Love only once : a Malory novel / by Johanna Lindsey.
      p. cm. — (Thorndike Press large print famous authors)
   ISBN-13: 978-1-4104-2727-4
   ISBN-10: 1-4104-2727-7
   1. Large type books. I. Title.
PS3562.I5123L6 2010
813'.54—dc22   2010008313

Published in 2010 by arrangement with Avon, an imprint of HarperCollins Publishers.

Printed in the United States of America
1 2 3 4 5 6 7 14 13 12 11 10

For my niece and nephew,
Raegina Kaohukaukuahiwiokaala
Howard
and Michael Lani Alii Howard

CHAPTER 1

1817 London

The fingers holding the brandy decanter were long and delicate. Selena Eddington was vain about her hands. She showed them off whenever a chance presented itself, as it did just then. She brought the decanter to Nicholas instead of taking his glass to the brandy. This served another purpose, as well, for she was able to stand in front of him as he reclined on the plush blue sofa, the fire at her back, her figure outlined provocatively through her thin muslin evening dress. Even a hardened rake like Nicholas Eden could still appreciate a lovely body.

A large ruby winked on her left hand as she steadied his glass and poured the brandy. Her wedding ring. She still wore it proudly, though she had been a widow for two years. More rubies circled her throat, but even spectacular rubies did not detract from her décolletage, exceedingly low, which allowed a mere three inches of material before the cinched high waist of the empire gown fell in straight lines to her trim ankles. The gown was a deep, dark magenta, and suited beautifully both the rubies and Selena.

"Are you listening to me, Nicky?"

Nicholas had that irritating pensive look about him that she recognized more and more of late. He was not listening to a word she was saying but was deep in thoughts that surely didn't include her. He hadn't even glanced at her while she poured his brandy.

"Honestly, Nicky, it's not at all flattering the way you go off and leave me when we're in a room alone together." She stood her ground in front of him until he looked up at her.

"What's that, my dear?" Her hazel eyes flashed. She would have stomped her foot if she'd dared let him see her vile temper. How provoking he was, how indifferent, how . . . impossible! If only he weren't such a good catch.

Mindful of her deportment, she said evenly, "The ball, Nicky. I have been going on about it, but you're not paying attention. If you like, I will change the subject, but only if you promise you won't be late coming for me tomorrow night."

"What ball?"

Selena gasped, truly surprised. He was not foxed, and he was not being blasé. The infuriating man really had no idea what she was talking about.

"Don't tease me, Nicky. The Shepford ball. You know how much I have been looking forward to it."

"Ah, yes," he said dryly. "The ball to outdo them all, and this only the beginning of the season."

She pretended not to notice his tone. "You also know how long I have waited for an invitation to one of the Duchess of Shepford's affairs. This ball promises to be her grandest in years. Simply everyone who is anyone will be there."

"So?"

Selena counted slowly to five. "So I will die if I am even the tiniest bit late."

His lips turned up in the familiar mocking smile. "You die much too often, my dear. You shouldn't take the social whirl so seriously."

"I should be like you?"

She would have called that retort back if she'd been able to. Her temper was very close to being unleashed, and that would be disastrous. She knew how he deplored excess of emotion in anyone — though it was all right for him to let loose his temper, which could be quite unpleasant.

Nicholas simply shrugged. "Call me eccentric, my dear, one of the few who doesn't give a bloody damn for the lot of them."

How true that was. He ignored and even insulted whomever he pleased. He made friends with anyone he pleased, too, even known bastards who were snubbed by society. And he never, ever, pandered to anyone. He was every bit as arrogant as people said he was. But he could also be devastatingly charming — when he wanted to be.

Miraculously, Selena kept a tight rein on her temper. "Nevertheless, Nicky, you did promise to escort me to the Shepford ball."

"Did I?" he drawled.

"Yes, you did," she managed evenly. "And you will promise not to be late in coming for me, won't you?"

He shrugged again. "How can I promise such a thing, my dear? I cannot foresee the future. There is no telling what might arise tomorrow to delay me."

She very nearly screamed. There was nothing to delay him except his own perfidious indifference, and they both knew it. It was not to be borne!

Selena made a quick decision and said nonchalantly, "Very well, Nicky. Since this is so important to me and I can't depend on you, I will find myself another escort and simply hope that you will eventually show up at the ball." Two could play his game.

"On such short notice?" he asked.

"You doubt I can?" she challenged.

He smiled, his gaze moving over her appreciatively. "No, indeed. I believe you will have very little trouble replacing me."

Selena turned her back on him before he could see how the remark affected her. Had that been a warning? Oh, how sure of himself he was. It would serve him right if she broke off their affair. No mistress of his had ever done so. He was always the one to end an affair. He was always the one in charge. How would he react if she dropped him? Would it throw him into a rage? Would it force his hand? This merited serious consideration.

Nicholas Eden stretched more comfortably on the sofa and watched Selena pick up her glass of sherry, then lie down on the thick fur rug in front of the fire, her back to him. His lips curled sardonically. How alluring her pose was, but of course she knew that. Selena always knew precisely what she

11

was doing.

They were at her friend Marie's townhouse, having enjoyed an elegant dinner with Marie and her current lover, played whist for an hour or so, and then retired to this cozy drawing room. Marie and her ardent gentleman had retired to a room upstairs, leaving Nicholas and Selena to themselves. How many other nights had been spent like this one? The only constant was that the Countess had a different lover every time. She lived life dangerously whenever her husband the Earl was out of town.

There was another difference tonight, though. The room was just as romantic, a fire burning, a lamp in the corner turned down low, good brandy, servants discreetly retired for the night, Selena as seductive as ever. But tonight Nicholas was bored. It was as simple as that. He had no wish to leave the sofa and join Selena on the rug.

He had known for a while that he was losing interest in Selena. The fact that he didn't especially wish to bed her tonight confirmed his feeling that it was time to end the affair. Theirs had lasted longer than most of his involvements, nearly three months. Perhaps that was why he felt ready to leave her despite the fact that he'd found no one to replace her.

There was no one he felt like pursuing just then. Selena quite outshined all the ladies of his acquaintance, except those odd few who were in love with their husbands and therefore not prone to his charm. Oh, but his hunting field was not limited only to married ladies bored with their husbands, not really. He did not scruple to leave untouched the sweet innocents out for their first or second seasons. If the tender young ladies were prone to succumb, they were not safe from Nicholas. As long as they were eager to be bedded, he would oblige them for however long the affair could escape the notice of their parents. These were quite his shortest dalliances, certainly, but his most challenging, too.

He had enjoyed three virgins in his younger hell-raising days. One, a Duke's daughter, was quickly married off to a second cousin or some such lucky gentleman. The other two had likewise been married off before full-scale scandals blossomed. Which was not to say the gossipmongers hadn't had field days with each affair. But without challenges issued from enraged families, the affairs remained only gossip and speculation. The fact was that the fathers in question were all afraid to face him on the dueling field. He had by that time already won two duels with irate husbands.

He was not proud of deflowering three innocents, or of wounding two men whose only error lay in having promiscuous wives. But he felt no guilt either. If the debutantes were foolish enough to give themselves to him without promise of marriage, well, so it went. And the wives of noblemen had known exactly what they were doing.

It had been said of Nicholas that he didn't particularly care who got hurt while he pursued his pleasures. Perhaps that was true, perhaps not. No one really knew Nicholas well enough to be sure. Even *he* wasn't sure why he did some of the things he did.

He paid for his reputation, in any case. Fathers with titles above his would not consider him for their daughters. Only the very daring and people looking for a rich husband kept Nicholas' name on their social lists.

But he was not looking for a wife. He had long felt he had no right to offer for a young woman of breeding and lineage that his title demanded. In all likelihood he would never marry. No one knew why the Viscount of Montieth was resigned to his bachelor life, so there were still countless hopefuls looking to snag him, to reform him.

Lady Selena Eddington was one of those hopefuls. She took pains not to show it, but he knew when a woman was after his title. Married to a Baron her first time around, she was looking higher now. She was strikingly beautiful, with short black hair surrounding her oval face with delicate curls, in the current fashion. Golden skin enhanced the expressive hazel eyes. Twenty-four, amusing, seductive, she was a lovely woman. It was certainly not her fault that Nicholas' desire for her had cooled.

No woman had ever managed to keep his ardor burning for long. He had expected this affair to fade. They all did. The only thing that surprised him was his willingness to end it before sighting a new conquest. The decision would force him to haunt the social scene for a while, until someone took his interest, and Nicholas hated having to do that.

Perhaps tomorrow's ball would be just the ticket. There would be dozens of new young ladies there, for the season had just opened. Nicholas sighed. At twenty-seven, after seven years of jaded living, he had lost his taste for young innocents.

He wouldn't break with Selena tonight, he decided, for she was already piqued with him, and she would unleash all of the temper he suspected she was capable of. That was to be avoided. He deplored emotional scenes, for his own nature was too passionate by half. Women could never stand up to his full rage. They were always reduced to tears, and that was just as deplorable. No, he would tell her tomorrow night when he saw her at the ball. She wouldn't dare make a scene in public.

Selena held her crystal glass of sherry up to the fire and marveled that the amber liquid was the exact shade of Nicholas' eyes when he was in an extreme mood. His eyes had been that honey-gold color when he first began to pursue her, but they were also that color when he was either annoyed or pleased about something. When he was feeling nothing special, was calm or indifferent, his eyes were more of a reddish brown, almost the color of newly polished copper. They were always disturbing eyes because even when they were a darker shade, they still glowed with an inner light. The unsettling eyes were offset by his swarthy skin and inordinately long dark eyelashes. His skin tone was dark gold to begin with, and he was bronzed by the sun as well, for he was an avid outdoorsman. He was saved from looking sinister by brown hair streaked with golden highlights. Worn in the currently fashionable windswept style and naturally wavy, his hair had a two-tone appearance in certain lighting.

It was detestable of him to be so handsome that the mere sight of him could start a girl's heart fluttering. She had seen it happen many times. Young girls became giggling ninnies in his presence. Older women offered blatant invitations with their eyes. No wonder he was so hard to handle. Lovely females had no doubt been throwing themselves at him since he'd come of age, or even before. And it was not just his face that was so entrancing. Why couldn't he be short, or even chubby, she asked herself, anything to take away from his devastating effect? But no, he fit the current mode of skin-tight trousers and cut-away coats as if the style had been created just for him. No having to nip in the coats or pad the shoulders for Nicholas Eden. His body was superb — muscular yet trim, tall yet graceful, the body of an avid athlete.

If only it weren't so. Then Selena's heart wouldn't throb whenever he looked at her with those sherry eyes. She was determined to bring him to the altar, for not only was he the best-looking man she had ever seen, he was also the Fourth Viscount Eden of

Montieth, and rich besides. Made to order was what he was, and arrogantly aware of the fact.

What, indeed, could bring him around? Something had to, for it was painfully obvious that he was losing interest in her. What could she do to reignite the flame? Ride naked through Hyde Park? Join one of the whispered-about Black Sabbaths that were said to be excuses for orgies? Behave even more scandalously than he did? She could break into Whites or Brooks — that would really shock him. Under no circumstances were women allowed in those all-male establishments. Or perhaps she could begin to ignore him. Or even . . . by God, yes, throw him over for another man! He would die! He would simply not be able to stand the blow to his vanity. It would arouse his rage and jealousy, and he would rashly demand that she marry him!

Selena became excited thinking about it. It would work. It had to. Anyway, she had no choice but to try. If it didn't work, she would have lost nothing, for she was losing him as it was.

She rolled over to face him and found him stretched out on the sofa with his feet propped up on one end, boots and all, his hands behind his head at the other end. Going to sleep on her! Famous! She could not remember ever being so insulted. Not even her husband of two years had ever gone to sleep in her presence. Yes, desperate measures were definitely called for.

"Nicholas?" She said his name softly and he answered her right away. At least he hadn't been asleep. "Nicholas, I have been giving our relationship a good deal of thought."

"Have you, Selena?"

She flinched at the boredom in his voice.

"Yes," she went on bravely. "And I have come to a conclusion. Due to your lack of . . . shall we say *warmth* . . . I believe I would be better appreciated by someone else."

"No doubt you would be."

She frowned. He was taking this awfully well. "Well, I have had several offers lately to . . . replace you in my affections, and I have decided" — she paused a moment before committing herself to a lie, then closed her eyes and blurted — "I have decided to accept one."

She waited several moments before she opened her eyes. Nicholas had not moved an inch on the sofa and it was another full minute before he finally did. He sat up slowly and his eyes fastened on hers. She held her breath. His expression was inscrutable.

He picked up his empty glass from the table and held it toward her. "Would you, my dear?"

"Yes, of course." She jumped up to do his bidding, not even thinking how autocratic it was of him to expect her to wait on him.

"Who is the lucky man?"

Selena started, spilling brandy on the table. Was his voice just a little sharp, or was that wishful thinking on her part?

"He would like our arrangement to be discreet, so you will understand if I don't divulge his name."

"He's married?"

She brought him his glass, which was precariously full, all the way to the brim, thanks to her nervousness. "No. In fact I have every reason to believe greater things will come of this relationship. As I said, he simply wants to be discreet — for now."

She should not have taken that tack, she quickly realized. She and Nicholas had also been discreet, never making love in her house because of the servants, though he did call for her there, and never using his house on Park Lane. Yet everyone knew she was his mistress. You only had to be seen with Nicholas Eden three times in a row for that assumption to be made.

"Don't ask me to betray him, Nicky," she said with a halfhearted smile. "You will learn who he is soon enough."

"Then, pray tell, why not give me his name now?"

Did he know she was lying? He did. She could tell by his manner. And who the devil *could* replace Nicholas? The men of her acquaintance had all steered clear of her once he became her escort.

"You are being obnoxious, Nicholas." Selena took the attack. "Who he is certainly can't matter to you, for although it hurts me to admit it, I have noticed a lack of ardor in you lately. What else can I think but that you no longer want me?"

Here was the opening for him to deny it all. The moment was lost.

"What is this all about?" his voice was sharp. "That blasted ball? Is that it?"

"Of course not," she replied indignantly.

"Isn't it?" he challenged. "You think to force me into giving you my escort to that affair tomorrow night by telling me this tale. It won't wash, my dear."

His colossal ego was going to be the death of her, it surely was. What conceit! He just couldn't believe that she might prefer someone else to him.

21

Nicholas' dark brow arched in surprise and Selena realized horribly that she had expressed her thoughts aloud. She was shocked, but then she stiffened her resolve.

"Well, it's true," she said boldly and moved away from him, back to the fireplace.

Selena paced back and forth before the fire, its heat nearly matching the heat of her anger. He didn't deserve to be loved.

"I'm sorry, Nicky," she said after a while, not daring to look at him. "I don't want our affair to end on a bad note. You really have been wonderful — most of the time. Oh, dear," she sighed. "You are the expert at this. Is that how it's done?"

Nicholas very nearly laughed. "Not bad for an amateur, my dear."

"Good," she said on a brighter note and risked a glance at him. She found him grinning at her. Damn, he still wasn't buying her story. "Doubt me, then, Lord Montieth, but time will tell, won't it? Just don't be too surprised when you see me with my new gentleman."

She turned back to the fire again, and the next time she turned toward him, he was gone.

CHAPTER 2

The Malory mansion on Grosvenor Square was brightly lit, and most of the occupants were in their bedrooms, preparing for the Duke and Duchess of Shepford's ball. The servants were busier than usual, running from one end of the mansion to the other.

Lord Marshall needed more starch in his cravat. Lady Clare wanted a light snack. She had been too nervous to eat all day. Lady Diana needed a posset to calm her. Bless her, her first season and first ball; she had not eaten for two days. Lord Travis needed help finding his new frilly shirt. Lady Amy simply needed cheering up. She was the only one in the family too young to attend the ball, even a masked ball where she wouldn't be recognized anyway. Oh, how awful to be fifteen!

The only person preparing for the ball who wasn't a son or daughter of the house was Lady Regina Ashton, Lord Edward

Malory's niece and first cousin to his large brood of children. Of course, Lady Regina had her own maid to fetch for her if she needed anything, but apparently she didn't, for no one had seen either of them for an hour or more.

The house had been humming with activity for hours. Lord and Lady Malory had started their preparations much earlier, having been invited to the formal dinner being given for a select few before the ball. They had left a little more than an hour ago. The two Malory brothers would escort their sisters and cousin, a major responsibility for the young men, one just out of university and the other still attending.

Marshall Malory hadn't been looking forward to escorting the family females until today when, unexpectedly, a lady friend had asked to join his party in the Malory family coach. A stroke of luck, receiving such a request from that particular lady.

He had been head over heels in love with her since he'd first met her, last year, when he'd been home for the holidays. She had not given him any encouragement then. But now he was through with school, twenty-one, a man on his own. Why, he could even set up his own household now if he was of a mind to. He could ask a certain lady to marry him. Oh, how wonderful to have reached his majority!

Lady Clare was also thinking about age. She was twenty, horrid as that was to contemplate. This was her third season and she had yet to win a husband or even an engagement! There had been a few offers, but not from anyone she could have considered seriously. Oh, she was pretty enough, with fair coloring, fair skin, fair everything. That was the problem. She was just . . . pretty. She was nowhere near as striking as her cousin Regina, and she tended to fade away when in the younger girl's company. Worst fate, this was the second season she would have to share with Regina.

Clare fumed. Her cousin should have married already. She'd had dozens of offers. And it wasn't as if she weren't willing. She seemed more than willing, seemed almost more desperate to get settled than Clare was. But one thing or another had brought all the offers to a dead end. Even a tour of Europe this last year had produced no husband. Regina had returned to London last week, still looking.

This year there would also be the competition of Clare's own sister, Diana. Just short of eighteen, she should have been made to wait another year before being brought out.

But their parents thought Diana was old enough to have some fun. She was expressly forbidden, however, to think seriously about any young man. She was too young to marry, but she could enjoy herself all she liked.

Next her parents would be letting fifteen-year-old Amy out of the schoolroom when she was sixteen, Clare thought, increasingly annoyed. She could just see it! Next year, if she still hadn't found a husband, she would have both Diana and Amy to contend with. Amy was just as striking as Regina, with that dark coloring only a few of the Malorys possessed. Clare would have to find a husband this season if it killed her.

Little did Clare know it, but those were her beautiful cousin's sentiments as well. Regina Ashton stared at her image in the mirror while her maid, Meg, rolled up her long black hair to hide its length and make it look more fashionable. Regina was not seeing the slightly tilted eyes of a startling cobalt blue, or the slightly pouting full lips, or the slightly too-white skin that set off her dark hair and long soot-black lashes so dramatically. She was seeing men, parades of men, legions of men — French, Swiss, Austrian, Italian, English — and wondering why she still wasn't married. It certainly wasn't for lack of trying.

Reggie, as she was always called, had had so many men to choose from it was actually embarrassing. There'd been at least a dozen she was sure she could be happy with, two dozen she'd thought she was falling in love with, and so many who just wouldn't do for one reason or another. And those whom Reggie had felt would do, her uncles felt would not.

Oh, the disadvantages of having four uncles who loved her dearly! She likewise adored them, all four. Jason, now forty-five, had been head of the family since he was only sixteen, responsible for his three brothers and one sister, Reggie's mother. Jason took his responsibilities seriously — too seriously at times. He was a very serious man.

Edward was his exact opposite, good-humored, jolly, easygoing, indulgent. A year younger than Jason, Edward had married Aunt Charlotte when he was twenty-two, much sooner than Jason married. He had five children, three girls and two boys. Cousin Travis, nineteen, was Reggie's age and in the middle of his family. They had been playmates all their lives, along with Uncle Jason's only son.

Reggie's mother, Melissa, had been far

younger than her two older brothers, nearly seven years. But then, two years after her birth, James was born.

James was the wild brother, the one who said to hell with it all and went his own way. He was thirty-five now, and his name was not even supposed to be mentioned anymore. As far as Jason and Edward were concerned, James did not exist. But Reggie still loved him, despite his terrible sins. She missed him sorely and got to see him only secretly. In the past nine years, she'd seen him only six times, the last time more than two years ago.

Anthony, truth to tell, was her favorite uncle. He was also the only one besides Reggie, Amy, and Reggie's mother who had the dark hair and cobalt eyes of Reggie's great-grandmother, whispered to have been a gypsy. No one in the family would confirm that scandalous fact, of course. Perhaps he was her favorite because he was so carefree, like Reggie herself.

Anthony, thirty-four and the baby of the family, was more like a brother than an uncle. He was also, quite amusingly, society's most notorious rake since his brother James had left London. But whereas James could be ruthless, having much of Jason in him, Anthony was gifted with some of

Edward's qualities. He was a dashing blade, an outrageous charmer. He didn't give a snort for anyone's opinion of him, but in his own way he did his best to please anyone who mattered to him.

Reggie smiled. For all his mistresses and outlandish friends, for all the scandals that flourished around him, the duels he had fought, the wild wagers he made, Anthony was sometimes the most lovable hypocrite where she was concerned. For one of his rogue friends to even look sideways at her was to receive an invitation into the boxing ring. Even the most lecherous men learned to hide their thoughts when she was visiting her uncle, to settle for harmless banter and nothing more. If Uncle Jason ever learned she had even been in the same room as some of the men she'd met, heads would roll, Tony's in particular. But Jason never knew, and although Edward suspected, he was not as strict as Jason.

All four uncles treated her more like a daughter than a niece because the four had raised her since her parents' death when Reggie was only two. They had literally shared her since she turned six. Edward was living in London by then and so, too, were James and Anthony. The three of them had a big row with Jason because he insisted on keeping her in the country. He gave in and allowed her to live six months of each year with Edward, where she was able to see her two younger uncles often.

When she was eleven, Anthony felt he was old enough to demand equal time with her. He was allowed the summer months, which were strictly for play. He was happy to make the sacrifice of turning his bachelor house into a home each year, and that was easily done, because along with Reggie came her maid, her nurse, and her governess. Anthony and Reggie had twice-weekly dinners with Edward and his family. Still, all that domesticity never gave Anthony a longing to marry. He was still a bachelor. And since her coming out, it was no longer proper for her to spend part of her year with him, so she saw him only irregularly.

Ah, well, she thought, soon she would be married. It was not what she particularly wanted. She would so much rather have enjoyed herself for a few more years. But it was what her uncles wanted. They assumed it was her desire to find a suitable husband and begin a family. Wasn't that what all young girls wanted? They had had a meeting to discuss it, in fact, and no matter how much she declared that she wasn't ready to leave the bosom of her family, their good intentions won out over her protestations until, finally, she gave up.

From then on she'd done her very best to please them because she loved them all so much. She brought forth suitor after suitor, but one uncle or another found fault with each of them. She continued her search through Europe, but by then she was so wretchedly tired of looking at every man she met with a critical eye. She couldn't make friends. She couldn't enjoy herself. Each man had to be carefully dissected and analyzed — was he husband material? Was he the magic one that all of her uncles would approve?

She was beginning to believe there was no such man, and desperately needed a break from this obsessive search. She wanted to see Uncle Tony, the only one who would understand, who would intercede for her with Jason. But Tony had been visiting a friend in the country when she returned to London and hadn't come back until last evening.

Reggie had gone by twice to see him that very day, but he was out both times, so she had left him a note. Surely he had gotten it by now. Then why hadn't he come?

Even as she had that thought she heard a carriage pull up in front of the house. She laughed, a merry, musical sound.

"Finally!"

"What?" Meg wanted to know. "I'm not done yet. I'll have you know it isn't easy gettin' this hair of yours tucked away. I still say you should cut it. Save me and you both time."

"Never mind that, Meg." Reggie jumped up, causing a few pins to drop to the floor. "Uncle Tony's here."

"Here now, where d'you think you're going like that?" Meg's tone was outraged.

But Reggie ignored her and rushed out of her room, hearing Meg's loud "Regina Ashton!" but paying no attention. She ran until she reached the stairs to the main lower hall, and then she became aware of her scanty attire and stopped. She drew back quickly around the corner, determined not to leave until she heard her uncle's voice. But she didn't hear it. She heard a woman's voice instead, and with a hesitant peek around the corner, she was greatly disappointed to see the butler admitting a lady, not Uncle Tony. She recognized the woman as Lady something-or-other, whom Reggie had met in Hyde Park a few days ago. Bother! Where the devil was Tony?

Just then Meg latched onto her arm and dragged her back down the hallway. Meg took liberties, that was a certainty, but no wonder, for she had been with Reggie as long as nurse Tess had, which was forever.

"If I ever saw anything as scandalous as you standin' there in your unmentionables, I'd like to know!" Meg scolded as she pushed Reggie back down on her stool in front of the small vanity. "We taught you better than that."

"I thought it was Uncle Tony."

"That's no excuse."

"I know, but I must see him tonight. You know why, Meg. He's the only one who can help me. He'll write to Uncle Jason and then I'll be able to relax, finally."

"And what do you think he can tell the Marquis that will do you any good?"

Reggie grinned. "What I'm going to suggest is that they find me a husband."

Meg shook her head and sighed. "You won't like the man they choose for you, my girl."

"Perhaps. But I simply don't care anymore," she insisted. "It would be nice to be able to pick my own husband, but I learned quickly enough that my choice doesn't matter if he's a bad choice according to them. I have been on display now for a full year, going to so many parties and routs and balls that I hate them already. I never thought I'd say that. Why, I couldn't wait to dance at my first ball."

"It's understandable, dear," Meg soothed.

"As long as Uncle Tony understands, and is willing to help, that's all I ask. I want nothing more than to retire to the country, to live quietly again — with or without a husband. If I could find the right man this evening, I would marry him tomorrow, *anything* to quit the social whirl. But I know that's not going to happen, so the next best thing is to let my uncles find him. Knowing them, that will take years. They can never agree on anything, you know. And in the meantime, I'll go home to Haverston."

"I don't see what your Uncle Tony can do that you can't do for yourself. You're not afraid of the Marquis. You can wrap that man around your little finger anytime you've a mind to. Haven't you done so often enough? Just tell him how unhappy you are and he'll —"

"I can't do that!" Reggie gasped. "I could never let Uncle Jason think he's made me unhappy. He would never forgive himself!"

"You're too kindhearted for your own good, my girl," Meg grumbled. "So you'll just go on bein' miserable, then?"

"No. See, that's why I want Uncle Tony to write Uncle Jason first. If I did, and he still insisted I stay here, where would that leave me? But if Tony's letter is scoffed at, then I'll know that plan won't work and I'll still have a chance to think of something else."

"Well, I'm sure you'll see Lord Anthony at the ball tonight."

"No. He detests balls. He wouldn't be caught dead attending one, even for me. Oh, bother! I suppose it will just have to wait until morning." Meg frowned then, and looked away. "What's this? What do you know that I don't?" Reggie demanded.

Meg shrugged. "It's . . . only that Lord Anthony's likely to be gone by mornin' and not back for three or four days. You can wait that long, though."

"Who said he was leaving?"

"I overheard Lord Edward telling his wife that the Marquis has sent for him. He's to be called on the carpet again for some trouble he's gotten himself into."

"No!" Then forlornly, "You don't think he's left already, do you?"

"No, indeed." Meg grinned. "That scamp won't be anxious to face his older brother. He'll put off leavin' as long as he can, I'm sure."

"Then I *must* see him tonight. This is perfect. He can convince Uncle Jason in person better than by letter."

"But you can't go to Lord Anthony's house now," Meg protested. "It's nearly time to leave for the ball."

"Then get me into my gown quickly. Tony is only a few blocks away. I can take the coach and be back before my cousins are ready to leave."

The others were in fact ready to leave then and were waiting for her when Reggie rushed down the stairs a few minutes later. This was unsettling, but not daunting. She pulled her oldest cousin aside as she entered the drawing room, giving the others a fleeting smile of greeting.

"Marshall, I really and truly hate to ask this of you, but I simply must borrow the coach for a few minutes before we all leave."

"What?"

She had been whispering, but his loud exclamation turned every eye their way. She sighed. "Honestly, Marshall, you needn't act as if I've asked for the world."

Marshall, aware at once that they were being watched, and appalled by his momentary lack of control, gathered all his dignity about him and said in the most reasonable tone he could muster, "We have been waiting for you for ten minutes already, and now you propose to make us wait even longer?"

Three more gasps of outrage came flying

at her, but Reggie didn't spare a glance for her other cousins. "I wouldn't ask if it weren't important, Marshall. It won't take me more than a half hour . . . well, certainly no more than an hour. I need to see Uncle Anthony."

"No, no, no!" This from Diana, who hardly ever raised her voice. "How can you be so thoughtless, Reggie? That's not like you at all. You'll make us late! We should be leaving right now."

"Stuff," Reggie replied. "You don't want to be the first ones there, do you?"

"We don't want to be the last to arrive either," Clare joined in peevishly. "The ball will commence in a half hour and it will take us that long to get there. What is so important that you must see Uncle Anthony now?"

"It's personal. And it can't wait. He's leaving for Haverston first thing in the morning. I won't be able to talk to him unless I go right now."

"Until he gets back," Clare said. "Why can't it wait until then?"

"Because it can't." Looking at her cousins set against her, and Lady what's-her-name looking just as agitated, Reggie gave in. "Oh, very well. I'll settle for a hired chaise or a chair, Marshall, if you'll just send one of the footmen to fetch one for me. I'll join you at the ball as soon as I'm finished."

"Out of the question."

Marshall was annoyed. It was just like his cousin to try and involve him in something foolish so that he, being the oldest, would be the one to get in trouble later. Well, not this time, by God. He was older and wiser, and she couldn't talk circles around him anymore the way she used to.

Marshall said adamantly, "A hired conveyance? At night? It's not safe and you know it, Reggie."

"Travis can come with me."

"But Travis doesn't want to," the escort in question was quick to reply. "And never mind turning those baby blues on me, Reggie. I've no mind to be late for the ball either."

"Please, Travis."

"No."

Reggie looked at all those unsympathetic faces. She wouldn't give in. "Then I shan't go to the ball. I didn't want to go in the first place."

"Oh, no." Marshall shook his head sternly. "I know you too well, dear cousin. No sooner do we leave here than you sneak out of the house and walk over to Uncle Anthony's. Father would kill me."

"I have more sense than that, Marshall," she assured him tartly. "I'll send another message to Tony and wait for him to come here."

"And if he doesn't?" Marshall pointed out. "He's got better things to do than jump at your beck and call. He may not even be at home. No. You're coming with us and that's final."

"I won't."

"You will!"

"She can use my carriage." All eyes turned to their guest. "My driver and the attendant have been with me for years and can be trusted to see her safely on her errand and then to the ball."

Reggie's smile was dazzling. "Famous! You really are a savior, Lady — ?"

"Eddington," the lady supplied. "We met earlier in the week."

"Yes, in the park. I do remember. I'm just terrible with names after meeting so many people this last year. I can't thank you enough."

"Don't mention it. I am happy to oblige."

And Selena *was* happy — anything to get them on their way, for heaven's sake. It was bad enough that she'd had to settle for Marshall Malory as escort to *the* ball of the season. But he was the only one of the dozen men she had sent notes to that morning who hadn't put her off with one excuse or another. Malory, younger than she, had been only a last resort. And there she was in the middle of a family squabble, all because of this young chit.

"There now, Marshall," Reggie was saying. "You certainly can't object now."

"No, I suppose not," he said grudgingly. "But just remember you said a half hour, cousin. You had better *be* at the Shepfords' before Father happens to notice that you're not. There will be the devil to pay otherwise, and you know it."

CHAPTER 3

"But I am serious, Tony!" Reggie exclaimed as she eyed him carefully across his sitting room. "How can you doubt me? This is an emergency, Tony." He was the only one of her uncles who insisted she call him simply by his Christian name.

She had had to wait twenty minutes for him to be roused from sleep, for he had spent the whole day at his club drinking and gambling, then come home and fallen into bed. Another ten minutes had been wasted just trying to get him to believe how serious she was. Her thirty minutes were already up and she'd barely begun. Marshall was going to kill her.

"Come now, puss. You wouldn't be a week in the country before you were missing gay old London. If you need a rest, tell Eddie boy you're sick or something. A few days in your room and you'll thank me for not taking you seriously about this."

"I have had nothing but the gay life for the last year," Reggie went on determinedly. "I traveled from party to party on my tour, not country to country. And it's not only that I'm tired of the constant entertainments, Tony. I could withstand that well enough. I'm not even suggesting I spend the whole season at Haverston, only a few weeks, so I can recuperate. It's this husband hunting that is going to be the death of me. Truly it is."

"No one said you had to marry the first man you met, puss," Anthony said reasonably.

"The first man? There've been hundreds, Tony. I'll have you know they now call me the 'cold fish.' "

"Who does, by God?"

"The name is perfectly appropriate. I have been cold and cutting. I've had to be, because I refuse to give a man hope when there is no hope."

"What the devil are you talking about?" Anthony demanded brusquely.

"I hired Sir John Dodsley long before the last season was over."

"That old reprobate? Hired him for what?"

"To act as, well, an adviser, you might say," she confessed. "That old reprobate, as you call him, knows everyone. He also knows everything there is to know about everyone. After my sixth serious suitor failed to pass muster with you and your brothers, I felt it was useless disappointing myself or any more young men by having to go through it all again. I paid Dodsley to attend every affair I did. He had a list of what you and your brothers might disapprove of in a man, and he shook his head at me for nearly every single man I met. It saved me time and disappointment, but it got me my quaint nickname, too. It's impossible, Tony. I can please Jason, but not you . . . you, but not Edward. Thank heaven Uncle James isn't also here to express his opinion. There isn't a man in existence who would please all of you."

"That's absurd," he protested. "I can think of a dozen off hand who would do very well."

"Would they, Tony?" she asked softly. "Would you really want me to marry any of them?"

He pulled an aggrieved face, then suddenly grinned. "No, I suppose not."

"So you see my predicament then?"

"But don't you want to marry, puss?"

"Of course I do. And I'm sure the man you and your brothers find for me will make me very happy."

"What?" He glared at her. "Oh, no you don't. You're not putting that responsibility on *my* shoulders, Reggie."

"All right then," she agreed. "We'll leave it to Uncle Jason."

"Don't be foolish. He'd have you married to a tyrant just like him."

"Come now, Tony, you know that's not true." She grinned.

"Well, close to it," he grumbled.

"You see, Tony, at least *I* wouldn't have to keep on summing up every man I meet. I want to enjoy myself again, be able to talk to a man without analyzing him, dance without wondering if my partner is husband material. It's gotten so that every man I look at, I ask myself, Shall I marry him? Could I love him? Would he be as good and kind to me as —" She stopped, blushing.

"As?" he prompted.

"Oh, you might as well know," she said with a sigh. "I compare every man to you and my other uncles. I can't help it. I almost wish you all didn't love me so well. You've pampered me outrageously. I want my husband to be a combination of all of you."

"What *have* we done to you?"

He was about to burst into laughter and she lost her temper. "You think it's funny,

44

do you? I don't see *you* facing this problem. And if I don't get a vacation from it, I swear I will try and reach Uncle James and have him take me away."

He sobered instantly. Though he was the closest to James, even he had been furious and unforgiving over what his brother had done.

"Don't say that, Reggie," he warned. "You're not thinking clearly. Calling James into this will make matters worse, not better."

She pressed the point mercilessly. "Then will you tell Uncle Jason I want to come home for a while? That I'm done with looking for a husband and will wait until the three of you can agree on whom I should marry?"

"Blister it, Reggie, Jason isn't going to like this any more than I do. You should be making your own choice, finding someone you love."

"I tried that." There was an awkward silence.

Anthony scowled. "Lord Medhurst was a pompous ass!"

"Did I know that? I thought he was quite the one. Well, so much for my falling in love."

"You could have had Newel if Eddie

hadn't been convinced he would make a terrible father." Tony continued to scowl.

"Yes, well, Uncle Edward was undoubtedly right. Again — so much for my falling in love."

"You certainly know how to depress a fellow, puss. We only wanted what was best for you, you know."

"I do know that, and I love you for it. I just know I'll adore whomever the three of you decide will make a perfect husband."

"Will you?" He grinned. "I'm not so sure. If Jason agrees to this, for example, he'll be determined to find a man who's nothing like me."

He was teasing. If there was anyone who would disapprove of someone like him for her, that someone was Tony himself. She laughed. "Well, you know you can always convert my husband, Tony — after I'm safely married."

CHAPTER 4

Percival Alden shouted in triumph as he reined in his horse at the end of Green Park, Piccadilly side. "That's twenty pounds you owe me, Nick!" he called over his shoulder as the Viscount came charging up behind him riding his bay. Nicholas Eden gave Percy a black scowl.

They began walking their horses around in a circle. The two friends had just come from Boodles, ending a perfectly good game of cards when Percy mentioned his new black stallion. Nicholas was just drunk enough to take up the challenge, and they sent for their horses.

"We could both have broken our bloody necks, you know," Nicholas pronounced quite sensibly, though his vision was blurred almost double. "Remind me not to do this again, will you?"

Percy thought that was terribly funny and began laughing so hard he nearly lost his balance. "As if anyone could stop you from doing what you've a mind to do, especially when you're foxed. But never mind, old chap. You probably won't remember this daring escapade come morning, and if you do, you won't believe your memory. Ah, where the bloody hell was that moon when it was needed?"

Nicholas looked up at the silver orb just coming out from behind a cloud bank. His head was spinning. Damnation! The race should have sobered him a little.

He fastened his wavering gaze on his friend. "How much do you want for that animal, Percy?"

"No wish to sell him. I'll be winning more races with him."

"How much?" Nicholas repeated obdurately.

"I paid two hundred and fifty for him, but —"

"Three hundred."

"He's not for sale."

"Four hundred."

"Oh, come now, Nick," Percy protested.

"Five hundred."

"I'll send him round in the morning." Nicholas grinned in satisfaction.

"I should have held out for a thousand." Percy grinned back. "But then, I know where I can get his brother for two fifty. And I wouldn't want to take advantage of you."

Nicholas laughed. "You're wasting your talent, Percy. You should get a job in Smithfield Market selling horseflesh."

"And give my dear mother yet another reason to curse the day she bore a son? No, thank you. I'll go on as I am, taking advantage of hard bargainers like yourself to turn a tidy little profit. It's more fun, anyway. And speaking of fun, weren't you supposed to put in an appearance at Shepford's tonight?"

"Bloody hell," Nicholas growled, his good humor disappearing. "Why did you have to remind me?"

"My good deed for the day."

"I wouldn't go near that place if my little bird didn't need her wings clipped," Nicholas confided.

"Ruffled your feathers, did she?"

"Would you credit she thinks to make me jealous?" Nicholas asked, outraged.

"You? Jealous?" Percy guffawed. "I would love to see the day, dearly I would."

"You're welcome to come along and watch my performance. I mean to give a very good one for Lady E. before I call it quits," Nicholas said darkly.

"You're not going to call the poor fellow out, are you?"

"Good God, over a woman? Of course not. But she will think so, while I will in fact give him my blessing of her. She'll be left to blame herself for her folly, for she will have seen the last of me."

"That's a novel way to go about it," Percy mused. "I must remember to try that. Look, why not give me your blessing of her? Fine-looking woman, Lady E. Oh, I say." Percy looked off across the street. "Speaking of . . . isn't that her carriage over there?"

Nicholas followed the direction of his nod to see the bright, outrageously painted pink-and-green curricle he knew so well. "Impossible," he muttered. "She would die rather than be late for that ball, and it's long since started."

"Don't know anyone else who owns such a smart-looking carriage," Percy remarked. "Been meaning to paint my own those colors."

Nicholas threw him a horrified look before glancing back at the street. "Who do we know who lives on this street?" he asked his friend.

"No one I can think of," Percy began. "Wait a minute! I think I know whose house she's stopped in front of. The house belongs to young Malory's kin — oh, what's his name? You know. Not the wild one who hasn't been around for years, but the other one, the one who's so good a marksman that no one will — oh, I have it! Anthony, Lord Anthony. Good God! You don't think she means to make you jealous with *him?* Even you don't dare mess with him, Nick."

Nicholas didn't answer. Slowly, very slowly, he left the park and crossed the street. If that was Selena, then she was right where she knew he would see her, because he passed this way every night on his way home from his club. As it happened, they had come out of the park that night near the end of Piccadilly, and if Percy hadn't spotted the carriage, he might not have either. But now his curiosity was aroused. Was Selena sitting inside the closed carriage, waiting for him to pass, unaware that he had already gone around her? Had she been unable to get an escort to her damned ball, and was again determined to drag him there with her? It was impossible that she could know Anthony Malory. He and his cronies were in a completely different league, rakehells all, thumbing their noses at society. Nicholas might have a tarnished reputation himself, but even he wouldn't be classed with that group of wastrels.

But what if she had somehow met Mallory? But she would not dally here tonight of all nights. The Shepford ball meant too much. It was all she had talked about for the last month.

Yet what if she had come here to tryst with Malory? Nicholas stopped by the curb three houses away. Percy caught up with him, looking alarmed. "That wasn't a dare I made back there, you know," Percy said earnestly. "You're not thinking of doing anything foolish, are you?"

"I've just been thinking, Percy." Nicholas was grinning. "If that is Lady E. in there, then she'll be coming out any moment now."

"How do you know that?"

"The ball. She might be late for it, but she isn't going to miss it, not she. However, maybe she *will* miss it after all. Yes, it would do her a world of good to miss it. A woman shouldn't get so involved with something that she ignores the man in her life. That lesson should be made clear to her, don't you think? Yes, quite clear. Very clear. So she won't make the same mistake again."

"Montieth! What the devil are you planning?" Percy demanded in alarm.

Nicholas didn't answer because his attention was drawn by the door opening down the street. His grin widened as Selena Eddington stepped outside. She was securing a short black domino over her eyes, and she had her hands raised to her face, but he would have recognized that black hair anywhere. She was wearing a long fur-edged cape secured at the throat. The cape was thrown back over her shoulders, revealing a lovely rose-colored gown. Nicholas was taken aback. Rose? That wasn't one of her colors. She contemptuously called it the color of innocence, a quality she had long ago lost without regret. He supposed she was out to impress the Duchess of Stepford with her youth.

She turned toward the man standing at her back and Nicholas recognized Anthony Malory. He knew those dark good looks well, saw him often enough at the clubs, though they were not exactly speaking acquaintances. Selena would find him very attractive, Nicholas admitted that. Well, he wished her luck. Malory was even more determined a bachelor than Nicholas. She would never bring that one to the altar. Did she realize that?

He watched in amusement as she embraced Malory, then gave him a quick kiss. He was obviously not taking her to the ball, for he was dressed in only a lounging robe.

"Well, what do you make of that?" Percy

said uncomfortably, bringing his horse a bit closer. "It is Lady E., isn't it?"

"Yes, and the carriage is facing this way, Percy, so I'll be going the other way. Do me a favor and hamper it from turning around as long as you can."

"Blister it, what are you going to do?"

"Why, take Lady E. home with me, what else?" Nicholas chuckled. "I'll go around the block and cut through Mayfair to get back to Park Lane with her. Meet me there."

"Damnation take you, Nick!" Percy exclaimed. "Malory's standing right there!"

"Yes, but he's not going to go chasing down the street after me on foot, now is he? And he won't have a weapon handy if he's just tumbled her. He may enjoy this entertainment."

"Don't do it, Nick."

But Nicholas wasn't sober enough to think. He started his mount down the street toward the carriage, picking up just a little speed before he reached it. When he veered off the street and onto the curb, he took everyone by surprise, riding right between the house and the carriage. Slowing for an instant, he grabbed Selena and yanked her across his horse.

Beautifully done, he congratulated himself. He couldn't have done it any better if he'd been sober. Shouting erupted behind him, but he didn't slow down. The woman across his horse started screaming, but he quickly stuffed his white silk handkerchief in her mouth to stifle her, then used his cravat to bind her wrists.

She was squirming so much that he was in danger of losing her, so he twisted her around until she was sitting in front of him, then whisked her cape over her head, bundling her tightly. Just as good as a sack, he thought with satisfaction. He chuckled as they rounded a corner and headed back toward Park Lane. "Sounds like no one's following, my dear. Perhaps your driver, Tovey, recognized me and knows you're in familiar hands." He chuckled again, hearing the muffled sounds she was making inside the cape. "Yes, I know you're miffed with me, Selena. But console yourself that you can give vent to a full temper tantrum when I let you go — in the morning."

She began to struggle again, but in another few moments he was stopping in front of his townhouse on Park Lane. Percival Alden was stationed by the great dark expanse of Hyde Park across the street, and only he saw Nicholas toss the bundle over his shoulder and carry it into the house. His butler tried not to look too startled.

STUTSMAN COUNTY LIBRARY
910 5 ST SE
JAMESTOWN ND 58401

Percy followed him inside and said, "They didn't even try to follow you."

"Ah, that means the driver did recognize me." Nicholas chuckled. "He's probably explained to Malory by now that the lady and I are friends."

"I still can't believe you did this, Nick. She'll never forgive you."

"I know. Now be a good chap and follow me upstairs so you can light a few lamps before I deposit my baggage." He paused just long enough to grin at his butler, who was staring at the feet hanging over his lordship's shoulder. "Tell my man to get my evening clothes out, Tyndale. I want to be out of here in ten minutes. And if anyone comes to call, for any reason, say that I left for the Duke of Shepford's ball an hour ago."

"Very good, my lord."

"You're still going?" Percy asked in amazement as he and the butler followed Nicholas upstairs.

"But of course," Nicholas replied. "I intend to dance the night away."

He stopped in front of a bedroom at the back of the house on the third floor, checking it quickly to make sure there was nothing of value in the room that Selena could destroy in anger. Satisfied, he told Tyndale to fetch the key, then nodded to Percy to light the lamp on the mantel.

"Be a good girl, my dear, and don't make too much fuss." He patted her backside in a familiar manner. "If you start screaming or do anything else foolish, Tyndale will be forced to put a stop to it. I'm sure you won't enjoy spending the next few hours trussed up on the bed."

He motioned for Percy to leave the room before he dropped her on the bed. Then he loosened her wrist bonds and left the room, locking the door with a soft click. He knew she would remove the gag sooner or later, but he wouldn't be around to hear her.

"Come along, Percy. I have extra evening clothes if you would like to join me at the ball."

Percy shook his head in confusion as he followed Nicholas back down to the second floor where his rooms were located. "I might as well, but I don't see why you're going on to the ball now that she won't be there."

"That's the crowning touch." Nicholas chuckled. "What's the point in Lady E.'s missing the ball unless she's told by her dear friends tomorrow that I danced every dance from the time I arrived until I departed."

"That's cruel, Montieth."

"No crueler than her throwing me over

for Malory."

"But you don't even care about that," Percy pointed out, exasperated.

"No, I don't. Still, it warrants *some* kind of reaction, doesn't it? After all, the lady would have been devastated if I'd done nothing."

"If she could choose how you would react, Montieth, I don't think she would choose this."

"Oh, well. Better this than my challenging Malory. Don't you think so?"

"Heavens, yes!" Percy was genuinely appalled. "You wouldn't stand a chance against him."

"You think not?" Nicholas murmured. "Well, perhaps not. After all, he *has* had more practice than I. But we'll never know, will we?"

CHAPTER 5

Reggie wasn't frightened. She had heard enough to know that her kidnapper was a nobleman. He assumed he'd been recognized by the driver of her carriage, so he meant no real harm. No, she wouldn't be hurt.

One other thing made Reggie smile with a deliciously wicked grin. The man had made a dreadful mistake. He thought she was someone else — Selena, he had called her. "It's only me," he had said, as if she should recognize his voice easily.

Selena? What made this man think she was Selena? He had simply picked her up off the sidewalk, so what made him . . . *"The driver recognized me"!* Good God, Lady Eddington! He knew the carriage so he thought she was Lady Eddington.

This was priceless. He would go to the Shepford ball — and *voilà,* there would be Lady Eddington with Reggie's cousins. Oh, how she wished she could see his face. It was just the sort of prank she might have played on someone in her younger years.

And then he would come racing back to his house, full of frantic apologies, begging her forgiveness. He would plead with her not to say anything. She would have to agree, for her reputation was at stake. She would go to the ball and simply say she had stayed longer with Uncle Anthony than she'd planned to. No one would ever know she had been abducted.

Having removed her gag and wrist bands, she stretched out on the bed, perfectly at ease, enjoying the adventure. It wasn't her first, not by any means. She'd had adventures all her life, beginning at age seven, when she'd fallen through the ice on Haverston Pond, and would have drowned if one of the stableboys hadn't heard her calling and pulled her out. The following year the same boy distracted a wild boar that had chased her up a tree. He'd been gored, and while he recovered quickly, happy to tell his friends all about the dramatic rescue, she was restricted from the woods for a year.

No, even her uncles' almost religious devotion to her upbringing hadn't been able to stand in the way of fate, and Reggie had seen more adventure in nineteen years than most men did in all their lives. Looking around her elegant, temporary prison, she smiled. She knew young women dreamed of adventure, yearned to be swept away by handsome strangers on horseback, but she had known the real thing. Twice, as a matter of fact, this evening's escapade being the second.

Two years before, when she was seventeen, she'd been attacked on the road to Bath by three masked highwaymen, and whisked away by the boldest of the three. Thank heaven her daring oldest cousin Derek had been in the coach that day and, taking one of the coach horses, had pursued her abductor furiously, rescuing Reggie from . . . whatever the stranger had had in mind.

And before that, when she was twelve, there had been her high-seas adventure. She was kidnapped for a whole summer, and endured terrifying storms at sea and even an incredible battle.

Well, she was having another adventure, an amusing and fairly safe one this time. And then she sat bolt upright. Uncle Tony! He knew about this! Suddenly it wasn't funny anymore. If he found out who her abductor was, he would come and break the door down. There would be no end of gossip, and then she would be ruined. Anthony

Malory wouldn't let it end easily, either. He would challenge the poor fellow and kill him, mistake or not.

Reggie got up and began to walk, barefoot, around the room. Oh, dear, this was becoming a dreadful predicament. She continued pacing, distracting herself by studying the room. It was done in muted greens and browns, and there were a few modern Chippendale pieces. Her cape was draped over an armchair, her slippers on the floor in front of it, her mask tossed on the padded seat. A single window looked out over a garden, dark and full of shadows. She repaired her hair using a mirror framed in the leaves and flowers of the Rocaille style.

She wondered if Tyndale really would tie her up and gag her if she started shouting for help. Better not to find out. She wondered, too, what was taking Nick so long to discover his mistake. The minutes continued to tick by on the Meissen clock on the mantel.

Nicholas watched her waltz by in the arms of some dandy wearing bright green satin that clashed horribly with Selena's plum-colored evening gown. With those colors, they were hardly a pair one could miss, even on that crowded dance floor.

"Bloody hell," Nicholas growled.

Percy, standing beside him, was more articulate. "Oh, good God! You've really gone and done it, haven't you? I knew you shouldn't have started this, and now you've really gone and done it."

"Shut up, Percy."

"Well, that *is* her, isn't it? Then for God's sake who's the bird you've got caged at home? You've stolen Malory's mistress, isn't that it? He'll kill you, Nick," Percy informed him. "He'll bloody well kill you is what he'll do."

Nicholas was ready to kill his excitable friend. "You do go on and on, don't you? The only thing that will come of this is my getting a tongue lashing from a furious woman I've never laid eyes on before. Lord Malory isn't going to call me out over a stupid mistake like this. What harm has been done, after all?"

"The lady's reputation, Nick," Percy began. "If this gets out —"

"How will it get out? Use your head, old boy. If she is Malory's mistress, what reputation has she to lose? What I *would* like to know, is what was she doing with Lady Eddington's carriage?" He sighed, very much the misunderstood, put-upon male. "I suppose I'd better run along home and let her out — whoever she is."

"Need help?" Percy grinned. "I'm rather curious to know who she is actually."

"She isn't likely to be in a receiving mood," Nicholas pointed out. "I'll be lucky if I only get a vase thrown at my head."

"Well, you can manage that on your own, thank you. Tell me all about it tomorrow, all right."

"I thought you'd feel that way," Nicholas said wryly.

Nicholas rode home as fast as he could. He was quite sober by that point and regretting the entire evening deeply. He prayed the mystery lady had a sense of humor.

Tyndale let him in and took his cloak, hat, and gloves. "Any problems?" Nicholas asked, knowing there would be a long list. But there wasn't.

"Not one, my lord."

"No noise?"

"None."

Nicholas took a long, deep breath. She was probably saving all her fury for him.

"Have the carriage brought round, Tyndale," he ordered before starting up the stairs.

The third floor was as quiet as a tomb. The servants had no reason to be in that part of the house after dark. Lucy, the pretty maid he'd been eyeing lately, wouldn't venture upstairs unless sent for, and his valet, Harris, would be sleeping on the second floor, expecting his master much later. At least no one in the house other than Tyndale knew about the lady's presence. That was a break.

Nicholas stood outside Reggie's door for a brief moment, then unlocked the door and opened it quickly. He was braced to receive a bash on the head, but the jolt he got at first sight of her was just as stunning.

She stood framed by the window, gazing at him in a startlingly direct way. There was no shyness in her look and no fear either on that exquisite, delicate, heart-shaped face. The eyes were disturbing, with an exotic slant. Such dark blue eyes in that fair face, so blue and clear, like colored crystal. The lips were soft and full and the nose was straight and slender. A thick fringe of sooty lashes framed those extraordinary eyes, while black brows arched gently above them. Her hair was raven black, too, in tight little ringlets surrounding her face, giving her fair skin a glow like polished ivory.

She was breathtaking. The beauty didn't stop with her face, either. She was petite, yes, but there was nothing childlike about her form. Firm young breasts pressed against the thin muslin of her rose gown. It was not cut as low as some gowns were and stopped short of being provocative, yet somehow it was as tantalizing as anything he'd seen in London. He wanted to pull the rose muslin down a few inches and watch those lovely breasts spring free. He received another jolt then, feeling his manhood rise against his will. Lord, he hadn't lost control like that since his youth!

Desperate to bring everything under control, he cast about for something — anything — to say. "Hello."

His tone implied "What have we here?" and Reggie grinned despite herself. He was gorgeous, simply gorgeous. It wasn't just his face, though that was striking. There was a sexual magnetism about him that was quite unnerving. He was even better looking than Uncle Anthony, whom she'd always considered the most handsome, compelling man in the world.

The comparison was reassuring. He reminded her of Uncle Tony, not only in height and appearance, but in the way his eyes assessed her. His mouth quirked upward in approval. How often she had seen her uncle look at women just that way. Well, he was a rake, she told herself. What other kind of man would abduct his mistress from the doorstep of another man's house? Had he been jealous, thinking his mistress and Uncle Anthony were . . . oh, this was becoming a most amusing situation.

"Hello, yourself," Reggie said impishly. "I was beginning to wonder when you would realize your mistake. You certainly took enough time about it."

"I am just now wondering if I have in fact made a mistake at all. You don't look like a mistake. You look very much like something I did right for a change."

He quietly closed the door and leaned back against it, those beautiful amber eyes boldly moving over her from head to foot. It was not at all safe for a young lady to be alone with a man of his stamp, and Reggie recognized that. Yet for some reason she couldn't fathom, she wasn't afraid of this man. Scandalously, she wondered if it would be such a terrible thing to lose her virtue to him. Oh, it was a reckless mood she was suddenly in!

She eyed the closed door and his large frame blocking that only exit. "Fie on you, sir. I hope you don't mean to compromise me more than you already have."

"I will if you will let me. Will you? Think carefully before you answer," he said with a devastating smile. "My heart is in jeopardy."

She giggled, delighted. "Stuff! Rakes like you don't *have* hearts. Everyone knows that."

Nicholas was enchanted. Could anything he said disconcert her? He doubted it.

"You wound me, love, if you compare my heart to Malory's."

"Never think it, sir," she assured him. "Tony's heart is as fickle as anyone's can be. Any man's heart would be more constant than his. Even yours," she said dryly.

This from the man's mistress? Nicholas couldn't believe his luck. She hadn't even sounded peevish about it. She simply accepted that Malory would never be faithful to her. Was she ripe for a change in lovers?

"Aren't you at all curious as to why I brought you here?" he asked. He was certainly curious. Why wasn't she upset?

"Oh, no," she replied lightly, "I have already figured that out."

"Have you?" He was amused, waiting to hear whatever outlandish explanation she had arrived at.

"You thought I was Lady Eddington," she said, "and you intended she miss the Shepford ball, while you attended and danced every dance. Did you?"

Nicholas shook himself. "What?"

"Dance every dance?"

"Not one."

"Well, you must have seen her there. Oh, I wish I could have seen your expression." She giggled again. "Were you terribly surprised?"

"Uh . . . terribly," he admitted. He was incredulous. How the devil had she put it all together? What had he said when he carried her up here?

"You have me at a disadvantage. I seem to have said a great deal to you earlier."

"Don't you remember?"

"Not clearly," he admitted weakly. "I'm afraid I was good and foxed."

"Well then, I suppose that excuses you, doesn't it? But you didn't really say all that much. It helps to know the people involved, you see."

"You *know* Lady Eddington?"

"Yes. Not well, of course. I only met her this week. But she was kind enough to lend me her carriage tonight."

He came away from the door suddenly then, crossing the room until he stood only inches away from her. She was even lovelier up close. She didn't move away, to his surprise, but looked up at him as if she trusted him fully.

"Who are you?" he asked in a hoarse whisper.

"Regina Ashton."

"Ashton?" He frowned thoughtfully. "Isn't that the family name of the Earl of Penwich?"

"Why, yes, do you know him?"

"No. He owns a piece of land bordering my own that I have been trying to buy for several years, but the pompous . . . he won't return my inquiries. You're not related to him, are you?"

"It is unfortunate, but yes, I am. At least the tie is quite distant."

Nicholas chuckled. "Most ladies would not think it unfortunate to be connected to an Earl."

"Really? Then they haven't met the present Earl of Penwich. I am happy to say I haven't seen the man for many years, but I doubt he has changed much. He is indeed a pompous . . ."

He grinned. "Who *are* your people, then?"

"I am an orphan, sir."

"I'm sorry."

"As am I. But I do have a loving family on my mother's side who saw to my upbringing. And now it is only fair for you to tell me who you are."

"Nicholas Eden."

"Fourth Viscount of Montieth? Oh dear, I *have* heard about you."

"Scandalous lies, I assure you."

"I doubt it." She grinned up at him. "But you needn't fear I'll think badly of you. After all, no one is quite as bad as Tony, or his brother James for that matter, and I love them both very much."

"Both? Tony *and* James Malory?" He was utterly stunned. "Good God, you don't mean you're James Malory's mistress, too!"

Her eyes widened for a moment. She bit her lip hard, but it didn't work. The laughter broke through in spite of her.

"I fail to see any humor," Nicholas began coldly.

"Oh, but there is, I assure you. I was afraid you might think Tony and I . . . oh, this is famous! I must tell Tony . . . no, I better not. He won't think it's funny. You men are so stuffy sometimes," she sighed. "You see, he's my uncle."

"If that is what you prefer to call him."

She laughed again. "You don't believe me, do you?"

"My dear Miss Ashton —"

"Lady Ashton," she corrected him.

"Very well — Lady Ashton. I'll have you know that Jason Malory's son, Derek Malory, is one of my closest friends —"

"I know."

"You do?"

"Yes, your best friend, actually. You went to school with him, though you finished a few years before he did. You took a liking to him when others did not. He loved you for that. I loved you, too, for befriending him, though I was only eleven at the time he told me about it and I had never met you. Where do you think I heard about you, Lord Montieth? Cousin Derek used to go on and on about you when he came home on holiday."

"Why didn't he ever mention you, then?" Nicholas snapped.

"Why would he talk about me?" she asked. "I'm sure you and he had better things to talk about than the children in your families."

Nicholas frowned darkly. "You could be making all of this up."

"Of course I could." She left it like that, without trying to convince him.

Her eyes sparkled with laughter. Damnation, she was beautiful.

"How old are you?" he asked.

"So you're not angry anymore?"

"Was I angry?"

"Oh, my, yes." She smiled. "I can't imagine why. *I* am the one who should have been angry. And I'm nineteen, if you must know, though you shouldn't have asked."

He began to relax again. She was wonderful. He couldn't bear much more. He wanted to hug her, yet he was loath to remind her of the impropriety of their situation.

"Is this your first season, Regina?"

She liked the way he said her name. "You are conceding that I am who I say I am?"

"I suppose I must."

"You don't have to sound so disappointed about it," she retorted.

"I'm devastated, if you must know." His voice became husky and he allowed himself to run a finger along her cheek, gently, so as not to frighten her. "I don't want you to be an innocent. I want you to know exactly what I mean when I tell you I want to make love to you, Regina."

Her heart began to beat faster. "Do you?" she whispered. She shook herself. She must not lose control. "Yes, of course you do," she teased him. "I thought I saw that look in your eyes."

His hand dropped to his side and his eyes narrowed. "How would you know that look?"

"Oh, my, you're angry again," she said innocently.

"Bloody hell!" he snapped. "Can't you be serious?"

"If I become serious, Lord Montieth, then

we'll both be in trouble."

Her dark eyes were inscrutable. Good Lord, there was another girl entirely beneath that effervescent surface.

She stepped past him and moved to the center of the room, and when she turned back to look at him, the gamin smile and teasing sparkle were back in place.

"This is my second season, and I have met many men just as improper as you," she assured him.

"I don't believe that."

"That there are men as improper as you?"

"That this is your second season. Are you married?"

"You imply that I should be, because I was brought out last year? Alas, as far as my family is concerned, there is no one good enough for me. A most annoying circumstance, I assure you."

Nicholas laughed. "It is too bad I sailed to the West Indies last year to inspect some property I have there. I would have met you sooner if I'd stayed here."

"Would you have tried for my hand?"

"I would have tried for — some part of you."

For the first time, Reggie blushed. "That was too bold."

"But not as bold as I would like to be."

Oh, he truly was dangerous, Reggie thought. Handsome, charming, wicked. Then why wasn't she frightened of being alone with Nicholas Eden? Common sense told her she should be.

She watched breathlessly as he came toward her, closing the space between them again. She didn't move away, and he smiled. A tiny pulse was beating at the base of her throat and he had an overwhelming desire to run his tongue over it, feel the pulse beating there.

"I wonder, are you as innocent as you claim to be, Regina Ashton?"

She couldn't give in to him, no matter how strongly he worked his magic on her. "Knowing who my family is, you really can't doubt me, Lord Montieth."

"You haven't been scandalized by my bringing you here," he blurted. "Why is that?" He studied her face closely.

"Oh, I suppose I saw the humor in it," she confessed, but then she added, "I was worried for a while, however, when I thought Uncle Tony might find out where you took me and come pounding on your door before you returned to let me go. That would have caused a fine commotion! I don't see how we could have kept a secret like that for long, and you might have ended up having to marry me. Such a shame, because we really wouldn't suit."

"Wouldn't we?" he asked, amused.

"Certainly not!" she said in mock horror. "I would fall madly in love with you, while you would continue to be a disreputable rake and break my heart."

"You are undoubtedly right," he sighed, playing along. "I would make a terrible husband. Nor am I likely to be forced into marriage, by the way."

"Not even if you have ruined my reputation?"

His mouth turned down. "Not even then."

She evidently didn't like his answer, and he was annoyed with himself for being so unnecessarily honest. Anger with himself made his bright amber eyes even brighter, as if an unnatural light glowed behind them. She shivered, wondering what he would be like if he really lost his temper.

"Are you cold?" he asked, seeing her rub the gooseflesh on her arms. Did he dare wrap his arms around her?

She reached for her cape and draped it loosely over her slim shoulders. "I think it's time —"

"I've frightened you," he said gently. "That wasn't my intention."

"I am afraid I know perfectly well what

your intentions are, sir," Reggie replied.

She bent down to put her slippers on, and when she straightened, she found herself in his arms. He did it so swiftly that she was being kissed before she could gasp. He tasted of brandy, sweet and intoxicating. Oh, she'd known it would be like this, so heavenly.

Never had she been kissed with such feeling, or such daring. He actually molded her small frame to his, letting her feel for the first time the state of a man's arousal. She was shocked and excited, and her breasts tingled where they pressed against his coat. What was this other, deeper feeling coming from way down inside her?

His lips trailed along her cheek and down to her throat, where he kissed the throbbing pulse, drawing the skin into his mouth, sucking ever so gently.

"You mustn't," Reggie managed to whisper. It didn't sound like her own voice at all.

"Oh, but I must, love, I really must." He scooped her in his arms.

She gasped. There was nothing amusing about what was happening now. His lips brushed her throat again and she groaned.

"Put me down," she said breathlessly. "Derek will hate you."

"I don't care."

"My uncle will kill you."

"It will be worth it."

That did it. "You won't think so when you see his weapon across a dueling field. Now put me *down,* Lord Montieth!"

Nicholas set her down slowly, carefully, causing her body to slide enticingly along his. "You would care, then?"

He was holding her close to him, and the steady heat of his body unsettled her. "Certainly. I wouldn't like to see you die because of a — a harmless escapade."

"Is that what you'd call my making love to you?" he chuckled, delighted.

"I was not referring to that, but to your bringing me here. As it is, I will have the devil's own time talking Tony round to forgetting this matter."

"You mean to protect me, then?" Nicholas said softly.

Reggie pushed away from him, unable to think clearly with her body against his. Her cape had fallen, and he retrieved it gallantly, handing it back to her with a bow.

She sighed. "If Tony doesn't know you are the one who absconded with me, then I shan't mention your name. If he does know, then, well, I suppose I will do my best to save your hide. But I insist you return me to him now, before he does something foolish, such as telling others I am missing."

"At least you give me hope." Nicholas smiled. "I may not make a good husband, but I have been told I make an excellent lover. Will you consider me?"

She was shocked. "I don't want a lover."

"I will have to follow you this season until I change your mind," he warned her.

He was incorrigible, she thought as, at last, he escorted her out of the house, incorrigible and very tempting. Tony had better be successful with Uncle Jason on her behalf, because Nicholas Eden could be a girl's downfall.

CHAPTER 6

"I'm sorry you missed the ball."

Nicholas stopped his carriage a few doors away from Anthony Malory's townhouse. His eyes caressed Reggie's face.

She grinned. "I'll wager you're even sorrier that Lady Eddington didn't miss it."

"You would lose the wager," he replied with a sigh. "I don't know why I did it anyway. The drink, I suppose. It's certainly doesn't matter one bit now."

"Stuff! You were jealous when you thought she was seeing Tony."

"Wrong again. I have never been jealous in my life, of anyone or anything."

"My, how fortunate for you."

"You don't believe me?"

"I don't see any other reason for your wanting to lock your mistress away for the evening. You didn't even plan to spend the evening with her."

He laughed. "You say that with such a

worldly air."

She blushed. "At any rate, you needn't be sorry that I missed the ball. I'm not."

"Because you met me instead?" he ventured. "You give me more and more hope, love."

She sat up stiffly. "I hate to disappoint you, Lord Montieth, but that is not the reason. I would as well have stayed at home tonight."

"As would I have, if you were with me. There's still time, you know. We can return to my house."

She shook her head at him, wanting to laugh. In fact, since meeting him, she had felt a continual ridiculous urge to laugh for the sheer joy of it. She was bubbling over. But she knew she had to leave him now and put this night behind her.

"I must go," she said softly.

"I suppose you must." His fingers closed over her gloved hand, but he made no move to help her down from the carriage. He exerted a pressure on her hand that held her in place. "I want to kiss you again before you go."

"No."

"Just a good-night kiss."

"No."

His free hand cupped her cheek. He

hadn't bothered to collect his gloves or hat before they left his house, and his bare fingers were hot against her skin. She couldn't move, and she waited breathlessly for him to steal the kiss she had refused him.

He did, his lips moving in to fasten on hers for a kiss that was nothing like any kiss she'd had before. Warm and masterful, his lips tasted hers until she thought she would explode.

"Come on, before I forget myself," he said roughly. Passion made his voice heavy.

Reggie was dazed as he helped her down from the carriage and led her toward her uncle's townhouse. "You'd better not come with me," she whispered. Lamps burned on each side of the door, and she could just picture the door opening and Tony facing Nicholas Eden with a gun in his hand. "It isn't necessary for you to accompany me."

"My dear, I may be many reprehensible things, but no one has ever said of me that I was not a gentleman, and a gentleman sees a lady to her door."

"Stuff! You're a gentleman only when it pleases you to be one, and now it pleases you to be obstinate."

Nicholas chuckled at her anxiety. "Do you fear for my safety?"

"Yes, I do. Tony is an agreeable fellow

most of the time, but there are occasions when he simply has no control over his temper. He mustn't see you until I have been able to tell him that nothing untoward has happened."

Nicholas stopped and turned her around to face him. "If he has such a violent temper, then I will not let you face him alone."

He thought to protect *her* from Tony. She might have laughed, but she suppressed the urge. "You would have to understand how it is between Tony and me to know that I am the last person who needs to fear him. We are very close, you see, so close that he regularly turns his life upside down for me when I stay with him. He always has, even abstaining from most of his usual pursuits for months at a time. *You* should be able to appreciate what that means," she finished dryly.

He led her forward again, grinning. "I concede your point. Nevertheless, there is a reason for everything I do, and I *will* see you to your door."

She started to protest again, but they were already there. She tensed, praying they hadn't been heard, that the door wouldn't open. She turned to face Nicholas, whispering, "What possible reason could you — ?"

But he interrupted roguishly, "You see, I now have an excuse to kiss you good night again."

He folded her in his arms, his mouth coming down to sear hers. This was passion, hot, blistering passion that melted her into him. Nothing else mattered. In that moment, she was his.

Nicholas ended the kiss with passion riding him hard. He nearly shoved her away from him, though without releasing her, his fingers biting into her upper arms. He held her there at arm's length, his breathing harsh, his eyes blazing.

"I want you, sweet Regina. Don't make me wait too long before you admit you want me, too."

It took Reggie a moment to realize that he had let her go and begun walking away. She had the wildest urge to run after him but steadied herself. It wasn't easy. Her heart was racing and her legs were wobbly.

Get hold of yourself, goose, she scolded herself. *You've been kissed before.* But oh, never like that!

Reggie waited until she saw Nicholas step into his carriage before she reluctantly turned away, opened the door, and went inside. The entry and hall were brightly lit and, thankfully, empty. The door to Tony's library-study was open and light spilled out of it. She moved toward it slowly, hoping Tony would be there and not out scouring London for her.

He was there, sitting at his desk with his head in his hands, the fingers twined in his thick black hair as if he'd been trying to pull it out. A decanter of brandy and a glass were beside him.

The sight of him looking so woebegone had a steadying effect on Reggie. Guilt helped her pull herself together. While she had been having the sweetest time of her life, the person who meant the most to her in all the world had been worried sick. And she hadn't even rushed back here. She'd taken her time, enjoying every moment spent with Nicholas. How could she have been so selfish?

"Tony?"

He looked up in shock. Then surprise washed over his handsome features, and relief. He hurried to her and gathered her into his arms, squeezing so tightly she thought her ribs would crack.

"Good God, Reggie, I've been half-baked with worry! I haven't been in such bad shape since James took you with him to — well, never mind that now." He set her away from him so he could look her over. "Are you all right? Have you been hurt?"

"I'm fine, Tony, really I am."

She looked fine too. No rents in her gown, no curls out of place. But she had been gone for three bloody hours, and the things he had imagined happening to her . . .

"I'm going to kill him first thing in the morning, as soon as I find out where the bloody hell he lives!"

So that's why there had been no pounding on the doors, Reggie realized.

"It was all perfectly innocent, Tony," she began, "a mistake —"

"I *know* it was a mistake, Reggie. That idiot driver of yours assured me of that. He kept insisting Montieth would bring you back at any moment, that he and Lady Eddington were, ah . . . that they . . . well, I think you know what I mean. Oh, bloody hell!"

"Yes." Reggie grinned at his discomfort. "I do know what you mean." Then she hastened to work him round. "The poor man thought you and his —"

"Don't say it! And that's no excuse anyway!"

"But can't you imagine his expression, Tony, when he saw that he had the wrong lady?" Reggie giggled. "Oh, I wish I could have seen him."

Anthony frowned. "How is it that you didn't see him?"

"I wasn't there. He left me at his house and went to the ball. You see his only intent was to make Lady Eddington miss the ball. You can understand how shocked he was when he saw her there. He didn't know who the devil he had locked up in his house."

"He locked you in his house?"

"But I was perfectly comfortable," she assured him quickly. "And so you see that I wasn't with him all this time — very little time in fact. No harm was done, and he brought me back here safe and sound."

"I can't believe you're defending him. If I had known where he lives, he'd be dead by now. The fool driver didn't know. I sent a man round to the clubs to make inquiries, but because of that blasted ball the clubs were nearly deserted. By the time my man got back to report that he hadn't learned anything, I was bloody well ready to hie myself off to Shepford's to find someone who could give me that scoundrel's address."

"And then Uncle Edward would have been alerted that I wasn't with you, and all hell would have broken loose," she finished for him. "It's a good thing you didn't do that. This way no one knows I haven't been

87

here with you all evening. Which means that all that is left to do is decide whether I should stay here or return to Uncle Edward's house. What do you suggest?"

"Oh, no you don't, my girl." He saw right through her ploy. "You are not going to get me to forget about this."

"If you don't, then I am ruined," she said quite seriously. "Because no one will ever believe that I spent three hours in Lord Montieth's house and came away with my virtue intact. It is intact, by the way."

He glared at her. "Then I won't kill him. But he will be taught a lesson he richly deserves."

"But no harm was done, Tony!" she insisted passionately. "And — and I don't want you to hurt him."

"You don't — by God, you'll tell me why!"

"I like him," she said simply. "He reminds me of you."

Lord Malory turned livid. "I *will* kill him!"

"Stop!" she cried. "You would never have forced yourself on an unwilling maid, and neither did he."

"Did he kiss you?"

"Well —"

"Of course he did. Only a fool wouldn't, and he's no fool. I'll —"

"No, you won't!" she cried again. "You

will pretend you never learned his name, and when you see him, you will ignore him. You will do that for me, Tony, because I don't know if I would be able to forgive you if you did anything to hurt Nicholas Eden. I enjoyed myself tonight, more than I have for a very long time." Having said so much, she pleaded with him, "Please, Uncle Tony."

He started to say something, clamped his mouth shut, scowled, sighed heavily, and finally said gently, "He's not for you, puss. You know that, don't you?"

"Yes, I do. If he were a little less disreputable, though, I would set my cap for him."

"Over my dead body!"

She gave him her sweetest smile.

"Somehow I knew you would say that."

CHAPTER 7

Reggie sat at her dressing table, staring dreamily at the little bruise on the base of her throat. Nicholas Eden's love mark. She touched the spot. It was fortunate she had not removed her cape when she returned to Tony's house last night. As it was, she would have to wear a scarf until the mark went away.

It was late in the morning, and she had slept much longer than was her habit. Her cousins would have breakfasted already, and if they were still at home, she would have to go through the story she and Tony had come up with last night.

Tony had sent a message to his brother Edward before she returned home, saying simply that Reggie would not be coming to the ball after all. Only that, no reason given. Their story was that Tony hadn't been at home when she got to his house, so she had waited for him for hours. When he did arrive, they had their talk. As it was so late after their conversation, she had simply gone home to bed. The servants at Uncle Edward's would confirm that Tony had brought her back there and she had indeed gone right to bed.

Reggie sighed and rang for Meg, then hastily went through her bureau in search of a scarf. Meg mustn't see her lovebite either.

When she came downstairs a half hour later, it was to find Aunt Charlotte and cousins Clare and Diana receiving. They were in the drawing room with their visitors — the Ladys Braddock, mother and daughter; Mrs. Faraday and her sister Jane; and two ladies Reggie didn't know. They all stared at her as she entered, and Reggie became most uncomfortable over the lies she was about to tell.

"My dear Regina," Mrs. Faraday spoke in a strangely sympathetic tone. "How divine you look — considering."

Reggie felt a tight knot forming in the pit of her stomach. No. It wasn't possible. Only her own guilty conscience made her think they could know about last night's escapade.

Nicholas Eden, Fourth Viscount Eden of Montieth, lay stretched out on his large bed, his arms tucked behind his head, only a thin sheet covering his nakedness. He had lain there after waking for nearly an hour, but made no move to get up and face the day. He had long since missed his usual morning ride through Hyde Park. There was nothing immediate that he needed to see to. Another letter to the Earl of Penwich demanding an answer about the land he wanted, but that could wait. It was bound to be only a source of irritation anyway, since he'd never received an answer from the man.

He needed to contact the manager of his shipping firm in Southampton to cancel the ship he had recently ordered made ready for him. He had planned to put London behind him for a few months, to sail to the West Indies again. But as of last evening, nothing could make him leave London.

Her name was Regina. He said the name aloud, letting it roll deliciously off of his tongue. Regina. Sweet, fair Regina with ebony hair and china-blue eyes. Those eyes. He had only to close his own eyes to see them smiling at him, laughing. Oh, they possessed such life. Regina, fairest of the fair, beauty beyond compare.

Nicholas chuckled at his fancy. Percy would say he had fallen head over heels.

Had he? Well, no, of course not. But he couldn't remember ever wanting a woman as much as he did Regina Ashton.

He sighed. Aunt Ellie would tell him to marry the girl and be happy. She was the only one since his father had died who cared a damn about Nicholas. Perhaps his grandmother did, or perhaps she didn't. It was hard to tell about Rebecca, the old tyrant.

And, of course, there was his "mother." She would be the last to wish him well. It was because of her that he couldn't — or wouldn't — marry Regina or any girl of good family. He wouldn't marry, at least not until the woman who was known to the world as his mother was dead. The threat she held over him would die with her.

Nicholas threw his sheet off and sat up, thoughts of the Dowager Countess ruining his pleasant idyll. It was because of her that he very seldom went home to Silverley, his country estate in Hampshire. Yet he loved Silverley, missed it to the point of bitterness. No matter, the only times he would go there were when the Countess was away. She was in residence most of the year, just to keep Nicholas away.

He rang for his man Harris and was informed that the Lords Alden and Malory were waiting for him in the breakfast room.

He gave no special thought to it, for those two friends often dropped by without prior notice.

When he joined them a short while later, Derek Malory was seated at the table with a large plate of food, and Percy stood by the sideboard sipping coffee. Derek offered a merry hello before he went back to teasing the young maid. Percy beckoned Nicholas to him with a conspiratorial grin.

"I know who the little bird is that you brought home to your nest last night," Percy whispered, then nodded toward Derek. "*He* doesn't know yet, but of course he will before the day is out."

Nicholas felt as if a mighty fist had been slammed into his midsection. He kept his voice calm when he whispered, "Be so good as to tell me how that information reached you?"

"It's not a secret," Percy chuckled. "In fact, I'll wager it will have made the complete rounds by the end of the day. I heard it on Rotten Row myself. Rode up to a couple of pretties I know and they couldn't wait to tell me the latest *on-dit.*"

"How?" This came out explosively, loud enough to gain a look from Derek, who then turned back to the maid.

"Lady E., don't you know. It seems her

driver thought she would be most interested in hearing all about your wicked scheme. And wouldn't you know, she was tickled pink to think you were jealous enough to do something so outrageous. She couldn't wait to tell all her dearest friends about it — and even those who are not so dear. Oh, she has had a busy morning of it."

"Damnation take the bitch!"

"Yes, well, if I were you, I would be leaving London for a while."

"And let the girl face this alone?"

"That never bothered you before."

For that remark Percy received the blackest scowl. "Don't bark at me, Nick. She'll fare better than you, no doubt get married off as your other innocents were, and live happily ever after. But there's Derek's uncle to think about, not to mention his father. This girl's got relatives who will demand your hide. You're not going to come off without a scratch for compromising this girl like you did the others."

"Blister it, I didn't touch the girl."

" 'Course you didn't, but who'd believe it?" Percy said pointedly. "Your best bet is to be gone before the challenge comes from one of her uncles."

At that moment Tyndale appeared at the door and announced, "Lord Malory's ser-

95

vant begs a word, my lord."

Derek looked up in surprise, seeing the servant standing behind Tyndale. "Oh, I say, Nicky, there must be some mistake. The chap doesn't work for me."

"I didn't think so," Nicholas muttered, and Percy groaned.

CHAPTER 8

"No!"

Anthony Malory looked up as his niece ran into the room and stared wide-eyed at the pistol he was cleaning at his desk. He gave her an impatient look before he went back to examining the weapon.

"It's too late for nos, Reggie."

"You've already killed him!" she cried.

He didn't look up, so he didn't see the color wash from her cheeks. "I've sent a man round to his house. I had no trouble learning the address this morning. He should be here soon to discuss the time and place."

"No, no, no!"

When he glanced up, her eyes were shooting sparks at him. "Now, Reggie —" he began, but she advanced on him.

"Is that your answer to everything?" She stabbed a finger at the weapon in his hands. "I thought we had this settled last night?"

"That was before Montieth's escapade became food for the gossipmongers. Or are you not aware that your name is on everyone's lips this morning?"

Reggie flinched but said evenly, "I do know it. I just left a room full of women who couldn't wait to offer their sympathies."

"And what did you tell them?"

"Well, I couldn't very well deny that it had happened, because Lady Eddington's driver witnessed the whole thing. But I did lie and say that I was brought right back, that Lord Montieth had realized his mistake quickly."

Anthony shook his head. "Which they didn't believe. Did they?"

"Well, no," she admitted reluctantly.

"Because that bloody driver waited a good hour for you to be returned, and everyone knows it. And it doesn't take an hour to do what is being said was done. Your lying about it only suggests that you have something to hide."

"But that's not true!"

"Since when does the truth matter to passionate gossips?"

"Oh, what am I going to do, Tony?" she cried miserably.

"You will do nothing. You will weather it, with the support of your family. *He* will pay the price for besmirching your good name."

98

"You will not challenge him."

Anthony's eyes narrowed. "If I don't, Jason will, and Jason will get himself killed. He's not the shot I am."

"No one is going to be killed, Tony." She said this as if the matter were entirely up to her. "There has to be another solution. That's why I came. I thought I would be too late to catch you before you left town, though. How did you find out?"

"I was, in fact, leaving town, and my old friend George hailed me to give me warning that the cat was out of the bag. It's bloody damned fortunate that I was late getting started this morning. Otherwise I'd be halfway to Gloucester by now, and old Eddie would have been left to deal with this. I can just imagine the mess he'd make of it."

"At least his answer wouldn't be to grab the nearest pistol," she retorted.

Anthony made a face. "Does he know yet?"

"No. He was closeted in his office all morning. He still is. Aunt Charlotte said she would try and keep it from him as long as possible. I thought maybe you wouldn't mind . . ."

"Coward. Eddie isn't the one you need to worry about, though. It's Jason who is going to fly through the roof."

"Well, at least he won't hear about it for some time."

"Don't count on that, puss. He'll know by the end of the day, tomorrow at the latest. You think he doesn't keep tabs on you when you're in wicked old London?"

"He doesn't!"

"Oh, but he does," Anthony assured her. "He had regular reports on you when you were in Europe, too. Nothing escapes Jason. Even I am not shielded from his all-seeing eye. How do you think he finds out so quickly about all my bloody scrapes?"

Reggie groaned. This was going from bad to worse. Jason could be just as hot-tempered as Tony. Besides that, he was a man of rigid principles. When there was any question of honor, his could not be tampered with.

For him there would be only one solution, and if that didn't work, he would be cleaning his pistols just as Tony was. But that first solution was intolerable. Nicholas Eden would never agree. He would rather face one of her uncles across the dueling field than be forced to marry, she was sure of it.

She worried at her lower lip. "There must be something we can do, Tony, some story we can invent."

"Any one of a dozen, puss, but not one

will be believed. The trouble is that Montieth has seduced innocents like you before. That he was alone with you — never mind that it wasn't you he meant to be alone with — implies that he took advantage of the situation. He is such a handsome devil, you couldn't have resisted him. That's what people will think. And say."

Reggie blushed and looked away uncomfortably.

"I don't know why I'm even discussing this with you," Anthony continued curtly. "There is only one thing to be done, and it's up to me to see it done."

Reggie sighed. "You're right, of course. I don't know why I've been resisting the idea so."

He raised a suspicious brow. "No tricks, Reggie."

"No tricks. You will see that he marries me. That is the only thing to be done."

"Bloody hell!" Anthony shot to his feet in full fury. "He's not good enough for you!"

"Nevertheless —"

"No! And no again! And don't think I'm not on to you, Regina Ashton. You think this will solve your other problem, and you won't have to look for a husband anymore."

"Now that you mention it . . . oh, Tony, I really wouldn't mind having him for a husband, really I wouldn't. And he reminds me of you."

"He is too much like me, which is exactly why he's not for you!"

"But he reminds me of Uncle Edward, too. And there's also a touch of Uncle Jason in him. Why, he was quite put out when I suggested that what he had done would ruin me and he would have to marry me."

"You said that?"

"I was in that kind of mood. And he got angry. He acted just as Uncle Jason would have."

"Why, that —"

"No, no, Tony. He's perfect, don't you see? A little like all of you — just what I have been looking for. And besides, it will be a challenge to reform him."

"He'll never change, Reggie," Tony insisted. "He'll never settle down."

"Oh, I don't know." She grinned. "We might make that statement about you, but we don't know for sure about him. And he did like me. That's a start."

"Don't let's put a nice face on it," Anthony said. "He wanted you. But he'll want other women, too, and he'll go after them. He won't be a faithful husband."

"I think I know that," she said quietly.

"And you still want him?"

She didn't want him dead. That was the alternative. "After all," she said quietly, "he should make things right. He has involved me in a scandal, so he should be the one to get me out of it. This is a peaceful solution, and I'm sure Uncle Jason will wholeheartedly agree."

"This is not what I would call Montieth getting his just deserts." Anthony glowered. "He'll be getting you into the bargain, while you will go on suffering."

"He won't see it that way, Tony. In fact, I'm positive he'll refuse."

"Good." Anthony smiled and went back to cleaning his pistol.

"Oh, no," Reggie said. "You must promise me you'll do your best to convince him, Tony."

"All right," he agreed.

He was smiling in a way that made her want to hit him. She knew that smile too well.

"I want Uncle Edward to be with you when you speak to him," she said suspiciously.

"But your Viscount will be here soon, puss," he reminded her.

"Then come with me to see Uncle Edward now. Leave a message for Lord Montieth to return this evening. And Tony," she added slowly, untying her scarf, "I think Uncle Edward should see this, to impress on him the importance of getting Montieth's consent."

Anthony's face darkened. "You said he only kissed you!"

She tied the scarf again, her look quite innocent. "Well, that *was* caused by a kiss, Tony."

"How dare he leave his mark on you?"

Reggie shrugged, carefully avoiding his eyes. "Do you think Uncle Edward will make too much of the mark and assume the worst? I suppose he will feel it's his duty to inform Uncle Jason of it. You don't think they'll want to rush the wedding, do you? I would rather wait a few months, just to be sure my first child is born after a decent interval of time."

"This is blackmail, Reggie."

She opened her dark blue eyes wide. "Is it?"

"Jason should have taken a switch to your backside when you first developed this talent for manipulating people."

"What a terrible thing to say!" Reggie gasped.

He laughed then, shaking his head at her. "You can drop the performance, puss. I'll get your Viscount to marry you, one way or another."

She hugged him, her delight evident. "And there'll be no more talk of killing?"

"None that will matter," he sighed. "Since Eddie is the logical, business-minded one of us, perhaps he can come up with something to bring the man round without resorting to violence."

He disengaged himself and turned to put the gun away. "You said Montieth wouldn't agree, Reggie, and when a man is stubborn, it takes persuasion to change his mind. You can still change *your* mind, you know." He looked at her intently.

"No. The more I think about it, the more I feel this is the right thing to do."

"He might hate you for it, you know. Have you thought about that?"

"He might, yes, but I will take the chance. I wouldn't consider marriage if he hadn't found me attractive. But he did try to seduce me — *try,* I said. No, he will be my husband, Tony. Tell Uncle Edward and Uncle Jason that I will have no other."

"Very well, then," Tony replied, then added with a sharp look, "but you will keep that blasted scarf on, hear? There is no point in my brothers thinking any worse of their future nephew-in-law than they have to."

CHAPTER 9

It was half past ten o'clock in the evening, and Nicholas sat in his carriage outside Edward Malory's house in Grosvenor Square, thirty minutes late for his appointment, but making no move to leave his carriage.

He had given up trying to guess what this was all about. He had understood that morning's summons from Anthony Malory perfectly well, but since that earlier meeting had not come to pass, he no longer knew what to think. He couldn't conceive of Derek's businesslike Uncle Edward demanding a duel, but what else could this be about? Bloody hell!

Reggie watched the dark carriage from an upstairs window, her nervousness having increased to terror. He was not going to like what she had set in motion. No, most assuredly not. He must suspect why he'd been called there. Why else would he hesitate to come inside?

Oh, Uncle Edward had had quite a lot to say about Lord Montieth, emphatic that she know exactly what she was letting herself in for. He had known the Eden family for years, had been very good friends with Nicholas' father, in fact. So Reggie knew it all now, including the stories of the other young women he had embroiled in scandal because they were weak enough to succumb to his charm. He was irresponsible, he was without conscience, he could be cold and arrogant, or ill-tempered. The charm he showed the ladies was not all there was to the man. Yes, she'd heard it all, but to Uncle Tony's disgust, she had not changed her mind.

Reggie was using Amy's room to peek out of the window, thanking her stars that she was alone upstairs. Aunt Charlotte had gathered her whole brood of children, all of them protesting vehemently, and descended on a friend outside London for the night. Reggie had been allowed to stay so that she would not have to wait until the next day to learn her fate. But she was to remain upstairs and not interfere in any way. Uncle Tony had been adamant about that. Even if she heard all hell breaking loose, she was not to venture downstairs.

Nicholas was relieved of his hat and gloves and escorted to the drawing room. The house surprised him by being much larger than it appeared on the outside. He knew that Edward Malory had several children; and the house was certainly big enough to accommodate a large family. The top two floors were probably all bedrooms, he thought, and the downstairs big enough to include even a ballroom.

"They are waiting, my lord," the butler announced as they reached the drawing room door. No expression crossed the servant's face, but his tone was disapproving. Nicholas nearly chuckled. He knew he was late.

All humor disappeared, however, when the butler opened the door, then closed it behind Nicholas. On a cream-colored sofa sat Eleanor Marston, his spinster Aunt Ellie; and beside her, Rebecca Eden, his formidable grandmother. At the moment, she looked ready to call down the wrath of God upon his head.

So. He was to be called on the carpet, was he? Lectured to by his own family as well as Regina's? His one surprise was that they hadn't summoned his "mother," Miriam. How she would have enjoyed this!

"So you finally mustered the courage to come inside, scamp?" the old dame began without preamble.

"Rebecca?" Eleanor admonished.

Nicholas smiled. He knew his grandmother didn't doubt his nerve any more than he did. She simply liked to ruffle his feathers. Aunt Ellie was always quick to come to his defense, bless her. She was, in fact, the only one who dared admonish the old dame. Aunt Ellie had lived with the old woman for twenty years as her companion, and he marveled at her stamina, for his grandmother was a true tyrant, ruling all around her with an iron will.

Long ago, Eleanor had lived with Miriam and Charles Eden at Silverley, in the first few years of his parents' marriage, before Nicholas was born. But the constant bickering between the two sisters had sent Ellie back to her parents. Later, she had gone to visit Charles' mother, Rebecca, out in Cornwall. She'd been there ever since that "visit," coming to visit Silverley often through the years, but only to visit, not to stay.

"How are you, madame?" he asked his grandmother.

"As if *you* care how I am," she retorted. "Do I come to London every year at this time?" she asked him.

"You have made that your habit, yes."

"But have you paid me a visit once since I arrived?"

"I saw you in Cornwall only last month," Nicholas reminded her.

"That is not the point." Then she leaned back and said, "Well, you surely have fallen into it this time, haven't you?"

"So it would seem," he replied dryly, then turned to face the two Malory men.

The older man came forward to greet him cordially. Big and blond and green-eyed, Edward Malory looked nothing like his brother Anthony, and everything like his brother Jason. He was an inch shorter than Nicholas' own six feet, but his build was stockier.

The younger Malory man stood rooted to his place by the fireplace. Dark blue eyes seemed to be envisioning Nicholas' dismemberment. Malory's vivid blue eyes and coal-black hair announced to Nicholas that Regina Ashton was Anthony's blood relation. It was more than that. She actually bore a startling resemblance to Anthony, even to the slight slanting of the eyes. Good God, he wondered, could Regina be his daughter? That would mean he'd sowed his oats a bit young, but it wasn't impossible.

"We haven't met, Nicholas," Edward Malory said and introduced himself. "But I knew your father Charles very well, and I've known Rebecca for some years."

"Edward invests my money for me, and very nicely, too," Rebecca explained. "Didn't know that, did you, scamp?"

Well, that explained how they'd gotten his grandmother here on such short notice. The proximity to family was starting to make him nervous.

Edward continued, "And I believe you know my youngest brother, Anthony?"

"We've crossed each other's paths in the clubs from time to time," Nicholas replied, making no move toward Anthony.

Anthony didn't acknowledge him at all except to fry him with his eyes. He was as tall as Nicholas, and just as broad in the shoulders, too. A hellion since he was sixteen according to Derek. Nicholas wagered there were worse scandals in Anthony's past than this silly flap over Regina. What the hell did Anthony have to look so condemning about?

"That one wants your head on a platter, scamp," his grandmother spoke in the growing silence. Ellie tried to shush her, but she wouldn't be shushed.

"I am already aware of that, madame,"

111

Nicholas said, facing Anthony. "Do we name the time, my lord?"

Anthony chuckled wryly. "By God, I really think you'd rather. But much as I would love to accommodate you, I have promised to let them deal with you first."

Nicholas looked around at the others. Sympathy poured from Ellie's brown eyes, and Edward looked resigned. Nicholas' nervousness increased suddenly, and he fixed his gaze on Anthony again.

"My lord," he said stiffly. "I would like to settle with you."

"My niece would have it otherwise."

"She what?"

"She's too kindhearted by half," Anthony sighed. "Doesn't want to see you hurt — more's the pity." He shook his head.

"Nevertheless, I do believe —"

"No, by God!" Rebecca thundered. "I wasn't around to stop those other duels you involved yourself in, but I'll stop this one. I'll have you thrown in jail first, my boy; see if I don't."

Nicholas tried to smile. "The man wants satisfaction, madame. I can offer no other."

"Lord Anthony will settle for something other than a duel because he loves his niece. We may be thankful for that."

"We? I cannot be thankful, madame."

"We can do without your satirical wit, too," she said. "You may be a damned arrogant, irresponsible pup, but you are the last Eden. You will get yourself an heir before you go throwing your life away on a dueling field."

Nicholas flinched. "Nicely put, madame. But what makes you think I don't already have an heir to give you?"

"I know you better than that. Although it often looks as though you're trying to populate the world, you have no bastards. And you know I would never accept one, anyway."

"Is this necessary, Rebecca?" Eleanor asked hastily.

"Yes, it is," the old woman replied, looking pointedly at the two Malory brothers.

"Nicky?" Eleanor beseeched him, and Nicholas sighed.

"Very well, I admit I have no bastards, either male or female. You are quite correct, madame. It is one thing I am most careful about."

"The only thing."

He gave her a slight bow but made no reply. His manner was casual, even bored, but Nicholas was seething inside. He enjoyed verbal battles with his grandmother when they were alone, but not in the company of others. She knew it and was baiting him just to be ornery.

"Oh, do be seated, Nicholas," Rebecca said testily, "I'm tired of craning my neck to look at you."

"Is this going to take long then?" He grinned maddeningly before taking the chair across from her.

"Please don't be difficult, Nicky," Eleanor beseeched again.

He was taken aback. This, from Ellie? She had always been the one he could talk to, the one who understood the bitterness just below his surface. While he was growing up, she'd always been a shoulder to cry on. How many times had he ridden the long road between Hampshire and Cornwall in the thick of night just to see her? After he grew up, she was still closer to him than anybody. She never even scolded him for the way he lived. It was almost as if she knew why he did the things he did.

She didn't, of course. Only Miriam knew the reason he was so reckless, why he forever walked a tightrope, never easing up.

Nicholas looked at his aunt tenderly. At forty-five, she was still good-looking, with light blond hair and soulful brown eyes. Her older sister Miriam had once been the prettier of the two, but bitterness had helped ravage Miriam's beauty. He liked to think Ellie's goodness had kept her so nicely.

This was the woman he had secretly pretended was his mother, all through childhood. Her expression told him many things, and she was as easy to read just then as she'd always been. She was sorry for his predicament. She was praying he wouldn't cause trouble. She was also in agreement with whatever had been decided behind his back. But would she side with his grandmother against him? She had never done that before. Did she really think he had ravished Regina Ashton? Oh, he might have seduced the girl if she'd been willing, yes, but the fact was that he hadn't seduced her. His conscience could overlook his intentions.

"Did they tell you all of it, Aunt Ellie?" he asked her.

"I believe so."

"They told you it was all a mistake?"

"Yes."

"And that I returned the girl unmolested?"

"Yes."

"Then what are you doing here?"

Rebecca frowned. "Leave her alone, scamp. It's not her fault you got yourself into this."

"We know whose fault it is," Anthony's

contemptuous voice sounded behind him.

Nicholas had had enough. "What is it to be then?" he demanded, turning around in his chair to look at Anthony.

"You already know what must be done, Nicky," Eleanor said with gentle reproof. "It is unfortunate that any of this happened. No one here believes that you meant to harm the girl, but the fact remains that her reputation *has* been irreparably damaged. She should not be made to suffer the humiliation of vicious gossip because one of your escapades went awry. You do see that, don't you?" She took a long, steadying breath. "You can do no less than accept responsibility for your actions. You must marry her."

CHAPTER 10

"I can't stand it, Meg, I really can't!" Reggie cried, agitation overcoming her.

The maid ignored the wail, just as she had ignored all the others. "Are you going to sleep in that scarf?"

Reggie put her hands to her throat. "Yes, of course. Uncle Edward may come to tell me what happened instead of Uncle Tony. I don't want anyone else to see it."

Meg frowned and went back to the sewing in her lap. She had seen the lovebite herself. Reggie couldn't hide anything from her, not for long anyway. She was outraged by the whole affair, and for once she was in complete accord with Anthony Malory instead of siding with the girl who sat cross-legged in the center of her bed, wringing her hands in an agony of suspense.

The Viscount Eden of Montieth should be shot, not given this treasure for a wife. Meg had never heard of anything so grossly unfair. Did you give the petty thief your purse with a thank-you-kindly? How could they give her precious Reggie to the man who was responsible for her shame?

"Will you go downstairs and see if you can hear anything, Meg?"

"No, I will not."

"Then I will."

"You will not either. You'll sit right there. Keep on worryin', if you like. Soon enough you'll be told he said yes."

"But that's the trouble." Reggie pounded her knees for emphasis. "He's going to say no."

Meg shook her head. "You won't convince me that you want him, my girl, so you can stop tryin'."

"But it's true, Meg."

"I know you too well, Reggie. You're just puttin' a good face on it, pretendin' for your uncles' sake, because this seems to be the only solution."

"Stuff." Reggie giggled, her humor breaking through. "You just won't admit that I'm wicked and shameful in wanting a man I only just met."

Meg looked up at her. "Now I see what you're about. You're for this because it will get you a husband quick and you won't have to be lookin' for one anymore. Admit it, my girl."

Reggie grinned. "That's an added bonus, yes."

"A bonus!" Meg snorted. "That's the only reason you want him. It must be."

"You won't say that after you get a look at him, Meg. I think I'm in love."

"If I believed that, I would go down there and kiss his feet. But you've got more sense than to think you're in love after one meeting."

"I suppose so," Reggie sighed, but her eyes twinkled. "It won't take long, though, Meg, really it won't. You wait and see."

"I hope I don't see it. I hope I don't see you married to him. It will be the sorriest day for you and if it happens, mark my words."

"Stuff," Reggie retorted.

"Just remember, I warned you."

"I won't marry her."

"Good." Anthony's smile was full of wicked pleasure. "I was against the idea from the start."

"Be still, Anthony," Edward warned him. "Nothing has been settled."

"I repeat, I won't marry her," Nicholas

said evenly, managing just barely to keep calm.

"You will be good enough to tell me why?" Edward's voice was also a study in tranquillity.

Nicholas said the first thing that came to mind. "She deserves better."

"Agreed," Anthony put in smoothly. "Under normal circumstances, you would never be considered."

Edward shot him a silencing look, then addressed Nicholas again. "If you are referring to your reputation, it precedes you. I am the first to admit it is unsavory. Yet such things must be overlooked now."

"I would make the girl miserable," Nicholas said quickly, with a bit more spirit.

"That is pure conjecture. You don't know Regina well enough to know what would make her happy or unhappy."

"You're just hedging, scamp," Rebecca said. "You have no good reason not to marry the girl, and you know it. And it's high time you were married, high time indeed."

"So I can produce your heir?" he replied.

"Now see here, Nicholas," Edward broke in. "Do you deny that you have embroiled my niece in a scandal?"

"Your niece?"

"Who the devil did you think she was, scamp?" Rebecca was exasperated.

Suddenly Anthony was laughing. "Tell me, Montieth, were you hoping she was illegitimate? A poor relation you could claim we were trying to foist off on you?"

"That will be enough," Edward warned again. "Nicholas . . . well, perhaps I shall have to concede that you didn't know who Regina was. Not many people remember Melissa, she died so long ago."

"Melissa?"

"Our only sister. She was much younger than Jason and I, the middle child. She was . . . well, I needn't elaborate on how precious she was to us, being the only girl in the midst of four boys. Regina is her only child."

"She's all they have left of Melissa," Rebecca added. "Do you begin to see how important Regina is to the Malory brothers?"

Nicholas was feeling sick.

"I should tell you, in regard to my brother's remark, that Regina is quite legitimate," Edward went on. "Melissa was happily married to the Earl of Penwich."

"Penwich!" Nicholas nearly choked on the name he had cursed so many times.

"The late Earl, Thomas Ashton," Edward

clarified. "Some obscure cousin has the title now. A disagreeable fellow, but he has no involvement with Regina. She has been under our care for the seventeen years since Melissa and Thomas died together in a terrible fire."

Nicholas' mind whirled. Bloody hell. She was in fact Derek's first cousin, the daughter of an Earl, niece to the Marquis of Haverston. He wouldn't be surprised to learn that she was also an heiress. She could easily have landed a husband with a better title than his. Could have. But now that he had linked her name to his, she wasn't quite the prize anymore, not to those families who wouldn't touch a girl with a scandal behind her. Everyone in the room knew it, including himself. Yet there were other men who would want her, regardless, men less rigid than some.

He said as much to Anthony. "*You* don't seem to think she has lost her chance at a good match, so why are you willing to settle for me?"

"Did I say I was, dear boy? No, no. She is the one who wants you, not I."

Nicholas cast about for a reply. "And as a favored niece, she gets want she wants?" he said.

"There is the simple fact," Edward intervened, "that if she married anyone else, the poor fellow would have to live with the scandal you have created being whispered behind his back for the rest of his life. That is a bit much for any man to take, and certainly wouldn't make for a happy marriage."

Nicholas frowned. "But she would tell her husband the truth."

"What does the truth matter when it is the untruth that is believed by everyone?" Edward replied testily.

"Am I to be held hostage to the narrow-mindedness of others, then?"

"What the devil is the matter with you, Nicholas?" Rebecca demanded. "I've met the girl and she is the loveliest little creature I've seen in a long time. You will never get a better match, and you know it. Why are you fighting this?"

"I don't want a wife — *any* wife," Nicholas said harshly.

"What you want became irrelevant," his grandmother retorted, "when you made off with an innocent girl whose family won't overlook it as others have. You're damned lucky they'll let you have her!"

"Be reasonable, Nicky," Eleanor chimed in. "You have to marry sometime. You can't go on forever as you've been doing. And this girl is charming, beautiful. She will make you a wonderful wife."

"Not my wife," he stated flatly. In the silence that followed, his hopes began to rise, but his grandmother dashed them.

"You'll never be the man your father was. Running off to sea for two years, coming back to live the life of a wastrel, delegating your responsibilities to agents and lackeys. By God, I'm ashamed to admit you're my grandson. And I tell you now, you may as well forget you know me if you don't own up and marry this girl." She stood up, her expression stony. "Come, Ellie. I have said all I will say to him."

Rebecca's face remained coldly unrelenting as she left the room, Ellie beside her. But once the door closed behind them, she turned to Eleanor and gave her a huge conspiratorial grin. "What say you, my dear? Do you think that did the trick?"

"That was a bit much about your being ashamed of him. You know you're not. Why, you delight in his wild escapade more than he does. I swear, Rebecca, you should have been a man."

"Don't I know it! But his little escapade is a godsend this time. I didn't think he would put up this much of a fight, though."

"Didn't you?" Eleanor retorted. "You

know why he won't marry. You know how he feels. Nicky refuses to force the stigma of his birth on an unsuspecting wife. He feels he cannot offer for a decent girl, yet his position makes it impossible for him to wed beneath his station. He decided simply never to wed. You know that."

Rebecca nodded, impatient, and said, "Which is why this is a godsend. Now he will have to marry, and into a good family, too. Oh, he doesn't like it one bit, but eventually he'll be glad. I tell you this girl won't give a toot if she ever learns the truth."

"Do you really believe that?"

"If I didn't, then she wouldn't be the one for him," Rebecca said stoutly.

They both knew exactly what motivated Nicholas, though he wasn't aware that they knew. To the world, Miriam was his mother, and the day she ended that pretense — as she often threatened to do — was the day he could stop living in dread of the revelation and become the pariah he was trying his best to become beforehand. He wanted to be thought wicked so as to become accustomed to the treatment he could expect if the truth came out.

"Someone ought to tell him that it probably wouldn't matter much if the truth did come out," Rebecca said. "No one would believe it anyhow, not after all these years."

"Why don't you tell him that?" Ellie asked, knowing the answer.

"Not me, my dear. Why don't you?"

"Oh, no." Eleanor shook her head emphatically. "He feels too strongly about it." She sighed. "We've been over this a hundred times, Rebecca. And besides, he's finally going to take a bride and settle down and have his own family."

"So we hope," Rebecca added. "But they haven't got a yes out of him yet."

"Your attitude is most puzzling, Nicholas," Edward was saying inside the drawing room. "If I didn't know for certain that you were a skirt man, I'd begin to wonder."

Nicholas had to smile at that remark, coming from this staid lord. "My inclinations are decidedly female, sir."

"Yet you don't want my niece?"

Anthony spoke up harshly. "Look me in the eye when you answer, Montieth, for I've seen the mark you put on her."

"What's this?" Edward demanded.

"Relax, Eddie. Just something between the Viscount and myself. But what's your answer, Montieth?"

Nicholas flushed darkly in anger. He felt

126

cornered and didn't like it at all. Had he really marked the girl? If so, what the bloody hell was she doing letting her uncle know about it? They said she wanted to marry him. Damnation, had she given Anthony the impression that their encounter was less than innocent? Was that why this youngest uncle was hell-bent on his blood?

"There is nothing wrong with your niece, my lords," Nicholas said tightly, his amber eyes glowing with anger. "But then, you surely know that better than I."

"Yes, it can be said without prejudice that she is desirable in every way. Still, we can't resolve this." Edward sighed here. "Jason isn't going to like this at all. He is her legal guardian, you see."

"Jason is going to tear him apart if there isn't an engagement by the time he gets here," Anthony said flatly. "Give it up, Eddie, and leave him to me. If Jason gets hold of him, there won't be anything left."

Nicholas sat down again and put his head in his hands as they went on arguing between themselves. He liked and respected Derek's father, Jason Malory, had hunted with him at Haverston and spent long evenings with him over good brandy and good talk. He admired the way Jason ran Haverston and dealt with his people. The last thing he wanted was for Jason to be angry with him. But he couldn't marry the girl, and he couldn't tell them why.

Never before had the bitterness of his parentage hurt him quite so much. The truth was that he was a bastard. And any woman who became his wife would suffer the stigma of his bastardy. He would be ostracized if the truth came out. Hadn't he seen it happen to Derek Malory, who was a known bastard? It was why he felt a closeness to Derek that he didn't feel with his other friends.

Edward's voice intruded on his thoughts. "I doubt Regina's financial status would impress you, Nicholas, for your father's wise investments and your own have made you a wealthy young man. Suffice it to say she is very well off. But . . . perhaps this *will* interest you."

Nicholas accepted the sheaf of papers that Edward brought out of his coat. Letters. *His* letters to the Earl of Penwich!

"How the devil do you come by these?" he demanded incredulously.

"They were forwarded to me just recently, as a matter of fact. The Earl is notorious for ignoring things that don't interest him, and that piece of land you want doesn't interest him."

"Why you?"

"Because it belongs to a trust that I manage. It's a nice little piece of land, with nearly a dozen tenants who all pay their rent regularly."

"It's a bloody large estate and you know it, and not nearly put to its full potential," Nicholas retorted.

"I didn't think you had such a fondness for land," Edward remarked shrewdly. "After all, you don't oversee Silverley."

A muscle jerked in Nicholas' jaw. Hell and fire! He stood a better chance against his old enemy Captain Hawke without a weapon than he did against these Malorys.

"Am I to understand I will never get my hands on that land if I don't marry your niece?"

"You might phrase it more delicately, but that's the gist, yes."

"Refuse, Montieth," Anthony tempted in a soft voice. "Meet me in the morning instead. I won't kill you. I'll aim a ways below your heart, so that the next girl you abscond with in the middle of the night will be believed when she says you've left her untouched."

Nicholas had to laugh. Gelding was the threat now? These were his options? He had no doubt that his grandmother could arrange jail, as she threatened. He'd be estranged from her, doubtless, and the truth was, he loved the old witch. Then there was death or grievous wounding if Anthony had his way. Those were the choices.

Or he could marry the loveliest creature he had ever set eyes on. He could probably have the land he wanted. Aunt Ellie was for this marriage. His grandmother and all the Malorys were for it.

Nicholas closed his eyes for a moment, apparently deep in thought. Then he opened them and stood up.

"My lords," he said evenly, "when is the wedding to be?"

Chapter 11

"So you've come to escort your fiancée to Vauxhall Gardens? To a concert? Never thought I'd see you attending a bloody concert, and in the daytime, at that!"

Derek Malory was enjoying himself immensely, and the look of pure disgust on Nicholas Eden's face was perfect. They were in the drawing room at Edward's house, in the very room where the infamous meeting had taken place the night before, and Nicholas had just arrived.

"This is apparently the only way I'll get to see her," Nicholas told Derek. "They wouldn't let me near her last night."

"Well, of course not. Wouldn't have been proper. She was told to go to bed."

"You mean she actually takes orders?" Nicholas said in mock astonishment. "I thought everyone followed hers."

"Oh, I say. You really are put out about this. I don't understand why. She's first rate, you know, a real gem. Couldn't do better."

"I would have preferred to pick my own wife, you understand, as opposed to having one forced on me."

Derek grinned. "Heard you put up quite a fuss. Couldn't believe any of this when they told me, especially that you'd given in. Know how you don't like to be told what to do, not one bit."

"Stop rambling, Derek," Nicholas demanded. "What are you doing here, anyway?"

"I'm to come along, don't you know. Cousin Clare and I are coming with you. Orders from Uncle Edward. Didn't think you'd get her alone, did you? Can't have any hanky-panky before the wedding."

Nicholas scowled. "What the hell difference would it make? I'm already supposed to have bedded her."

"No one believes that, Nick, at least no one in the family."

"Except your Uncle Anthony?"

"Don't know what he thinks," Derek said more soberly. "But you'd best watch out for him. They're especially close, you know, he and your intended."

"She's his favorite niece?"

"It's more than that. He was only three years younger than Aunt Melissa, you see, and they were always inseparable. When she died, he was only seventeen. Her daughter kind of took Melissa's place in his affections. All my uncles felt that way, including my father. But Uncle Anthony, being the youngest, was more like a brother to Regina. You wouldn't believe the fights he had with my father once he came of age and moved to London, because the old man wouldn't let him have her part of each year the way Uncle Edward does." Derek chuckled. "The old man finally gave in because she wanted it, too, and there isn't much she wants that he doesn't give her."

Nicholas grunted. Regina was going to be impossibly spoiled. "Why is it I never met her at Haverston?"

"She was always with Uncle Edward or Uncle Anthony when you came. They each had her for four months of the year by the time you started visiting me." Derek laughed. "But you did meet her once, that first time I brought you home. She was the little hoyden who spilled the bowl of pudding in your lap when you teased her."

"But you called the child Reggie!" Nicholas cried.

"We all call Regina Reggie, and she's grown now. Do you remember her?"

He groaned. "How could I forget? She

133

stuck her tongue out at me when I threatened to blister her bottom."

"Yes, well, she didn't like you at all after that. She was at the house once more, I believe, when you came to visit, but she stayed out of your way."

"She told me that, when you told her about me, she loved me," Nicholas said dryly.

"Oh, she did love you then, I'm sure," Derek chuckled. "But that was before she *met* you. She was especially fond of me, you see, and she was pleased with anyone who befriended me."

"Bloody hell. Next you'll tell me she was your playmate."

"Shouldn't surprise you, old chap. After all, I was only six when she came to Haverston. I admit I led her astray, there being only the two of us. Dragged her everywhere with me. 'Course the old man had a bloody fit when he finally realized she was fishing and hunting instead of sewing, out climbing trees and building forts in the woods instead of tending to her music. Did you know he married just to give us a mother? Hoped it would have a steadying influence. Poor choice though. Love the old girl, but sickly, you know. Spent more time at Bath getting the cure than she did at Haverston."

"Are you telling me I'm marrying a tom-boy?"

"Heavens no! Remember, she's spent part of every year with Uncle Edward's family for the past thirteen years, and Edward's got three girls near her age. When she was here with them, she was brilliant at her studies, an angel of decorum and all that. Of course, we still had our fun when she was at Haverston. I can't even count all the times we got called on the carpet by the old man. And *she* never got the worst of it, I did. By the time she was fourteen, she had lost her hoydenish ways, though. She was even running the household by then, for our mum was hardly ever there."

"So she was running one household, studying at another, and what, I'd like to know, did she learn at the third?"

Derek chuckled at his vicious tone. "Now don't eat me. Actually, her time with Uncle Anthony was like a holiday. He did his best to see she enjoyed herself. And he prob'ly taught her how to deal with chaps like us." Then he said seriously, "They all love her, Nick. You won't get around that, no matter what."

"Am I then to be burdened with interfering in-laws the rest of my life?" Nicholas asked coldly.

"I doubt it will be so bad. After all, you'll have her to yourself out at Silverley."

The thought was worth relishing, but it would never come to that. Nicholas had given in to their bullying, but he actually had no intention of marrying Regina Ashton. Somehow he had to make her break their engagement. She might have a cousin who was a bastard, but she wouldn't have a husband for one as well.

Derek was luckier than Nicholas, for he had lived his twenty-three years knowing what he was and not letting it bother him. But Nicholas hadn't found out about his birth until the age of ten. And before the revelation, the woman he'd thought was his mother had made his life miserable simply because he did believe her to be his mother. He had never understood why she hated him, treated him worse than a servant, continually belittling him, berating him. She'd never even pretended to like him, not even in his father's presence. It was more than any child should have endured.

One day, when he was ten years old, he'd innocently called her "mother," something he rarely did, and suddenly she screamed at him, *I am not your mother! I am sick of pretending to be. Your mother was a whore trying to take my place — a whore!*

His father had been there, the poor man. Little did his father know that nothing could have made Nicholas happier than to learn that Miriam was not his mother. It was only later that he realized how cruelly the world treated bastards.

His father was forced to tell him the truth that day. Miriam had had many miscarriages in the first four years of her marriage to Charles, and the doctor's warning that it might always be so strained the marriage badly. Charles didn't actually say so, but Nicholas figured out that Miriam acquired an aversion to the marriage bed. Charles found comfort elsewhere.

Miserably, Charles explained that Nicholas' real mother was a lady, a good, kindhearted woman who had loved Charles. He had taken advantage of that love in one night's drunkenness, the only time he and she allowed themselves that freedom. Nicholas was conceived that night. There was never any chance that the woman might keep the child. She was unmarried. But Charles wanted the child, wanted it desperately. Miriam agreed to go away with the woman until the child was born. When she returned, everyone believed the baby boy was hers.

Nicholas understood her bitterness, her

resentment of him, though understanding didn't make it easier to live with. He endured Miriam for another twelve years, until his father died. He left England then, at twenty-two, intending never to return. His grandmother never forgave him for those two years of disappearance, but he'd loved sailing the seas on his own ships, living through one adventure after another, even fighting in a few sea battles. He finally came home to England, but he couldn't ever go home to Silverley. He couldn't live with Miriam and her hate and her continual threats to tell the world the truth about his birth.

To date, no one knew except the two of them and his father's lawyers, for Charles had had Nicholas declared his legal heir. And it wasn't that Nicholas couldn't withstand the scorn if the truth came out; he had prepared himself for it. But his father had taken great pains to keep it a secret, to keep the family name pure. He didn't wish to damage his father's reputation.

He couldn't trust Miriam, however. She might speak out eventually. For that reason, he had no right to marry a girl of good family who would become an outcast if Miriam chose to betray him.

No, Regina Ashton was not for him. He

would give anything to possess her, he acknowledged. But he would also give anything not to marry her, not to risk putting her through the horror in store for her if his secret was revealed. He had to find some way out of it.

CHAPTER 12

"I'm sorry to have kept you waiting, my lord."

Nicholas whirled around at the sound of her voice. A jolt passed through him. He had forgotten how truly ravishing she was. She stood hesitantly in the doorway, a little afraid. Her cousin Clare was behind her. Tall and blond like most of the Malorys, she was pretty enough, but she faded away next to the exotically beautiful Regina.

Once again he was shocked to feel his body affected by the sight of Regina. Bloody *hell.* He would have to end their engagement quickly or bed her.

She continued to stand there in the doorway, and he said, "Come, I won't bite you, love."

She blushed at the endearment. "You haven't met my cousin Clare," she offered, coming forward slowly.

He acknowledged the introduction, then

said to Regina, "Derek has just been refreshing my memory of you. You should have told me we met before."

"I didn't think you would remember," Regina murmured, thoroughly embarrassed.

"Not remember getting pudding dumped in my lap?" he said, eyes wide in mock wonder.

She smiled despite her nervousness. "I won't say I'm sorry for that. You deserved it."

Seeing the twinkle in her cobalt-blue eyes, he asked himself how he was ever going to make her believe he didn't want her when he did want her. She delighted him in every way. Just the sight of her was enough to heat his blood. He had an overwhelming desire to kiss her, to taste the sweetness of her lips again, feel the pulse beating at her throat. Damnation take her, she was too desirable by half.

"Come along then, children," Derek teased. "This is a lovely afternoon for a concert. Egad! I'm really going to a day concert — and as chaperon, to boot." He walked out the door, shaking his head comically.

Nicholas would have stolen a word with Regina, but cousin Clare made that impossible, her critical eye never leaving them for a moment. He sighed, hoping Derek would be able to arrange something for him later.

Regina seemed in uncommonly good spirits during the ride to Vauxhall Gardens, keeping up a steady flow of nonsensical chatter with her cousins. Was it nerves or was she really so happy? He enjoyed watching her. Was she really pleased about the marriage? Why had she told her uncles she wanted him? Why *him?*

Reggie was astonished by Nicholas' friendliness. After being told how many times he had refused to marry her before finally giving in, she'd expected bitterness, even anger. Why was he so warmly accepting? It couldn't be the land, could it? It wasn't at all flattering to know it had taken a piece of land to sway him. Tony bellowed that he'd been bought. But Tony hadn't yet seen the way Nicholas Eden looked at her. *Was* he bought? And why had he fought so hard against the marriage, then given in?

He must want her; the way his eyes smoldered told her he did. Really, it was shameful the way he looked at her, and he did it even in front of her cousins. She'd seen Clare's shocked expression and Derek's amused one. But Nicholas didn't seem to be aware of what he was doing. Or was he doing it intentionally, to embarrass her? Was his amiability being faked? His desire for her wasn't faked, she was sure of that.

They left the carriage and walked along a flowered path, music growing louder as they neared the large area where an orchestra was set up. Nicholas was looking at Derek so intensely that the younger man finally got the message and hurried Clare ahead of them to buy pastries from the vendors circulating through the audience. Reggie laughed as Derek pulled his cousin along against her protests.

The moment he could, Nicholas whisked her off the pathway and behind a large tree. They were not alone. They were shielded from the crowd of people ahead, but not from those still coming up along the path. But it was secluded enough for a few private words.

He had his chance. She was backed up against the tree, his arms braced on each side of her, a captive audience, forced to listen to his every word. She looked up at him expectantly, and he thought, *Hate me, woman. Despise me. Don't marry me.* It was all there in his mind to say, but he lost himself in her eyes.

Without even realizing he was doing it, he bent his head and touched his lips to hers, feeling the petal softness, the sweetness as her lips opened. Fire rushed through him, and he leaned into her, pressing her between him and the tree. Yet even this wasn't close enough. He needed to be closer. . . .

"Lord Montieth, please," she managed, gasping. "We can be seen."

He leaned slightly away, just far enough that he could see her face.

"Don't be so formal, love. You are entitled to call me by my given name, don't you think?"

Did she hear bitterness in his voice? "You don't . . . *why* did you agree to marry me?"

"Why did you want me to?" he snapped.

"It seemed the only solution."

"You could have brazened it out."

"Brazened it — ? Why should I have to? I warned you what would happen if we were found out."

"You were joking!" he reminded her harshly.

"Well, yes, because I didn't think we *would* be discovered. Oh, I don't want to argue. What's done is done."

"No it's not," he said tightly. "You can break the engagement."

"Why would I want to do that?"

"Because you don't want to marry me, Regina," he said in a soft, almost threatening voice. "You don't want to." Then he smiled tenderly, his eyes caressing her face. "You want to be my lover instead, for I will love you to distraction."

"For a time, my lord?" she asked curtly.

"Yes."

"And then we'll go our separate ways?"

"Yes."

"That won't do."

"I will have you, you know," he warned her.

"After we are married, yes."

"We won't marry, love. You will come to your senses long before the wedding day. But I will have you anyway. You know we are inevitable, don't you?"

"You seem to think so."

He laughed. How charming she was. His laughter froze when he heard the deep voice behind him.

"I won't say I'm sorry for interrupting, Montieth, because it appears you need interrupting."

Nicholas stiffened. Reggie peaked around Nicholas' shoulder to find her Uncle Tony and a lady holding tightly to his arm. Oh, no! Not her! Nicholas was going to be furious for he would be sure to think Tony had brought Selena Eddington there on purpose.

"*You* in Vauxhall, Tony?" She tried to

sound disbelieving. "I don't believe it."

"Spare me your mockery, puss. I've heard raves about this particular orchestra."

She held her breath as Nicholas' gaze fell on his mistress, who was looking confused and angry. Reggie almost felt sorry for the woman, but her sympathy didn't quite surface. After all, Selena had thought nothing of tossing Reggie's name to the scandalmongers.

"We meet again, Lady Eddington," Reggie said with false sweetness. "Now I can thank you for the loan of your carriage the other night."

Anthony cleared his throat loudly and Nicholas laughed unpleasantly. "I, too, must thank you, Selena. Why, I wouldn't have met my future bride if it hadn't been for you."

A myriad of emotions washed over Lady Eddington's face — none of them pleasant. She was calling herself a thousand kinds of a fool. When she'd learned what happened, she was so pleased that Nicholas had meant to kidnap her that she'd told all her friends how romantic her lover was . . . and how unfortunate to have nabbed the wrong female. Her bragging had resulted in disaster for herself.

Anthony said firmly, "You will be coming along now, won't you? Perhaps I should start chaperoning you myself. I must have a talk with that errant nephew of mine. Derek should know better than to leave you two alone. Being engaged is not a license to behave badly. Remember that."

With that he departed, whispering something in Lady Eddington's ear as he ushered her away, more than likely encouraging her not to make a scene. Nicholas' mouth was set in a hard line as he watched them go. "Didn't your uncle trust me to tell her of my engagement myself? I would have, with great pleasure. If it were not for her and her uncontrollable conceited bragging —"

"You wouldn't be marrying me," Reggie finished softly.

The fury went out of him. His expression became maddeningly unreadable. "And you would be my lover instead of my wife. A preferable arrangement."

"Not for me."

"Are you saying you wouldn't succumb, love?"

"No, I'm not sure, not sure at all," she answered truthfully. There was sadness in her admission, and he was instantly remorseful.

"I am sorry, love," he said gently. "I shouldn't be badgering you. I should simply tell you that I don't want to marry you."

She gazed at him unwaveringly. "Am I to be grateful for your honesty?"

"Blister it! Don't take it as an insult. It has nothing to do with you!"

"It has everything to do with me, my lord," Reggie said angrily. "You have linked my name to yours whether you meant to or not. *You* did that, not I. Also, you agreed to marry me. You were coerced into it, yes, but if you had no intention of honoring that agreement, then you should not have been seen in public with me today. Our public appearance binds me more firmly to you. I am afraid I am stuck with you now, whether *I* like it or not. And I am beginning not to like it at all." Without giving him a chance to recover, she turned and walked away.

Nicholas didn't move. He felt ridiculously pleased when she talked of being stuck with him, and then ridiculously hurt when she said she didn't like it. He had no business feeling like this about her. They were not stuck with each other, and he'd damned well better remember that.

CHAPTER 13

"Uncle Jason!"

Reggie threw herself into her uncle's outstretched arms, thrilled to see him. Jason Malory, Third Marquis of Haverston, was a big man, as all her uncles were big men. She liked that.

"I've missed you, my girl. Haverston isn't the same when you're away."

"You say that every time I come home." She smiled at him fondly. "Actually I did want to come home for a while before all this happened. I still do." She looked around the drawing room and saw Uncle Edward and Uncle Tony.

"And leave your bridegroom cooling his heels here in London?"

"Somehow I don't think he would mind," she replied softly.

He led her to the cream-colored sofa where Anthony was sitting. Edward was standing by the fireplace, as was his habit.

They had more than likely been having a family discussion before her arrival. It must have been about she-knew-what. Nobody had even told her that Uncle Jason was there.

"I was afraid I wouldn't have time to talk to you before you were due to leave," Jason began. "I'm glad you came down early."

Reggie shrugged. "Well, I kept Nicholas waiting yesterday when he took me to Vauxhall, and I didn't want to do that again."

Jason sat back, looking very solemn. "I can't say as I like having this matter settled before I even got here. My brothers took a lot upon themselves."

"You know we had no choice, Jason," Edward defended himself.

"A few days wouldn't have made any difference," Jason returned.

"Are you saying you will withhold your consent now, after the engagement has been decided on?" Reggie exclaimed.

Anthony chuckled. "I warned you, Jason. She's got her heart set on the young rake, and there's nothing you can do to change that."

"Is that true, Reggie?"

It had been true, yes, but . . . she wasn't so sure now, not after yesterday. She knew Nicholas still wanted her. He had made that plain. And she wanted him. Why pretend otherwise? But marriage?

"I do like him very much, Uncle Jason, but — I'm afraid he doesn't really want to marry me."

There. It was said. Why did it make her feel so desolate?

"I have been told that he refused adamantly before he agreed," Jason said gently. "That was only to be expected. No young man likes to be forced into anything."

Her eyes filled with hope. Could that be the only reason?

"I forget that you do know him," she said, "better than the rest of us."

"Yes, and I've always liked the boy. There is a lot more to him than he allows the world to see."

"Spare us, brother," Anthony said sardonically.

"He'll make her a good husband, Tony, despite what you seem to think."

"Do you really think so, Uncle Jason?" Reggie asked, hope rising.

"I do indeed," he said firmly.

"Then you approve of my marrying him?"

"I'd have preferred to see you married under normal circumstances, but as this unfortunate situation has come upon us, I can't say I'm unhappy that the fellow is

Nicholas Eden, no."

Reggie grinned happily, but before she could say any more, her cousins started drifting in. They were all going with her to the Hamiltons' rout, Amy with her and Nicholas, the others with Marshall in his smart new four-seater. Amidst all the merry chatter as Jason was greeted by his nieces and nephews, Nicholas arrived and stood in the doorway unnoticed. Panic washed over him as he viewed this large family. He was supposed to marry into this overwhelming brood? God help him.

It was Reggie who approached him first. He smiled down at her, determined to keep a tight rein on his emotions this time. She was stunning in a cream day gown that complemented her transluscent complexion. The style was unusual, for while most London women delighted in exposing as much of their bosom as possible, she had contrived to cover hers with a gauze insert that rose all the way to her neck, ending in a thick lacy band around her throat. He was amused. Perhaps he *had* marked her there and this was her clever way of concealing it. He wondered.

"Nicholas?" she asked, curious as to what he was thinking.

"So you have decided to have done with

formality?" he said softly. "I feared you wouldn't be speaking to me at all today."

"Are we to argue again, then?" She looked crushed.

"Perish the thought, love."

She blushed prettily. Why did he persist in calling her that? It wasn't proper and he knew it wasn't. But that was Nicholas.

The Marquis greeted Nicholas warmly and without mentioning the wild escapade that accounted for the engagement. The ride to the Hamiltons' country house a few miles outside of London went smoothly, too, young Amy filling each lapse in conversation with excited chatter, for she wasn't often allowed to go to late-night parties.

It remained then to see what reactions the engaged couple would receive at the Hamiltons' for Nicholas' engagement to Regina was overtaking the subject of their first improper meeting in the gossip mills. He had found that out the previous evening, at a dinner party.

The Hamilton soirée wasn't a large gathering. There were only a hundred people present in the large country house, so there was plenty of room to move around. Guests sampled the array of food set out on long tables, danced in a salon cleared for that purpose, or chatted in small groups. A few stodgy ones glared at the sight of Nicholas and Regina together, but most engaged in wild speculation concerning their first unorthodox meeting.

It had always been arranged that they marry, was the *on-dit*. He had only been amusing himself with Selena while waiting for Regina to return to London. They had met on the Continent, you know. No, no, my dears, they met at Haverston. He and the Marquis' son have been quite chummy for years, don't you know.

"Have you heard what they're saying, love?" Nicholas asked as he claimed her first waltz. "They have us betrothed since you were in swaddling."

Reggie had heard some of the more outlandish speculations from her cousins. "Never say so," she giggled. "My other beaux will be devastated that they never had a real chance."

"Other beaux?"

"The dozens and dozens who sought my hand." A few glasses of champagne had brought out the imp in her.

"I hope you are exaggerating, Regina."

"I wish I were," she sighed, blissfully unaware of his changing temper. "It has been most tedious, you know, trying to make a choice from so many. I was quite ready to give up . . . and then you came along."

"How fortunate for me." Nicholas was furious. He had no idea that he was jealous. Without another word, he maneuvered them to the side of the room, where he abruptly left her with Marshall and Amy, giving her a curt bow in parting. His back to her, he headed for the card room, where he could get a more potent libation than champagne.

Reggie frowned, utterly bewildered. To tease her about the new gossip, smile at her with great tenderness, warm her with his honey-gold eyes, and then become so angry without reason. What was the matter with him?

Reggie smiled, determined not to let him make her miserable. She was asked to dance again and again, and she renewed acquaintances with the young men who had flocked around her last season. Basil Elliot and George Fowler, two persistent admirers, now dramatically professed their lives at an end because of the Viscount's good fortune. Both young men swore they would love her forever. Reggie was amused and flattered, for George and Basil were both wildly popular. Their attentions made up for Nicholas' rudeness.

It was some two hours before the errant Lord Montieth decided to join Reggie again. She had not seen him in all that time, but he had seen her. Time and again he had stood in the door of the card room and seen her laughing up at a dancing partner, or surrounded by ardent beaux. The sight sent him right back for another drink. He was pleasantly foxed by the time he approached her.

"Will you dance with me, love?"

"Will we *finish* this dance?" she rejoined.

He didn't answer. He didn't wait for her to accept either but clamped his hand onto her waist and moved her out onto the dance floor. It was another waltz, and he held her much too close this time.

"Did I tell you yet this evening that I want you?" he asked her suddenly.

She had been aware that there was something different about him, but it wasn't until he leaned close that she smelled the brandy. She wasn't worried though. No one who could move around a dance floor so gracefully could be foxed.

"I wish you wouldn't say that kind of thing, Nicholas."

" 'Nicholas,' " he repeated. "Sweet of you to call me by my given name, love. After all, most everyone here thinks we are already lovers, so it would seem a bit odd for you to call me Lord Montieth."

"If you don't want me to —"

"Did I say that?" he interrupted. "But something like 'beloved' would be even nicer than just 'Nicholas.' I suppose you must love me if you want to marry me. And I don't want to marry you, but I do want you, love. Never doubt it."

"Nicholas —"

"It's all I can seem to think about," he went on. "I am found guilty, yet I have not been permitted to enjoy my crime. Hardly fair, don't you agree?"

"Nicholas —"

"Beloved," he corrected. Then he changed the subject.

"Let's go see the Hamiltons' lovely gardens." Before she could protest, he led her off the dance floor and out of the house.

The gardens were brilliantly landscaped into rolling lawns dotted with trees, man-made ponds, flower beds, a topiary garden, and even a gazebo, so thickly covered by flowering vines that it resembled a tree.

They did not pause to appreciate these beauties. In a twinkling Reggie found herself inside the gazebo, wrapped in Nicholas' arms, being kissed so thoroughly she was close to fainting.

Moonlight spilled in through the hanging vines, bathing them in soft silver light. Padded benches hugged each short, trellised wall. The floor was wood, smooth and polished. There were large potted plants scattered between the benches, their leaves rustling gently in the warm night air.

Deep down Reggie knew that Nicholas was not going to be satisfied with just kissing her, not this time. It would be up to her to stop him. But a voice inside her demanded to know why she wanted to stop him.

He was going to be her husband, wasn't he? Why should she deny him anything — especially when she didn't *want* to deny him anything? And wasn't it possible that his attitude toward their marriage would change if they . . . ? Well, wasn't it?

How conveniently the mind works to get what it wants. And how predictably the body reacts to pleasant feelings, wanting more and more. Her mind and her body conspired against Reggie, and soon there was no fight left in her. She wrapped her arms around Nicholas in surrender.

He carried her to a bench, sat down, and cradled her in his lap. "You will not be sorry, love," he whispered, and then his warm mouth claimed hers again.

Sorry? How could she be when she was so excited and happy?

He supported her back with one arm while his other hand moved slowly along her neck, then lower, making her gasp as it passed over her breasts. On it went, over her belly, down her thigh. He was feeling her hesitantly, as if he couldn't quite believe she would let him. But as his hand began to trace that same path upward, he became bolder, more possessive.

Through the thin silk of her gown, her skin began to burn. The gown was in the way, a nuisance. He thought so too. The button at her throat came undone first, then the tie that held the gown beneath her breasts. In another moment they were standing and he had it removed completely.

Nicholas gasped at the sight of Regina in silk underclothes that clung, molding her gentle curves. She looked right back at him, unashamed, which fanned the flames licking at him. Her eyes were black in the shadowy light, her young breasts straining at the lacy chemise. She was the most beautiful creature he had ever seen.

The small bruise at the base of her throat drew his gaze and he smiled. "So I did put my mark on you. I suppose I should say I'm sorry."

"You might be sorry if you knew how difficult it has been to conceal. You won't give me any more like it, will you?"

"I can't make any promises," he whispered hoarsely.

Then he looked at her shrewdly and asked, "You aren't frightened, are you, love?"

"No — at least I don't think so."

"Then let me see all of you," he persuaded gently. She let him come to her again, and he began removing the rest of her clothing until she was naked. His eyes explored her slowly, hungrily, and then he pulled her close to him and fastened his mouth on her breasts. His tongue, his teeth, his lips all came into play, making her gasp and cry out again and again. She wrapped her arms around his head, holding him to her. Her head fell back as he began kissing her belly. Good God, she couldn't take much more. . . .

"Shouldn't you . . . Nicholas . . . your clothes, Nicholas," she finally managed.

In seconds he was bare-chested, and Reggie's eyes widened, so amazed was she at what his clothes had concealed. She had known his chest would be broad, but now it seemed so huge. He was darkly tanned all over, the mat of hair on his chest golden brown.

She ran her fingers over his muscular upper arm. Her touch scorched him, making him groan.

"The rest now," she pleaded softly, wanting to see all of him, as he had seen all of her.

She moved away and sat down to watch as he undressed. She didn't feel at all awkward, naked though she was. She feasted her gaze on him, a man in all his glory.

When he was finally naked, she went to him and touched him, first his narrow hip, then his long, thick thigh. He grasped her hand, stopping her.

"Don't, love." His voice was harsh with passion. "I am near to exploding now, yet I must go slowly."

Then she saw what was near to exploding. Unbelievable. Beautiful. Extraordinary.

Slowly she raised her eyes to his. "How am I to learn what pleases you if I can't touch you?"

He cupped her face between his hands. "Later, love. This time it will please me to please you. But I must hurt you first."

"I know," she said softly, shyly. "Aunt Charlotte told me."

"But if you trust me, Regina — if you relax and trust me — I will prepare you.

There will be only a little pain, and I promise you will enjoy what comes after."

"I have enjoyed what comes before." She smiled up at him.

"Oh, sweet love, so have I."

He kissed her again, his tongue parting her lips to plunge inside. He was on the very edge of losing control. Her eagerness inflamed him, made him fight for precious time. He caressed her belly, then drifted lower to her parted thighs.

She moaned as he touched the warm essence of her. And then she jerked in surprise when he thrust a finger deep inside her. Her back arched, breasts pressing against his chest. She tore her lips away from his.

"I am . . . prepared, Nicholas, I swear I am."

"Not yet, love," he cautioned.

"Please, Nicholas," she gasped.

That undid him. He glanced down at the narrow bench in frustration. He refused to take her maidenhead on the floor, but — damnation, he should never have brought her to this place, not for her first time.

"Nicholas!" she beseeched him passionately.

He positioned himself and then leaned into her as gently as he could. He heard her gasp as her warmth closed around him. She surged forward until her maidenhead was reached. The pressure stopped her, but in their position, he could not breech her quickly enough to minimize the pain.

There was no help for it. He closed his mouth over hers to receive her cry and then, without warning, he lifted her up and pulled her down hard onto him. He held her like that, impaled.

It took only moments before her nails eased out of his shoulders and she sighed with pleasure again, relaxing against him.

"Nicholas?"

His name had never sounded sweeter. He smiled with relief and answered her without words, clasping her buttocks to lift her, then letting her slide back onto him slowly.

She quickly increased the tempo, clinging to him tightly. A thousand fires were ignited in her, joining into one flame that soon could not be contained. It washed through her, drowning her in sweetest fire.

Nicholas could not remember ever being so sated, or feeling such tenderness after making love. He wanted to hold Regina forever and never let her go.

"Was that . . . normal?" she asked dreamily.

He laughed. "After what we just experienced, you want mere normalcy?"

"No, I suppose not." She lifted her head from his chest, sighing, "I suppose we must go back to the house."

"Oh, bloody hell," he growled. "I suppose we must."

She gazed at him, love and longing lighting her beautiful face. "Nicholas?"

"Yes, love?"

"You don't think they'll guess, do you?" The truth was, she didn't care if they did, but she believed she should ask.

Nicholas grinned at her. "No one would dare suggest we had made love out of doors. It isn't done, love."

Between dressing, teasing, and stealing kisses, it was another twenty minutes before they were on their way walking around the pond toward the house. Nicholas' arm was draped over her shoulder, holding her close, when Amy rushed out at them from behind a wall of shrubbery.

"Oh, Reggie, I'm so glad it's you!" she called breathlessly.

"Have I been missed?" Reggie asked, preparing herself for an ordeal.

"Missed? I don't know. I've been out . . . walking, you see, and I didn't realize so much time —" Amy started to cough, a bad acting job, as the shrubbery behind her began to rustle. "Marshall will be so angry," she said. "Would you mind terribly if I told him I'd been with you?"

Reggie managed to suppress her grin. "Of course not, if you promise not to let the — time — get away from you again. Nicholas?"

"Not at all," he agreed. "I know how easy it is to lose track of time myself."

All three of them managed to keep straight faces as they hurried back to the house.

CHAPTER 14

The engagement party, given by Edward and Charlotte Malory, was a complete success. The whole family and all of their close friends were there. Even Jason's wife had been persuaded to leave the cures at Bath and be there for the event. Nicholas' grandmother and Aunt Eleanor enjoyed themselves immensely, and Reggie got the impression that they had despaired of Nicholas' ever marrying. His mother, of whom he never spoke, was conspicuously absent.

Nicholas was on his best behavior, and everything went beautifully. The party had taken two weeks to prepare, and all the meticulous attention to detail, all the effort paid off.

Alas, smooth sailing doesn't last. Two months after the party, Regina Malory was at the very bottom of despair. It didn't help that she had reached this level of misery by slow degrees.

It was all for nothing.

She wouldn't have believed it possible, not after he had made love to her. She had been so certain he would be happy to marry her after that night. He had been so wonderful, so incredibly patient and tender with her that night. Certainly he had had too much to drink, but was that enough to make him forget the evening?

Oh, they were still to be married. And he always let her know when he was leaving town. He went to Southampton for weeks at a time, claiming business. He always let her know when he returned to London, but in the last two months, she had seen him no more than five times. And those five times were terrible, every one.

He was never late to call for her each time he escorted her to a party, but he'd brought her home only three times. The other two times she had let her temper get the best of her and left without him. It wasn't that he deserted her to spend the entire evening in the card room or embroiled in political discussions, but he often spent more time with Selena Eddington than with her. When he made an obnoxious fool of himself by following her around, well, that was the outside of enough.

Intentional, all of it. She knew very well he was playing the cad for her benefit. That was what hurt so much. If she for a minute thought he was showing his true colors, well, she would let Tony have at him, just see if she wouldn't. But he was not a cad. He was waging a ruthless campaign to make her cry off. Just as he had been forced into the engagement, so he meant to force her out of it.

The very worst of it was that no matter how much it hurt, she couldn't break with him. She no longer had just herself to think of.

Nicholas removed her short black lace cape and handed it to the footman, along with his own red-lined dark cloak and his top hat. Reggie was wearing a white gown trimmed with thin gold tassels along the hem and short sleeves. The neckline was fashionably low, barely covering her breasts, and she was uncomfortable in the gown because of that and because white was reserved for innocent maids.

She had managed to coax her Uncle Edward into trusting her without a chaperon this once. Not since the engagement party had there been any pleasantness between her and Nicholas.

Whatever she had hoped for, she was already disappointed. They had been alone in his closed carriage on the short ride, and he hadn't tried to get close to her, hadn't said a single word to her.

She stole a glance at him as they walked side by side to the music room, where a young couple, friends of Nicholas', were entertaining the twenty or so dinner guests. Nicholas looked exceptionally fine tonight in a long-tailed dark green coat, embroidered cream waistcoat, and frilled shirt. His cravat was loosely knotted, and he wore long trousers instead of the knee breeches and silk stockings preferred by dandies for evening dress. The material clung to his long legs, revealing the powerful thighs and calves. Just looking at his long, graceful body made her feel embarrassed.

His hair was a riot of short, dark brown waves, with so many golden streaks running through it that it sometimes looked copper, or even blond. She knew it was soft to the touch, knew too that his lips were soft, not the hard, rigid line they had been lately. Oh, why wouldn't he talk to her?

A gleam entered her eyes. She stopped in the hall with a tiny gasp, forcing Nicholas to stop as well. He turned back toward her, and she bent over to adjust her shoe. Clumsily, she lost her balance and swayed toward him. Nicholas caught her under her arms, but she fell onto him anyway, her hands gripping his shoulders to steady herself, her breasts pressing into his chest. He gasped as though hit in the stomach by a powerful blow. Indeed, it was a powerful blow. Heat surged through his body, and the fire entered his eyes, banking them like smoldering coals.

Reggie's dark blue eyes smoldered. "Thank you, Nicholas."

She let go of him and walked on as if nothing had happened while he stood there, eyes closed, teeth clenched, trying to regain some control. How was it that such a tiny incident could snap the tight rein he kept on himself? It was bad enough that the sight of her and her voice and scent took a constant toll, but her touch . . . that was the one weapon that shattered his defenses totally.

"Oh, look, Nicholas. Uncle Tony's here!"

Reggie smiled across the room at Anthony Malory, but her smile was as much for herself as for him. She had heard Nicholas' gasp, felt him tremble, saw the desire in his amber eyes. Deceitful man. He still wanted her. He didn't want her to know it, but now she did know. The knowledge warmed her, made up for a good deal of his abominable treatment.

Nicholas reached Reggie at the entrance to the music room, his eyes falling instantly on the dark head of Anthony Malory, bent toward the lady he was sitting next to. "Bloody hell! What's he doing here?"

Reggie wanted to laugh at his tone, but she managed to keep a straight face. "I wouldn't know. The hostess is your acquaintance, not mine."

His eyes fixed on hers intently. "He doesn't often attend these affairs, invitation or not. He came so that he could keep an eye on you."

"Oh, unfair, Nicholas," she chided. "This is the first time we've come across him."

"You are forgetting Vauxhall."

"Well, that was an accident. I don't believe his intention that day was to keep an eye on me."

"No. We both know what his intention was that day."

"My, but you *are* angry," she murmured, and then she let the subject drop. She knew why her uncle was there. He had heard that Nicholas was being seen with other women, and he was furious. Apparently he had decided his presence might help.

The young couple at the piano ended their

duet, and some of the guests began to rise from their chairs to stretch their legs before the next song began. Bright satin coats and matching knee breeches graced the more fashionable men. The married women were distinguished by bold color, because maidens wore pastels or white.

Reggie knew everyone except their hostess, Mrs. Hargreaves. George Fowler was there with his sister and younger brother. She had recently met Lord Percival Alden, Nicholas' good friend. She even knew Tony's current ladylove, who was sitting next to him. And to her profound irritation, Selena Eddington was there, too, her escort an old chum of Tony's.

"Nicholas." Reggie touched his arm gently. "You must introduce me to our hostess before George's sister begins her recital."

She felt him stiffen under her fingers, and she smiled as she walked ahead of him toward Mrs. Hargreaves. My, but she must make a point of touching him more often, she thought.

The evening didn't progress as she wished. At dinner, she found herself placed well away from Nicholas at the long table. He was seated next to their hostess, an attractively voluptuous woman, and he put himself out to be charming, captivating his hostess and all the other women around him.

She talked as graciously as she could to George, but it was hard to bubble when she felt so sad. The rakish Lord Percival, on her right, didn't help at all, continually making comments about Nicholas that drew her eyes to him again and again, forcing her to recognize all the signs she'd witnessed before. Nicholas wasn't just being charming to Mrs. Hargreaves, he wore the look of a man in hot pursuit.

As the evening wore on, Reggie forgot her earlier triumph in discomfiting Nicholas. He did not look at her once during the meal. She found it difficult to summon even the briefest of smiles for her companions, and she thanked heaven that Tony was not nearby. If she'd had to endure his snide comments just then, she would have burst into tears.

It was with profound relief that Reggie at last retired from the room with the other ladies. She had only a few minutes to compose herself, however, before the men sauntered into the drawing room. She held her breath, waiting to see if Nicholas would continue to ignore her. He made his way straight to Mrs. Hargreaves without giving Reggie a glance.

It was the outside of enough. Her pride wouldn't let her stay. And if her uncle said even one word to her about Nicholas, she would explode. She couldn't do that in public.

When she asked George Fowler to take her home, his limpid green eyes widened in delight. Then he said, "But your uncle?"

"I'm rather annoyed with him." She was and she wasn't, but it served as an excuse. "And he has brought a lady with him, anyway. I hate to impose on you, though, George. You have your sister with you."

"My brother can see to her, never fear," he declared, smiling.

Well, she thought crossly, it was nice that *some*body liked her.

CHAPTER 15

"Why is it, I wonder, that you notice the minute she leaves the room with someone?"

Nicholas swung around to meet the level gaze of Anthony Malory. "Following me, my lord?" he asked.

"No point in staying now that the entertainment is over," Anthony replied agreeably. "And a grand show it was too. Only ten minutes gone, and off you go too. Bad effect that."

Nicholas glared at him. "I'm surprised you didn't follow her to make sure Fowler takes her right home. Isn't that what a good watchdog would do?"

Anthony chuckled. "Whatever for? She will do what she wants to do, no matter what I say. And I trust her more with Fowler than I do with you" — he paused and cleared his throat — "even if he was one of the chaps after her last season. If he doesn't take her right home, well, you can't very well blame him, can you? You're doing your best to give these young bucks the impression she's still available." He waited a moment. "Aren't you?"

Nicholas' eyes flared. "If you take exception to my behavior, you know what you can do about it."

"Indeed," Anthony said coldly, all humor gone in an instant. "If I didn't think Reggie would make a fuss about it, I'd see you in the ring quickly enough. When she stops defending you, we'll make that appointment — you may depend upon it."

"You're a bloody hypocrite, Malory."

Anthony shrugged. "Yes, I am, when one of my own is involved. You know, Montieth, Jason may think highly of you, but Jason knows only the more positive aspects of your character. He doesn't know what you're trying to do, but I do."

"Do you?"

They stopped talking as Percy came in. Anthony left the scowling Nicholas, and Percy approached his friend sympathetically. "So you've had another run-in with him, have you?"

"Something like that," Nicholas bit out.

Percy shook his head. Nicholas' problem was that he rarely had any opposition in his life. He was big enough and reckless enough that no one cared to match words with him, let alone fight him. Now he had Lady Ashton's relatives forcing their collective will on him, and the frustration was doing him in.

"You shouldn't take it so hard, Nick. You've just never come up against anyone as formidable as yourself before, and now you've got a whole passel." When Nicholas did not reply, he went on, "It'll be better once you're married."

"Bloody hell!" Nicholas swore. He left Percy and went to fetch his cloak.

Nicholas took a deep breath of the night air as he stepped outside to await his carriage, which was across the street. Then he took another deep breath. It did not calm him.

"Wait up, Nick." Percy came down the stairs. "It might help if you talk to a friend."

"Not tonight, Percy, I'm on the short end of my temper."

"Because of Malory?" Nicholas grunted. "Oh, it's because she left with Georgie, then, is that it?"

"*She* can leave with whomever she bloody well pleases, for all I care!"

"Gad, don't eat me," Percy protested, backing away a little. "Old George is really . . . not actually harmless, but . . .

well, dash it all, she's engaged to you. She —" He saw he was only making matters worse. "I don't believe it. Can the unfeeling Montieth really and truly be jealous for a change?"

"Of course I'm not jealous," Nicholas snapped. "I simply hoped tonight would be the end of it."

Except that he had seen red, dark red, when George Fowler put his hand to Regina's elbow. Fowler was young, he was handsome, and damn Malory for saying he had been after Regina last season!

"What the devil are you talking about, Nick? End of what?"

"This farce of an engagement. You didn't really think I would marry the girl just because I was browbeaten into agreeing to it?"

Percy whistled softly. "So that's what you were doing, sniffing round Mrs. H. I knew she wasn't your type." Nicholas shook his head. "But I thought you were trying to make your lady jealous."

"Furious, enough to jilt me. It's not the first time I've chased after another skirt with her there watching. I even gave my full attention to Selena, as disgusted as I am with her. But Regina has not spoken up about it once."

"Maybe the girl loves you," Percy said simply.

"I don't want her love, I want her hate," Nicholas growled. Now, he told himself, not after he was used to her love, had come to depend on it and returned it. He couldn't bear her hate then.

"Well, you're in a fine pickle. What if she doesn't break off with you? Will you jilt her?"

Nicholas looked skyward. "I gave my word I'd marry her."

"Then you might end up doing just that."

"I know."

"Would it be so bad?"

He was afraid it would be heaven, but he wasn't going to say that to Percy. His carriage pulled up to the curb then and he asked, "Do me a favor, Percy? Go back in there and give my future in-law a message for me. Tell him he had better have a talk with his niece about who she lets take her home." He chuckled. "If he thinks it matters to me, he might redouble his own efforts to get her to jilt me. If nothing else, the message will irritate him. That makes me happy." And he did look better.

"Thanks much, old man. He's liable to take *my* head off, getting a message like that," Percy said.

"Depend upon it." Nicholas smiled. "But you'll do it for me anyway, won't you? That's a good fellow."

Nicholas laughed at the expression on Percy's face, and waved as his carriage moved down the driveway.

It took only a moment for his good humor to flee. Tonight was proof that he couldn't take much more of Regina's presence. Her touch alone had brought him to his knees. Damnation! He had tried staying away from her as much as possible, but while that was more comfortable, it didn't change his predicament. They were still, in fact, engaged.

"End of the road, mate," broke into his reverie.

Mate? From *his* staid driver?

Nicholas glanced out the window and saw, not his house, but trees close at hand. Nothing but dismal black lay beyond. How had he been so preoccupied as not to know he was being taken outside London to the countryside? Or was he in one of London's huge parks? If so, it might as well be the bloody countryside for all the traffic that might pass at night.

What the devil had Malory done, hired a thug to deal with him so Anthony could swear to Regina that he had not touched

180

Nicholas? He could just see her uncle laughing about it with his friends.

Nicholas smiled grimly. This was one way to let off steam. Why hadn't he thought of it himself?

CHAPTER 16

Earlier in the evening, just after Nicholas and Regina arrived at Mrs. Hargreaves' in the West End, a short, stocky fellow named Timothy Pye hailed a passing hack and gave the driver the address of a tavern near the waterfront.

Timothy did odd jobs, from an honest day's work on the docks to slitting a man's throat. He admitted to a partiality for easy jobs, and this one was about as easy as they got. His friend Neddy was working with him. All they had to do was follow this nabob wherever he went and every so often report the lord's whereabouts to their employer.

It was Timothy's turn to report, and it didn't take long to reach the better-class tavern where the bloke was staying. Upstairs, he pounded on the door. It took only a moment to open.

Two men were in the room. One was a

tall, thin fellow with a huge, bushy red beard. The other was a young man of medium height, a boy really, pretty in a girlish sort of way, with black hair and darkest blue eyes. Timothy had seen the younger fellow only once before in the half-dozen times he had reported to the older man. Their names had never been given, nor did Timothy care to know who they were. He simply did as he was paid to do, no questions asked.

" 'E's settled in fer the evenin', so it 'pears," Timothy began, speaking to the red-bearded one. "Some party o'er the West End. Lots o' fancy hacks linin' the street both sides."

"Alone?"

Timothy grinned here. "Brought the fancy piece wi' 'im in his carriage, same as before. Took her inside. I saw 'em."

"Are you certain it's the same lady, Mr. Pye, the one who left without him last time?"

Timothy nodded. "Can't rightly ferget that'n, sir. She's a bleedin' beauty, she is."

The younger man spoke. "Must be his mistress, don't you think? Me father said he's not the type to waste his time on anyone he's not beddin'."

"Blast it, boy!" Red beard growled. "*My*

father. *My,* not *me.* Why is it you never make these slips when your old man is around? It's only my ears that are cursed."

The young man flushed red all the way down his chest, a fact revealed by his loose shirt. His dark blue eyes averted in embarrassment, he moved over to a table where a deck of cards was spread out next to a bottle of wine and two glasses. He sat down there and shuffled the cards, intending to ignore the rest of the report after being humiliated.

"You were saying, Mr. Pye."

"Right, sir." The "sir" came naturally, for the bloke might not look exactly like a gentleman with that bushy red beard, but he talked like one. "I know'd ye want ter be 'earin' 'bout the fancy, 'case she leaves wi'out 'im agin t'night."

"How is the lighting on the street?"

"Fair. But not so bright me and Neddy can't take down the driver nice an' quiet-like."

"Then perhaps tonight is the night." Red beard smiled for the first time. "You know what to do if the opportunity presents itself, Mr. Pye."

"Right, sir. You don't want the fancy involved, I know, sir. If 'e comes out alone, we 'ave 'im."

The door closed behind Pye and Conrad

Sharpe laughed. It was a deep resounding laugh for such a thin man. "Oh, don't sulk, lad. If all goes well, we may be on our way home tomorrow."

"You didn't have to go correcting me in front of the likes of him, Connie. My father don't correct me in front of others."

"Doesn't," Conrad corrected again. "Your father is a fairly new father and, so being, he takes pains to spare your feelings, Jeremy."

"And you don't?"

"Why should I, brat?"

There was genuine affection in the older man's manners, and young Jeremy grinned at last. "If they get him tonight, will I get to go along?"

"Sorry, lad. It will be a messy business that your father won't want you to see."

"I'm sixteen!" Jeremy protested. "I've lived through a *sea battle.*"

"Just barely."

"Regardless —"

"No," Conrad said adamantly. "Even if your father agreed, I wouldn't let you. You don't need to see your father at his worst."

"He's only going to teach him a lesson, Connie."

"Yes, but because you were hurt, the lesson will be harsh. And his pride is involved, too. You didn't hear the slurs and taunts the young lord rubbed into the open wound. You were flat on your back with a near-mortal wound."

"Thanks to him! Which is why —"

"I said no!" Conrad cut him short again.

"Oh, all right," Jeremy grumbled. "But I still don't see why we've gone to all this fuss and bother, having him trailed in Southampton to no luck, then wasting two weeks here in London doing the same thing. It would have been much more fun just to sink one of his ships."

Conrad chuckled. "Your father should hear your idea of fun. But as for that, this lord may have only six ships to his merchant line, but losing one wouldn't tickle his pocket. Your father is determined to even the score on a more personal level."

"And then can we go home?"

"Yes, lad. And you can get back to your proper schooling."

Jeremy made a face and Conrad Sharpe laughed. Then they heard a female giggle coming from the room next door, where Jeremy's father was, and Jeremy's grimace turned to a hot blush, making Conrad laugh all the harder.

Chapter 17

Still baked from the day's heat, the ground was warm beneath his cheek. Or perhaps he had lain in that spot for hours and his own body heat had warmed the ground, he didn't know. These thoughts went through Nicholas' mind when he came to and opened his eyes.

He next called himself a fool, ten kinds of a fool. Gentleman that he was, he had simply stepped out of his carriage, never dreaming he would be attacked even before his foot touched the ground.

He spat dirt out of his mouth. They had apparently left him lying where he'd fallen. Careful movement told him his hands were tied behind his back, and nearly numb besides. Famous. With sharp stabs shooting through his head, he would be lucky if he could get to his knees, let alone his feet. *If* they had left him his carriage, he wouldn't be able to drive it without the use of his hands. Had they left the carriage?

Twisting his head agonizingly to the side, Nicholas saw one of the carriage wheels — and a pair of boots beside it.

"You're still here?" he asked incredulously.

"An' where would I be goin', mate?"

"Back to your den of thieves, I assume," Nicholas answered.

The fellow laughed. What the devil did this mean? Wasn't this just a common robbery, then? He thought of Malory again, but try as he might, he couldn't conceive of the fellow hiring someone to rough him up.

"Have I been unconscious long?" Nicholas asked. His head throbbed.

"A good hour, mate, ter be sure."

"Then would you mind telling me what the bloody hell you're waiting for?" Nicholas growled. "Rob me and be about your business!"

Again the fellow laughed. "Did that, mate, right off. Wasn't told I couldn't, so I did. But me business is right 'ere, seein' ye stay put."

Nicholas tried to sit up, but a wave of dizziness toppled him. He cursed, trying again.

"Steady, mate. Don't be tryin' no tricks now, or I'll 'ave ter let yer 'ave another taste o' me cudgel."

Nicholas sat up, his knees bent to support

his chest. Deep breathing helped. He finally got a look at the slovenly creature. He wasn't impressed. If he could just get to his feet, he would make short work of the fellow even with his hands tied.

"Be a good fellow and help me up, will you?"

"That's funny, mate. Yer twice the size o' me. I weren't born yesterdy."

So much for that, Nicholas thought. "What have you done with my driver?"

"Dumped 'im in an alley. Ye needn't worry. 'E'll wake up wi' a 'eadache, same as ye 'ave, but he'll be a'right."

"Where are we?"

"I liked ye better when ye were asleep," the footpad answered. "Too many questions."

"You can at least tell me what we are doing here," Nicholas asked impatiently.

"Yer sittin' in the middle o' the road, and I'm makin' sure ye stay there."

"No, what you're doing is making me angry!" Nicholas snapped.

"That worries me, mate," the fellow snickered, "it surely do."

With just a little leverage and effort, he could plow his head right into the ignominious bastard's belly, Nicholas thought. But his planning was interrupted by the sound of another carriage approaching. Since the footpad was not making haste to leave the scene, Nicholas concluded uncomfortably that the carriage was expected. What bloody next? "Friends of yours?"

The fellow shook his head. "I told ye, mate, ye ask too many questions."

The outside lamp on the approaching carriage illuminated the area and what Nicholas saw was naggingly familiar. Hyde Park? He rode the paths there every morning and knew them as well as the grounds of Silverley. Would they dare accost him so close to his home?

The carriage stopped twenty feet away, and the driver got down and brought the carriage lantern forward. Behind him two men left the carriage, but Nicholas could see only vague shapes because the light was thrust toward his own face. He tried to stand, but Pye's cudgel pressed down on his shoulder warningly.

"A very pretty picture, eh, Connie?" he heard, and then, "Indeed, yes. All trussed up and awaiting your pleasure."

Their laughter grated on Nicholas' oversensitive nerves. He didn't recognize the voices, but they were cultured accents. What enemies had he made recently among the fashionable set? Good God, dozens! All the past suitors of his bride-to-be.

"A splendid job, my good fellows." A purse was tossed to the cudgel-wielder, and another to the short, stocky carriage driver. "Just light that lamp there for us, and then you may return the hired hack. We'll make use of this carriage since his lordship won't be needing it."

The light moved out of his eyes and Nicholas got his first good look at the two men. Both were tall and bearded, both well dressed, the thinner man in a double-breasted redingote; the other one, with a huge beard, in a several-tiered Garrick coat. He saw dark trousers and well-polished boots. But who were they?

The broader man, slightly shorter than the other, sported an ivory-handled walking stick. That plus his bushy beard gave him a caricaturelike appearance. He was older than his companion, possibly in his early forties. He seemed vaguely familiar, but for the life of him, Nicholas couldn't place either of them.

"Bring that other lamp over here before you go."

Nicholas' own carriage lamp was set on the back of the carriage, casting light on him, but leaving the two gentlemen in shadows. The driver and the thug left in the hired carriage.

"He looks confused, doesn't he, Connie?" the younger man said when the carriage had rumbled away. "You don't think he's going to disappoint me by saying he doesn't remember me?"

"Perhaps you should refresh his memory."

"Perhaps I should jar it."

The boot caught Nicholas on the jaw. He fell back on his bound arms, grunting in pain.

"Come, lad, sit up. That was barely a tap."

Nicholas was hauled roughly to his feet by his bound wrists, wrenching his arms. He swayed for a moment, overcome by a wave of dizziness, but a heavy hand steadied him. Fortunately his jaw was already turning numb. He barely felt a twinge when he parted his lips. "If we are supposed to have met —"

The fist knocked the breath out of him as it slammed into his stomach. He doubled over, gasping for air that eluded him.

The hand that slipped beneath his chin to draw him back up was almost gentle. "Don't disappoint me again, lad." The voice was soft with warning. "Tell me you remember me."

Nicholas flushed with impotent anger as he stared at the man. He was only a few inches shorter than Nicholas. The light brown hair was long and tied back with a ribbon, though shorter, blonder locks fell over his ears. The beard was the same light brown shade as the hair. When he moved his head to the side to study Nicholas, a flash of gold appeared at his ear. An earring? Impossible. The only men who wore earrings were . . . uneasiness began to replace his anger.

"Captain Hawke?"

"Very good, lad! I would hate to think you had forgotten me," Hawke chuckled. "You see what the right prodding can do, Connie? And it was a darkened alley where we last met. I doubt the boy got a good look at me then."

"He saw you well enough on the *Maiden Anne.*"

"But do I look the same on board ship? No. He's a clever lad, that's what. It was a matter of deduction, see? I doubt he has another enemy like me."

"I hate to disappoint you," Nicholas said wearily, "but you no longer have a monopoly on hating me."

"No? Splendid! I wouldn't like to think of you having too easy a time of it once I'm gone."

"Then I shall live to see another day?"

Nicholas asked.

Connie laughed. "He's as arrogant as you are, Hawke, damned if he isn't. I don't think you frighten him at all. He'll be spitting in your eye next."

"I don't think so," Hawke replied coldly. "I might pluck out his own in that case. How d'you think he'd look wearing a patch like old Billings?"

"With that pretty face?" Connie snorted. "It would only enhance his superb looks. The ladies would love it."

"Well, perhaps I should see to his face, then."

Nicholas did not even see the blow. Fire exploded on his cheek, the impact staggering him. Connie was there to hold him up, however, and then the other cheek received the same powerful blow.

When his head cleared, Nicholas spat blood. His eyes glowed with a murderous light as he met the pirate captain's stare.

"Are you angry enough now to fight me, lad?"

"You need only have asked," Nicholas managed.

"You needed a bit of motivation. I'm here to even the score, not play with you. I demand a good showing, or we'll only have to do this again."

Nicholas snorted, though it hurt to make the effort. "Even the score? You forget who attacked whom on the open sea."

"But that's my trade, don't you know."

"Then how do you dare speak of revenge simply because you were bested?" Nicholas demanded. "Or do I have the honor of being the only man ever to come away with a whole ship after an encounter with the *Maiden Anne*?"

"Not at all," Hawke said honestly. "We have limped into port before. I myself have received wounds in the heat of battle. Though I did not take kindly to having my son injured when you felled my main mast. But even that had to be accepted for having the boy on board. However, as one gentleman to another —"

"A gentleman pirate?" It was dangerous, but Nicholas had to say it.

"Sneer as you will, but you are clever enough to comprehend why we had to meet again."

Nicholas nearly laughed. It was incredible. The pirate had attacked him first, intending to win the cargo Nicholas was carrying. Nicholas had won that sea battle. He supposed he shouldn't have taunted Captain Hawke when he sailed away. That had been hitting below the belt. But, it had happened four years ago, and he'd been young and reckless, heady with victory. Still, those taunts were apparently what had goaded Hawke into evening the score. What gentleman could ignore an insult?

Gentleman! They had met in a darkened alley in Southampton after Nicholas returned to England, three years ago. He had been unable to see his assailant that night, though Hawke took pleasure in introducing himself. That encounter had been interrupted.

Then there'd been a letter, a *letter,* waiting for Nicholas when he returned from the West Indies last year, expressing regret that Hawke had been unable to renew their acquaintance when he was in London. The letter convinced Nicholas that he had made a terrible enemy. Why, oh, why, was he so blessed as to have a scum of the earth thirsty for his blood?

"Cut him loose, Connie."

Nicholas tensed. "Do I fight you both?"

"Come now," Captain Hawke protested. "That would hardly be sporting, would it?"

"Bloody hell," Nicholas growled. "Striking a defenseless man isn't sporting."

"Did I hurt you, lad? You must accept my apologies, but I thought you were made of sterner stuff. And you must understand, I feel justified after all the bother you've cost me waiting for this moment."

"You will understand if I don't agree?"

"Certainly," Hawke replied with a mock bow.

Hawke removed his Garrick. He was dressed for easy movement in a flowing shirt tucked into his trousers. Nicholas was encumbered with cloak, coat, and waistcoat. He saw that he wouldn't be given the opportunity to remove any of these as he watched the pirate flex his fingers impatiently.

Nicholas couldn't stop the groan from escaping as his bonds were finally severed and his arms dropped painfully to his sides. There was no feeling in his fingers for several moments, and then too much feeling as the blood rushed into them. And he had assumed correctly. He was not given a moment's grace to recover before the first staggering blow caught him under the chin. He landed hard.

"Come on, lad," Hawke complained with a weary sigh. "We won't be interrupted this time. Give me a good showing and I'll call it quits."

"And if I don't?"

"Then you may not walk away from here."

Nicholas took the warning. He threw off

his cloak while he was on the ground and then propelled himself at the older man, catching him in the midsection and knocking them both to the ground. He followed with a hard right to Hawke's jaw, but the impact so jarred his throbbing hand that he was the one who cried out in pain.

Nicholas gave it his best, but Hawke was relentless, and despite Nicholas' injuries, Hawke was the more furious of the two. He was also heavier and more muscular. His hamlike fists were merciless on Nicholas' already bruised face and body. The fight was a hard one for both, however, and as Nicholas lay bleeding in the dust, he knew the older man was hurting, too. Even so, Hawke could laugh.

"I must hand it to you, Montieth," Captain Hawke panted. "You probably could have beaten me if you'd had a fresh start. I am satisfied now."

Nicholas heard only some of it before he passed into blessed unconsciousness. Conrad Sharpe leaned over and shook him, but he didn't stir.

"He's out, Hawke. You have to take your hat off to the boy, though. For a pampered nabob, he lasted much longer than I would have expected." Conrad chuckled then. "How does your own body feel now about settling scores?"

"Do be quiet, Connie. Hell and fire, the chap's got a nasty right."

"I noticed," Conrad laughed.

Hawke sighed. "You know, under different circumstances I could almost like him. It's a shame I had to come across him when he was such a sharp-tongued young pup."

"Weren't we all at that age?"

"Yes, I suppose we were. And we all must learn from it." Hawke tried to straighten to his full height but groaned and doubled over. "Get me to a bed, Connie. I think I'll need at least a week's rest after this."

"Was it worth it?"

"Yes, by God, it sure as hell was!"

CHAPTER 18

The last of the officials and the doctor filed out of the room, and Nicholas' valet, Harris, closed the door. Nicholas allowed himself a smile, but the movement turned to a grimace as the cut on his lip stretched.

"If you don't mind, sir, I'll manage that smile for the both of us," Harris offered. And then he actually did, his drooping mustache leveling out as he smiled widely.

"It did end better than I could have hoped, didn't it?" Nicholas said.

"That it did, sir. Instead of coming before the magistrate on a simple matter of assault, he'll face the charge of piracy."

Nicholas wanted to smile again, but thought better of it. Now he knew how Captain Hawke felt about evening scores. Well, Hawke's victory had been very, very short-lived.

"I suppose I shouldn't gloat, but the fellow deserves no better," Nicholas said.

"Indeed not, sir. Why, the doctor said you're lucky your jawbone is still intact. And I never in all my days saw so many bruises and —"

"Oh, that doesn't matter. You don't think *he's* not suffering now, too? It's the principle of the matter. I never would have met the cur if he hadn't attacked my ship to begin with. Yet *he* held a bloody grudge! But I don't think he's laughing about it now, sitting in jail."

"It's fortunate the watch found you when they did, sir."

"Yes. Pure luck, that."

Nicholas had regained consciousness a few moments after Hawke and the red-haired Connie left in Nicholas' carriage. And it was only a few more moments when he heard horses' hooves not too far away. He managed to call out, and the two night watchmen heard him. It took some convincing to get them to leave him and go after his carriage instead. Thirty minutes later they came back for him with the happy news that his carriage was recovered and the injured assailant apprehended — though the other one managed to outrun capture.

Nicholas told the whole story to the good fellows who brought him home, and Hawke's name nagged at one of them. Sure enough, a host of officials descended on Nicholas while the doctor was still working on him. They announced that Hawke was a felon wanted by the Crown.

"It is also fortunate, sir," the valet continued chattily as he straightened the bedcovers over Nicholas, "that Lady Ashton was not with you when you encountered the thugs. I assume the evening went as planned and she left without you again?"

Nicholas did not answer. When he thought of what might have happened . . . no, it did not bear thinking about. She was safe because George Fowler had taken her home.

Hmm. George Fowler indeed. Unreasonable anger, hot and vicious, took hold of him.

"Sir?"

"What?" Nicholas barked, then recovered. "Ah, yes, Harris, the evening went as expected where the lady is concerned."

The middle-aged valet had been with Nicholas for ten years and was privy to his thoughts and feelings the way no one else could be. He knew Nicholas didn't want to marry Regina Ashton, though he didn't know why — nor would he dream of asking. He and Nicholas had discussed the strategy Nicholas was employing to deal with the commitment.

"Lady Ashton had words with you, sir?"

"It didn't go *that* well," Nicholas replied tiredly. The sedative the doctor had given him was starting to take effect. "I am still engaged."

"Well, surely next time . . ."

"Yes."

"But there's not much time before the wedding," Harris added hesitantly. "The doctor wants you to have three weeks' bed-rest."

"Bother that," Nicholas retorted. "I will be up and about in three days, no more."

"If you say so, sir."

"I do say so."

"Very good, sir."

Never having suffered such a beating before, Nicholas had no way of knowing he would feel ten times worse the next day. He roundly cursed Captain Hawke and would have liked the pirate hanged.

It took a full week before he could move even slightly without pain. And though he was finally up and moving in another week, the cuts on his face were still raw.

He was in no fit condition to see Regina. But he couldn't afford to lose any more time.

The wedding was only a week away. He

had to see her.

He called at the Malory house in Grosvenor Square despite his appearance. He was told Regina was out of the house, shopping for her trousseau. This information increased his panic. He waited for an hour, and when she arrived he very rudely whisked his fiancée away from her cousins the moment she walked in the door.

He led her through the garden and on into the square, saying nothing, his stride long and fast, his expression darkly brooding. Her soft voice breaking into his thoughts brought him to a halt.

"You are recovered?" she asked. A brisk autumn breeze whipped leaves through the air and played havoc with the feathers on Regina's bonnet. Her cheeks were flushed, her eyes sparkled with blue lights. She was too damnably lovely by far, blooming with health and vitality. She was still the most beautiful woman he had ever encountered.

"Recovered?" Nicholas demanded, wondering how on earth she had found out about the attack when he had avoided her these last two weeks just so she wouldn't find out.

"Derek told us of your illness," she explained. "I am sorry you were not well."

Damnation! So he was to receive her

sympathy, thanks to Derek's coloring the truth. He would have preferred her anger.

"Actually, I was visiting a favorite tavern of mine on the waterfront and was set upon by ruffians who beat me soundly for my purse. Still, there is a certain excitement in frequenting unsavory places."

She smiled tolerantly. "Tony was sure you would use your illness as an excuse to postpone the wedding. I told him that wasn't your style."

"You know me so well, love?" Nicholas asked sardonically.

"You may be many things, but cowardly isn't one of them."

"You presume —"

"Oh, stuff," she interrupted. "I won't believe it if you try to convince me otherwise, so you needn't try."

Nicholas gritted his teeth and she flashed him an amused grin. Looking at her beauty affected him strongly, as it always did, and his thoughts were quite scattered for the moment.

"I suppose I should ask how you have been getting on?"

"You should, yes," Reggie agreed. "But we both know that what I do with my time doesn't interest you. For instance, you wouldn't be wounded, would you, if you knew I have been so busy I haven't missed you? And you wouldn't care if you knew that other men have escorted me to the affairs my cousins insist I attend?"

"George Fowler?"

"George, Basil, William —"

"Careful, or I will begin to think you are trying to stir my jealousy in retaliation."

"Retaliation? Oh, I see, you judge me by your own behavior. How amusing, Nicholas. Just because you find other women fascinating —"

"Blister it, Regina!" Nicholas finally lost all patience. "Why do you wrap your anger up in polite nonsense? Scream at me!"

"Don't tempt me."

"Aha!" he exclaimed triumphantly. "I was beginning to think you had no spirit."

"Oh, Nicholas." Reggie laughed softly. "Am I supposed to call you a foul, despicable creature, and swear tearfully that I wouldn't marry you if you were the last man and so forth?"

Nicholas glared furiously. "You mock me, madame?"

"What makes you think that?"

She said this with such an innocent expression that he put his hands on her shoulders, ready to shake her. But her magnificent blue eyes widened in surprise as her own hands came up to brace against his chest, and Nicholas flushed red hot.

He stepped back from her, nearly trembling. "The press of time forces me to be blunt, Regina," he said coldly. "I asked you before to end this farce of an engagement. I am asking you again. Nay, I am begging you. I do not want to marry you."

She dropped her gaze, staring fixedly at the high polish of his Hessian boots. "You don't want me . . . in any way then? Not even as a lover?"

His honey-gold eyes flashed at the turmoil the question caused, but he said only, "You would no doubt make a fine mistress."

"But you are not interested?"

"Not any longer."

She turned her back on him, her shoulders drooping, a dejected little figure. Nicholas had to restrain himself with every ounce of will from reaching out and gathering her into his arms. He wanted to take it all back, to show her what a lie it had been. But it was better for her to be disillusioned for a time, and then to forget him. He could not let this lovely woman marry a bastard.

"I really thought I could make you happy, Nicholas." Her words floated to him over her shoulder.

"No woman can, love, not for any length

of time."

"I'm sorry then. I really am."

He didn't move. "You *will* jilt me then?"

"No."

"No?" He stiffened, disbelieving. "What the devil do you mean?"

"The word no means —"

"I know what the bloody word means!"

She finally turned around. "You don't have to shout at me, sir."

"Formal again, are we?" he cried, his temper cresting.

"Under the circumstances, yes," she answered curtly. "You have only to absent yourself from London next week. I assure you I am quite strong enough to bear up under the humiliation of being jilted."

"I gave my word!" he exclaimed.

"Ah, yes, the word of a gentleman — who is a gentleman only when it suits him to be one."

"My word is my bond."

"Then you must stick to it, Lord Montieth."

She started to walk away, but he caught her arm, his fingers hard. "Don't do it, Regina," he warned darkly. "You will regret it."

"I already do," was the whispered reply. It took him aback.

"Then *why?*" he asked desperately.

"I — I must," she replied.

He let go of her arm and stepped away, his face a mask of fury. "Damnation take you then! I will be no husband to you, this I swear. If you persist in this farce, then that is what you will have, a mockery of a marriage. I wish you happy."

"You don't mean that, Nicholas!" There were tears in her eyes.

"I give you my word, madame, and a last warning: Do not come to the church."

CHAPTER 19

"Ah, don't cry any more, sweetheart," Meg pleaded. "Your cousins will be here in a moment to help with the dressin'. You don't want them to see you like this."

"I can't help it," Reggie sobbed miserably. "And aren't brides supposed to cry on their wedding day?"

"But you've been cryin' for a week. It hasn't helped, has it?"

"No." Reggie shook her head.

"And you don't want your eyes to be all puffy, not today of all days."

Reggie shrugged wearily. "I don't care about that. I'll have the veil on."

"But you won't be wearin' a veil tonight."

There was a silence, and then Reggie whispered, "Will there be a wedding night?"

"You can't be thinkin' he won't show up?" Meg gasped, outraged.

"Oh, he'll be there," Reggie sighed. "But I told you what he said."

"Nonsense. Some men are just scared to death of marriage, and your Viscount appears to be one of them."

"But he swore he wouldn't be a husband to me."

"He said that in anger," Meg said patiently. "You can't go holdin' a man to what he says in anger."

"Yet he can hold himself to it, don't you see? Oh, how could I have been so wrong about him, Meg?" Reggie cried. "How could I?" She shook her head. "To think I once compared him to Tony. Nicholas Eden is nothing like my uncle. He hasn't an ounce of feeling — except between his legs," she added bitterly.

"Reggie!"

"Well, it's true," she retorted. "I was just a game to him, another conquest."

Meg stood looking down at her, hands on her hips. "You should have told him about the baby," she said for the hundredth time. "At least he would have understood why you must go through with this."

"He probably wouldn't have believed it. *I* am even beginning to wonder. Look at me! Four months gone and I'm still not showing even a little. And there's been no sickness, no . . . Am I binding myself to this man for nothing? What if I'm not carrying his child?"

"I wish it weren't so, my girl, but you know it is. And I still say you should have told him."

"Fool that I was, I thought his despicable behavior was only a ruse," Reggie said bitterly. She sighed. "You know, Meg, I do still have some pride left."

"Sometimes we must swallow every bit of pride, sweetheart," Meg said gently.

Reggie shook her head. "I'll tell you just what he would have said if I had confessed. He would have told me to stop wasting time on a lost cause and find a father for my child."

"Maybe you should have."

Reggie's eyes flashed. "I would never force one man's child on another! Nicholas Eden has a child on the way, and he can pay the price for it, not someone else."

"You're the one payin', Reggie, with heartache and misery."

"I know," she sighed, the fire gone. "But only because I thought I loved him. Once I see how wrong I was, I will manage."

"It's not too late, you know. You can leave for the Continent before —"

"No!" Reggie said so forcefully the maid jumped. "This is *my* child! I won't hide in shame until it's born and then give it up, just to save myself an unpleasant marriage." Then she elaborated, "I don't have to live with the man, you know, not if it proves too difficult. I don't have to stay with him forever. But my child will bear his father's name. Nicholas Eden will share the responsibility, as he should."

"Then we had best be gettin' to the church on time," Meg sighed.

Nicholas was already at the church, silently raging and despairing by turns. Family and friends were arriving, proving that this was really happening. His grandmother and aunt were there, but Miriam Eden was conspicuously absent again. It reinforced his conviction that he had done the right thing in warning off his fiancée.

His heart sank when Jason Malory entered the church, the bride a few steps behind him. Exclamations ran through the crowd, for she was truly breathtaking in a silk gown of powder blue and silver, with tiers of white lace trimming. It was strikingly old-fashioned, tight-waisted, long-sleeved, and reaching to the floor. Though the bell of the skirt was not as full as the gowns of the last era had been, the outer skirt was split on both sides and trimmed with lace, revealing wide panels of silver underskirt. There was lace beneath the rounded bodice and at the neck. A circlet of silver and diamond chains held in place a white veil which covered her face to her chin, draping in back nearly to the floor.

She stood in the church door for several long moments, facing Nicholas at the end of the aisle. He couldn't see her face or her eyes, and he waited breathlessly, willing her to turn around and flee.

She didn't. Regina placed her hand on her uncle's arm and began the long walk down the aisle. Cold, calm anger settled inside Nicholas. On the whim of this small child-woman, he was being forced into marriage. Very well, let her have her day of triumph. It would not last long. When she learned she had married a bastard, she would wish she had heeded his warnings. Ironically, Miriam would help. She would take a malicious delight in apprising Regina of all Nicholas' faults. He thought with grim humor that this would be Miriam's first act of kindness toward him. Of course, she wouldn't know it for what it was.

Chapter 20

Reggie stared out the coach window, but all she could see was her own reflection. She flushed as her belly growled with hunger but didn't look at Nicholas to see if he had heard. He was across from her in the plush coach, which bore his coat of arms.

The interior lamp had been burning for two hours, but still they hadn't stopped at an inn for dinner. She was hungry, but she was damned if she'd beg.

The wedding guests had been served a huge luncheon at Malory house, but Reggie hadn't been there for it. Nicholas took her home directly from the church, telling her to pack an overnight bag and order the rest of her things sent on to Silverley. The two of them were gone even before their guests arrived.

He had made her ride all afternoon and into the evening, but she didn't feel like complaining, not when he sat there so pensively, never once looking her way. He hadn't spoken a word since leaving London.

He was married and furious about it. Well, she'd expected he would be. But it boded well, didn't it, that he was taking her to his country estate? She hadn't expected that. She didn't know what she had expected.

Her stomach growled again and she finally decided to ask, "Will we be stopping soon for dinner?"

"The last inn was in Montieth. Silverley is just up ahead," Nicholas replied brusquely.

It would have been nice if he'd told her that sooner.

"Is Silverley large, Nicholas?"

"About as large as your own estate, which borders mine."

Her eyes widened. "I didn't know that!"

"How could you not?"

"Why are you angry? Why, it's perfect. The estates will now be combined —"

"Which is what I have wanted for years. But surely your uncle told you about that. He used your estate as the inducement to get me to marry you."

Reggie blushed furiously. "I don't believe it."

"That I wanted the land?"

"You know what I mean!" she snapped. "Oh, I knew there was some land involved, and Tony even said it was what swayed you, but — but I didn't believe it. No one told me about this. I didn't know your estate borders the land that came to me through my mother. I haven't lived there since — my parents died, in the fire that destroyed the house. I was only two at the time. I have never returned to Hampshire. Uncle Edward has always seen to what was left of the estate, as well as to the inheritance I got from my father."

"Yes, a tidy sum that, fifty thousand pounds, which he was happy to point out has tripled due to his wise investments, giving you a sizable yearly income."

"Good God, are you angry about that, too?"

"I am not a fortune hunter!"

Her own grievances were riding very close to the edge. "Oh, bother. Who in his right mind could accuse you of that? You're not exactly a pauper."

"It is no secret that I wanted your land, land I assumed belonged to the Earl of Penwich, since the Earl was the last to be in residence there."

"My father was, not the present Earl. But as the land came to him through my mother, it was not entailed to Penwich and it was their wish it come to me."

"I *know* that now! Your Uncle Edward thought it quite amusing to inform me as I left the church that I no longer needed to worry about buying the estate. He couldn't wait to tell me. Wanted to relieve my mind, he said. Bloody hell. Do you know how it looks, madame?"

"Do you realize you are insulting me, sir?"

He had the decency to look surprised. "I didn't mean to imply —"

"Of course you did. That is what you are complaining about, isn't it? That people will say you married me for my inheritance? Well, thank you very much. I was not aware this was the only way I could get a husband."

His brows narrowed and he said coldly, "Shall we *discuss* how you got a husband?"

Her eyes flashed blue sparks, and for a moment she feared she would lose all control. She managed, just barely, to keep silent, and Nicholas refrained from goading her. Both were relieved to find the coach stopping just at that moment.

He stepped outside and extended a hand to help her down. But as soon as she was standing on the ground, he got back into the coach. She stared up at him, her eyes widening in disbelief.

"You wouldn't!" she gasped.

He said bitterly, "You can't be surprised. I am a man of my word, after all."

"You can't just leave me here — not tonight."

"Tonight, tomorrow — what difference?"

"You know what difference!"

"Ah, yes, the wedding night. But we have had ours, haven't we, love?"

She gasped. "If you do this, Nicholas," she said tremulously, "I swear I will never forgive you."

"Then we are well met, aren't we, if we both honor our oaths? You have what you wanted. You bear my name. I give you now my home. Where is it written that I must share it with you?"

"You expect me to stay here while you go on as before, living in London and . . ."

He shook his head. "London is too close for our arrangement. No, I'm leaving England altogether. Would that I had done so before we met!"

"Nicholas, you can't. I am —"

Reggie stopped herself before making the one declaration that might change his mind. Her pride stubbornly reasserted itself. She would not follow the path of thousands of other women, just to keep a man by her side. If he wouldn't stay because he wanted to . . .

"You are — what, love?"

"Your wife," she said smoothly.

"So you are," he agreed, his mouth tightening into a hard line. "But you will recall I didn't ask you to be, and I warned you not to press the marriage. I have always been plainspoken about this, Regina."

He closed the coach door then and tapped on the roof to signal the driver. Reggie stared incredulously as the vehicle moved away.

"Nicholas, come back!" Reggie shouted. "If you leave . . . Nicholas! Oh! I hate you! I hate you!" she cried in frustration, knowing he couldn't hear her anyway.

Stunned, she turned around to face the large gray stone house. It looked like a miniature castle, a gloomy one, in the dark night, with its central tower and corner turrets. This was only a close view, however, so she did not see how it spread out behind and on the sides of the main block in asymmetrical heights and shapes. There even was a large domed conservatory at the back of the house, towering over the servants' wing on the right.

The arched windows on either side of the door were dark. What if there was no one at home? Famous. Abandoned on her wedding night, and to an empty house!

Well, there was nothing for it. Squaring her shoulders, she forced a smile and approached the front door as if there were nothing odd about a bride arriving without her bridegroom. She knocked, first quietly and then loudly.

When the door finally opened, Reggie saw the startled face of a young girl, a maid. She was not at all confident about answering doors. That was Sayers' duty. He took himself so seriously. He would have her hide to know she has usurped his place.

"We weren't expectin' company, my lady, or I'm sure Sayers would've been waitin' round to let you in. But you've such a soft knock . . . gor, listen to me ramblin'. What can I do for you?"

Regina grinned, feeling ever so much better. "You can let me in, to begin with."

The girl opened the door wider. "You've come to call on the Countess, Lady Miriam?"

"I guess I've come to live here — for a while, at least. But I suppose I can start with seeing Lady Miriam."

"Gor! You've come to live here? Are you sure you want to?"

This was said with such patent surprise that Reggie laughed. "Why? Are there dragons and goblins here?"

"There's one I could speak of. Two if you count Mrs. Oates." The girl gasped, then went vivid red. "I didn't mean . . . oh, forgive me, my lady."

"No harm done. What's your name?"

"Hallie, mum."

"Then, Hallie, do you think you could inform Lady Miriam that I have arrived? I am the new Countess of Montieth."

"Gor!" Hallie squealed.

"Precisely. Now, will you show me where I can await Lady Miriam?"

The maid let Reggie in. "I'll just tell Mrs. Oates you're here, and she'll go up and tell the Countess."

The entry hall was marble-floored and narrow, with only a single long refectory table up against a wall. An ornate silver platter was positioned in the center of the table for calling cards, and a lovely tapestry hung behind. A large Venetian mirror dressed the opposite wall with a brace of wall candles on each side, and a pair of double doors directly facing the front door.

Hallie opened the double doors, and a much larger hall was revealed, two stories high, with a magnificent domed ceiling way above. The main staircase was in the center of the right wall. And at the end of the hallway were opened doors that led into an antechamber, and Reggie caught a glimpse of stained-glass windows nearly covering the outside wall. The impression was of an extremely large house.

At the far end of the hall on the left was the library, and this was where Hallie led her. Forty feet long and twenty wide, the library had tall windows along the far wall, giving ample light in the daytime. The other three walls were covered with books, and huge portraits hung high up above the bookcases.

There was a fireplace, and sofas to either side of it. Beautifully crafted chairs, lounges, and tables were spaced near the windows for reading. There was an ancient reading stand in gold lacquer. A carpet in rich browns, blues, and gold covered the floor. A pedestal desk occupied the far end of the room, with chairs around it, and there was a painted leather screen which would turn that far corner into a cozy study set off from the rest of the room.

"It shouldn't be long, mum," Hallie said. "The Countess . . . oh, dear, the Dowager Countess now, isn't she? Just like the old one, his lordship's grandmother. But Lady Miriam will be eager to welcome you, I'm sure," she said politely, not sounding at all convinced. "Can I get you something?

There's brandy there on the table, and mulberry wine, too, that the Countess likes."

"No, I'll just make myself comfortable, thank you," Reggie replied with a smile.

"Very good, mum. And can I be the first to say I'm glad you've come? I hope you like it here."

"I do too, Hallie," Reggie sighed. "I do too."

CHAPTER 21

Reggie looked at the morning sun that was just barely peeking into the corner of her bedroom. Directly below her south windows was the round dome of the conservatory. Beyond was the servants' court, and beyond that, hidden behind a clump of trees, the stables and carriage house.

She was in the master bedroom in the rear right corner of the central block of the house. That allowed her two walls of windows, all draped in bloodred velvet with gold fringe and tassels. All the colors in the room were dark except for the powder blue wallpaper. Still, when it got later and all the windows let in light, the room would be cheery.

Her other wall of windows looked out over a vast parkland. The view was stunning — trees dotting the lawns, a forest to the left full of orange-and-gold autumn leaves. A small lake to the right was a riot of color, too, with a carpet of late-blooming wildflowers lining its banks and the blue lake sparkling in the sunshine. What a peaceful, tranquil scene, undisturbed at this early hour. It might almost have made Reggie forget her troubles. But not quite.

She rang for a maid, hoping she would *not* get Mrs. Oates, the housekeeper, who was just as Hallie had described her, a dragon. What a crass, pretentious, annoying creature she was. Imagine, insisting on showing Reggie to a guest room, and a small one at that. Reggie had set her straight quickly. Conceding that the rooms meant for the lady of the house were occupied by Miriam Eden, who couldn't be expected to vacate them overnight, she pointed out that the master's rooms were empty and would do very well.

This had appalled the housekeeper. Only a sitting room separated the two large bedrooms, each of which had a door into the sitting room. Lady Miriam had one of the bedrooms.

Reggie won her way after subtly reminding Mrs. Oates that she was the new mistress of the house. Miriam Eden might have continued to run Silverley after her husband's death, but Silverley actually belonged to Nicholas, and Reggie was Nicholas' wife.

Mrs. Oates cautioned her to be quiet when they passed through the sitting room next to Miriam's room. Reggie was told that Miriam wasn't feeling well and had retired early, which was why Reggie hadn't been properly greeted.

Truth to tell, Reggie was relieved. She was exhausted, embarrassed by the absence of her husband of only a few hours, and so full of bitterness that she was unfit to meet anyone.

She settled into Nicholas' room, and found it was utterly devoid of personal items. Somehow, that made everything worse.

The servant who answered Reggie's call was dark-haired and dark-skinned and just the opposite of talkative Hallie. She said hardly a word as she helped Reggie dress and arrange her hair, then showed her to the breakfast room.

This room was at the front of the house and had full benefit of the morning sun. The table was set for one. A slight? On a side wall was a large rosewood china cabinet filled with fine gold-rimmed china with a floral design of pink and white. Between the windows on the back wall was a lovely carved oak and ebony buffet.

Hallie came in, smiling brightly, carrying

a large covered platter which she set on the buffet.

"Mornin', mum. Hope you had a pleasant night."

"Indeed I did. Has the Countess come down yet?" Reggie indicated the single setting.

"She's off on her mornin' ride. She never eats this early, mum."

"Neither do I, really. Why don't you show me the rest of the house now instead?"

"But there's all this food," Hallie said in surprise, removing the lid on the platter to reveal eggs, sausage, kippers, ham, jellies, toast and rolls, even two delicious-looking tarts.

"Heavens!" Reggie gasped. "I wasn't supposed to eat all of that, was I?"

Hallie giggled. "Cook was out to make a better impression, seein' as how she only sent up cold dishes for you last night."

"Well, then I'll just take this with me, and one of these," Reggie said, wrapping a fat sausage in a roll and taking one of the tarts. "And now we can have that tour."

"But shouldn't Mrs. Oates — ?"

"Yes," Reggie interrupted conspiratorially, "I suppose she should. But I can let her show me around again later. Right now I would like to see just how big Silverley is, and I would like pleasant company along."

Hallie giggled again. "There's none of us likes Mrs. Oates too well, but she does run a tight ship, as she's so fond of sayin'. Come along then, your ladyship. But if Mrs. Oates should come upon us —"

"Not to worry," Reggie assured her. "I'll think of something to explain why you're with me. You won't be blamed."

The house was indeed big. Near the entryway they passed a billiard room with not one but three tables in it. There were more rooms than Reggie could remember, each filled with lovely Chippendale furnishings and Queen Anne pieces. Many of the high ceilings were arched and decorated with lovely gilded plasterwork. Some had large, gorgeously crafted chandeliers.

There was a music room decorated in green and white and, to the right of the drawing room, an antechamber with floor-to-ceiling stained-glass windows bathing the room in colors which were sharply set off against the white marble floor. Plush red benches hugged the walls. Reggie was astonished by the beauty of the place.

At the back of the house, off the large, formal dining room, was the conservatory. Along a walkway that circled the room were chairs and sofas and statues on pedestals.

There were potted plants at the sides of wide stone steps leading down to a fountain in the center of the room. Everywhere were trees and autumn flowers. Reggie was sorry she had missed seeing the room in summer when the indoor garden would have been in full bloom.

Upstairs, the whole length of the back of the house was taken up by the master suites. From right to left were the lord's chamber, the sitting room, the lady's chamber, and then a nursery. There were rooms for a nurse and lady's maid.

The tour took just under an hour, and Hallie was able to escape back to the servants' domain in the center of the house right of the main hall before anyone discovered what they had been doing. Reggie settled in the library then to await Lady Miriam.

Her wait was short. The Countess came in straight from her riding excursion, dressed in a deep violet habit and still carrying a riding quirt. She showed only a moment's surprise at finding the room occupied. She then proceeded to ignore Reggie while she removed her hat and gloves.

So that was the way it was to be? Well, it helped explain Nicholas' propensity to rudeness.

Reggie was able to study Miriam Eden while she was being ignored. For a woman likely nearing fifty, she was holding up remarkably well. She was trim and youthful, her posture stiffly erect. Her tightly wound blond hair was fading, but there was no gray in it. Her eyes were a wintry gray. Hard, cold eyes, but perhaps they smiled sometimes? Reggie thought not.

There was a slight physical resemblance to Miriam's sister Eleanor, but the physical similarity was where it began and ended. The younger sister exuded warmth and gentleness, and there was none in the Countess. How could she possibly live with this woman?

"Should I call you Mother?" she asked suddenly, and there was a perceptible start from the Countess. She turned and looked at Reggie squarely. The gray eyes were frigid, the lips pursed. She most likely wasn't used to being addressed before she condescended to speak, Reggie reflected.

In a brittle voice Miriam replied, "Don't. I'm not your mother any more than I'm —"

"Oh, dear," Reggie interrupted, "I gathered there was an estrangement between you and Nicholas when you didn't come to our wedding, but I —"

"I was needed here," Miriam said stiffly.

"— didn't realize you had disowned your son," Reggie finished.

"What are you doing here, and without Nicholas?" Miriam asked.

"Nicholas and I simply don't suit, you see, and so we couldn't possibly live together," Reggie replied.

There was an astonished pause. "Then why marry?"

Reggie shrugged and gave her a dazzling smile. "It seemed a good idea. For me anyway. I was tired of the constant whirl of parties and such. I much prefer the country life."

"Which doesn't explain why Nicholas would marry."

Reggie raised a brow. "Surely you know why. I wasn't present myself when Nicholas agreed to marry me, but your sister and mother-in-law were there."

Miriam frowned. Of course she wouldn't ask the same question again. Nor would she admit that she didn't communicate with Eleanor or Rebecca. She was being left to wonder about the marriage, which was just what Reggie had intended.

"We are rather isolated here," Miriam warned.

Reggie smiled. "That sounds wonderful. My only regret is that I must ask you to select other rooms for yourself."

Miriam drew herself up stiffly. "I am told you have taken over Nicholas' rooms."

"But they won't do for long, you see. I must have the nursery close at hand." She patted her belly lovingly.

The Countess appeared ready to choke. "Nonsense. You can't be expecting. You were married only yesterday, and even if you stopped at some inn after the wedding, you couldn't possibly know —"

"You are forgetting your son's reputation, Lady Miriam. Nicholas is an expert seducer. I was quite helpless against his charm. I am now four months along."

The Countess stared at Reggie's belly, and Reggie said, "Isn't it fortunate I am not showing?"

"I don't see how you can think any of this fortunate in any way," Miriam said with stiff hauteur. "People can count, you know. It's shameful that you don't even blush when you — just shameful."

"I don't blush, madame, because I feel no shame," Reggie replied coldly. "No shame, no guilt. And if my child is born five months after the marriage, well, other babies have been born early. At least I have a husband, even if he won't be around very much. And my child has a name. Considering your son's reputation, no one will be surprised that Nicholas could not be held off for the four long months of our engagement."

"Well, I never!"

"Haven't you?"

Miriam Eden turned crimson at the innuendo and stalked out of the room. Reggie sighed. Well, she had made her own bed, so to speak. She shouldn't have alienated the sour old bird, but . . . Reggie smiled. That last look of outrage on the Countess' face had been worth whatever unpleasantness she could expect from the woman.

CHAPTER 22

"Putting on a little weight, aren't you, puss?" Anthony asked as he kissed Reggie's cheek and then sat down next to her on the lawn. "Must be eating because you're miserable. And no wonder, living with that cold fish."

Reggie put down her sketch pad and smiled fondly at her uncle. "If you mean Miriam, she's not so bad. After our first two rows, we reached an agreement. We simply don't speak to each other."

"I suppose that's one way to get along with someone," Anthony replied in his driest tone.

Reggie laughed delightedly. "Oh, Tony, I've missed you this last month. I really did expect you sooner. Everyone else has been here."

"You wouldn't have cared to see me right after I heard what was going on. It has taken me this long to cool off."

She sighed. "I suppose you wanted to kill him again?"

"Damned right. I tried to find the blackguard but he has disappeared."

"I could have saved you the trouble of looking," she told him levelly. "He told me he was leaving England. I guess he meant it."

Anthony's temper rose. "We had better talk of something else, puss. Your husband is not my favorite subject. What is that you're drawing?"

Reggie handed over her sketch pad. "Just a hound chasing falling leaves. He ran off into the woods a few minutes before you arrived. I've been getting some good poses of the gardeners, though, and the grooms exercising the horses." He turned the pages and admired her work. "That's Sir Tyrwhitt, a neighbor," she said when he got to her sketch of a middle-aged dandy. "Would you believe he and the Countess — ?"

"No!"

"Well, I don't know for certain, mind you, but she's like a different person around him, actually girlish, if you can believe that."

"I can't," he said firmly.

Reggie laughed. "And that's Squire Gibbs and his young wife Faith. I like her a lot. Miriam is furious that she and I have become friends. An invitation to Silverley has always been an honor, you see, and so when I gave Faith an open welcome, the Countess took to her room for two days to express her displeasure."

"Likes to lord it over the lesser gentry, does she?" he asked.

"Oh, she's very serious about it, Tony."

Anthony turned another page. "Good God, who are those characters?"

"Two of the gardeners, I guess. There are so many servants here I haven't met them all yet. I drew these men yesterday down by the lake."

"You must have been particularly gloomy yesterday. You made them look so sinister."

Reggie shrugged. "It wasn't my mood. They *were* sinister-looking. They moved on when they saw me drawing them, so I had to finish the sketch from memory."

"They look like waterfront brawlers," he said, "not gardeners."

"Oh, stuff. All the people here are really nice, once you get to know them."

"Except the cold fish."

"Don't be unkind, Tony. I don't think she's led a very happy life."

"That's no excuse for forcing her unhappiness on others. And speaking of —"

"Don't," she said stonily. "I'm perfectly

fine, Tony, really."

"You can't lie to me, puss. Look at you. You wouldn't be putting on weight if you were exercising, and the only time you mope about and ignore your health is when you're unhappy. I know you, remember? You're just like your mother in certain ways. But you don't have to stay here, you know that. You can come home."

"I know I've made a mistake, Tony, but I don't want the world to know it. Do you understand?"

"For his sake?" he asked sharply.

"No," she replied, then added hesitantly, "The weight you keep harping on isn't what you think, Tony. I'm pregnant."

There was a moment's startled silence. Then he said, "You can't know this soon. You've only been married a month."

"I *am* pregnant, Tony. Very, very pregnant."

His cobalt-blue eyes, so like hers, grew wide, then narrowed furiously. "He didn't! I'll kill him!"

"No, you won't," she replied, vetoing his favorite solution. "This is going to be your first great-nephew or -niece. How could you explain to the child that you'd killed his father?"

"He deserves a sound beating at the very least," growled her uncle.

"Perhaps," she agreed. "But not for seducing me before the wedding. I was a willing participant in the making of this child."

"Don't bother defending him, puss. You forget he's just like me and I know *all* the tricks. He seduced you."

"But I knew exactly what I was doing," she insisted. "I . . . it was foolish in the extreme, I know that now, but I thought it would help to change his attitude. He kept trying to get me to break the engagement, you see. He never deceived me into thinking he was willing to marry me."

"He agreed!"

"Yes, but he thought he could make me jilt him before the wedding."

"You should have."

"Should haves don't count, Tony."

"I know, I know, but blister it, Reggie, how could he desert you, knowing —"

"I never told him! You don't think I would try to keep a man *that* way, do you?" She sounded genuinely shocked.

"Oh," Anthony said, brought up short. Then he said somberly, "Honestly, puss, you really are just like your mother. Melissa gave birth to you only a few months after her wedding, too."

Reggie gasped. "Really? But . . . why didn't any of you tell me that?"

239

Anthony turned red and looked away. "Well, were we to say, 'By the way, dear, you only just made legitimacy.' "

She giggled and leaned over to kiss his cheek. "Well, thank you for telling me. I'm glad to know I'm not the only promiscuous one in the family — besides Uncle Jason, I mean," she teased.

"Promiscuous! At least your father didn't desert Melissa. He adored her. He would have married her sooner if her stiff-necked pride hadn't kept them apart."

"I never heard any of this," she whispered, shocked.

"They had some terrible rows, they did. She broke the engagement three times, swearing each time that she never wanted to see him again."

"But everyone always told me how much they loved each other," Reggie protested.

"They did, puss," he assured her. "But she was as hot-tempered as I am. The slightest little disagreement got out of hand. Thank God you didn't inherit *that* from her."

"Oh, I don't know," Reggie mused. "If he ever does come back, I'm not going to forgive him. He made me love him, and then he wouldn't even give our marriage a chance. I do have some pride, even if I did practically beg him not to leave. My love has turned to . . . well, it infuriates me even to think about him."

"Good for you. Think about coming home, will you? There's no reason you can't be with your family for the birth. We'll keep outsiders well away from you."

"Well, I do have Meg, and I —"

"Think about it," he ordered sternly.

She grinned at him. "Yes, uncle."

CHAPTER 23

It was another damp November morning, and Reggie walked down to the lake with her sketch pad. Uncle Tony had spent the night, and she had seen him off early, promising again to think about coming home. She would think about it, or at least think about returning to London, where she would be closer to the family. She could keep up appearances by moving into Nicholas' townhouse. That was an idea. And it would even give her something to do, now that she was restricted as to physical activities. She could redecorate his London house, spend some of his money.

Trouble was, she had come to enjoy the tranquillity of Silverley. At least it was tranquil when Miriam wasn't around. Reggie got along well with the servants, too. Even Mrs. Oates had unbent surprisingly the moment she learned Reggie was expecting a baby. It seemed Mrs. Oates loved babies. Who would have guessed?

Reggie looked at the gray mansion wistfully. She might have been truly happy there. She pictured her children running across the Silverley lawns, sailing little boats on the lake in summer, ice-skating in winter. She even pictured their father giving them their first ponies and showing them their paces. Somehow she knew Nicholas would have a gentle hand with children. She sighed, a deep, long sigh, pulling up the hood of her fur cloak and casting a look at the heavy bank of clouds above her. Meg was right. It was getting too cold to be sketching outdoors.

She tucked her sketchbook under her arm and turned to go back to the house. She would sketch the lake another time. It was then that she saw one of the servants hurrying toward her, coming not from the house but from the woods.

On the other side of those woods lay her own estate. She hadn't gone there yet. The melancholy caused by thinking about that place where her parents had died was too much. She would go there eventually, she told herself. Eventually, yes. And someday she would show it to her child. The estate had belonged to his . . . her grandparents.

As he got closer she recognized the servant

as one of the men she had sketched the other day. He was carrying an oversized sack used, she guessed, to gather dead leaves. He looked as strange as she remembered. A vague sense of danger rose in her.

Maybe it was the full, unkempt beard and long shaggy hair. Or maybe it was his bold demeanor. Whatever, she decided not to wait for him to reach her. She would run to the house.

She stopped, calling herself a ninny. She was letting her imagination run wild. Silly of her. He was only a gardener, after all.

Reggie had no sooner finished the thought than the man reached her, took a moment to catch his breath, then smoothly yanked the sack he carried over her head and shoulders. Her first impulse was to scream, but surprise overtook her until the sack was yanked all the way down her body, and her scream was only a tiny muffled sound.

Her assailant wasted no time shouldering his prize and rushing back into the woods. An expensive, well-sprung coach waited there, hidden, with two high-stepping grays straining to be off. A man was in the driver's seat, ready to crack the whip at the first sign of pursuit. The man on the ground glared up at him.

"Ye could at least get your arse down 'ere

and open the bleedin' door, 'Onry. She might look like a light bit of fluff, but after that long trek she don't feel light."

Henri, or 'Onry, as his English friends were wont to call him, chuckled at Artie's surliness, a sure sign that he was no longer worried about their mission. "Then no one is giving chase?"

"Not as I saw. Now give us a 'and. Ye know the cap's orders about treatin' 'er real gentle."

They laid Reggie on a thickly padded seat and quickly wrapped a rope around her knees to hold the sack in place. "This will sweeten his temper, yes? Never thought we would catch our fish this soon."

"Give it up, Frenchy. Ye'll never sound like an Englishman, so stop tryin'. And I bet ye thought we'd be freezin out 'ere in these woods for weeks, eh?"

"Well, did you not?"

"Yeah, but I tol' ye it pays to be ready, and see if she didn't come right out to us. A fine piece of luck! If this don't please the cap'n, what will, I ask ye?"

"The little fish catching the bigger one."

"Right ye are. Let's just 'ope that don't take too long either."

"You will ride back here with her to see

she does not fall off the seat, or do you wish me —"

"Ye can 'ave the pleasure. I don't trust ye gettin' this lumberin' land ship out o' these woods in one piece. That'll be my job." He chuckled. "I take it ye fancy that arrangement?"

"As you please, Artie." The young Frenchman flashed a grin at the Englishman.

"Just don't get a mind to sample the goods, mate. Cap'n wouldn't like that a'tall," the man said seriously before climbing into the driver's seat again. The coach rocked forward.

Reggie's mind was racing. This had to be a simple kidnapping. A demand for money would be met, and then she would be returned home. Nothing to worry about.

She wished her body would see it that way. She was trembling violently. They were taking her to a captain who didn't want her roughed up. Yes, a kidnapping. And he was a sea captain, she surmised, because there was a large harbor in Southampton. Why, Nicholas' own shipping firm was located there.

She forced herself to recall every word they'd spoken. What was that about the little fish catching the bigger one? She strained all her senses, alert to every sound, every movement.

It wasn't more than half an hour before their pace slowed and she knew they were in Southampton.

"A few more minutes, *chérie,* and we will have you inside and more comfortable," her captor assured her.

"Inside?" Not "on board?" Well, he was French, after all, so maybe that had been a language problem. Oh dear. The tight sack around her cloak was beginning to make her itch and sweat. And to think she'd believed there would be no more adventures once she was grown!

The coach stopped and she was carefully lifted out, the Englishman carrying her this time. There were no sounds of a waterfront, no waves lapping against a ship, no creak of nearby timber at anchor. Where were they? There was no gangplank to maneuver across, either, but steps were mounted. Then a door was opened.

"Hell's bells, Artie, you got her already?"

"Well, this ain't ballast I'm totin', lad. Where do I put 'er?"

"There's a room ready for her upstairs. Why don't you let me carry her?"

"I can box yer ears and not drop 'er, lad. Want to test me?"

There was a deep chuckle. "You're too

touchy by half, Artie. Come on, I'll show you where the room is."

"Where's the cap'n?"

"He's not expected back until tonight. I guess that means I get to take care of her, don't it?"

"Will ye listen to this young cockerel, 'Onry?" Artie demanded. "Not on yer life, lado, will we be leavin' ye alone with the likes o' 'er. Yer the only one round 'ere who might think 'e can get away with a little hanky-panky 'cause the cap's yer old man. Don't ye be thinkin' about it while I'm around."

"I said take care of her — not take *care* of her," the boy shot back.

"Is the lad blushin', 'Onry? Is that a real blush I see?"

"Run along, *mon ami,*" Henri said to the boy. "You questioned his strength, and he will not let up on you today."

"Well, at least let me see what she looks like."

"Oh, she's a pretty one, lado." Artie grinned. "In fact, when the cap sets eyes on 'er, 'e's likely to forget what 'e wanted 'er brought 'ere for. Might just keep 'er for 'imself. Might just indeed."

They carried her to her upstairs room, and then she was set down on her feet. She

248

swayed and nearly fell. The rope at her knees was removed, and the sack lifted off. But the little room was so dark, its windows boarded up, that she had trouble seeing for a moment.

A deep breath of air was her first order of business. Then she focused on the three men, her captors and the boy, moving toward the door. The younger one was looking at her over his shoulder, his mouth hanging open.

"Just a minute, *if* you please," she called to the departing men. "I demand to know why I was brought here."

"The cap'n will be tellin' ye that when 'e gets 'ere, m'lady."

"And who is the captain?"

"No need for names," the brawnier of the two answered, offering a placating tone in response to her haughty one.

"Yet I know your name, Artie. And I know your name, Henri. I even —" She stopped before telling them she had sketched both of them. "I wish to know why I am here."

"Ye'll 'ave to wait and talk to the cap'n. Now, there's a lamp there on the table, and ye'll be fed shortly. Just settle down and make yourself comfy-like."

She swung around, furious, her back to them. The door closed and a key was turned in the lock. She let out a sigh. Where had she gotten the nerve to act so hoity-toity? They were sinister-looking characters despite their bantering manner and placating voices. Well, at least she hadn't shown them any fear. They wouldn't see a Malory cringe. That was a huge satisfaction.

She sat down warily on a rickety chair, wondering forlornly if that might just be her last moment of satisfaction for a long while.

CHAPTER 24

The food was delicious, even in Reggie's nervous state. She ate her fill of squab pie, rice pudding, and saffron cakes. There was a delicate wine, too. But once the distraction of dining was over, she went back to worrying.

Henri had brought her the food. He had put on a very rakish ruffled silk shirt; black breeches with high, wide-topped boots; and a long, coatlike vest. Good Lord, all he lacked was an earring. He had even shaved everything except his tightly curled mustache. Why?

What *had* she gotten herself into this time? Feminine clothes were laid out on the bed, brand-new from the look of them, silk robe, a more discreet linen nightgown, furry bedroom slippers, and, embarrassingly, underthings. On a vanity were toilet articles, brush, comb, a very expensive perfume, all new.

The young man had come in to start a fire for her early in the afternoon, and Artie stood guard at the door. He smiled timidly at her. She glared back frostily. She ignored the boy entirely.

It was night now, but she refused to make use of the large bed. She would stay awake all night if she had to, but she wouldn't relax until she had met the captain and given him a piece of her mind.

She fed the fire with wood the boy had left her, then drew a chair up to it, tucking her feet beneath her dark blue velvet skirt. The room was warm and she began feeling sleepy.

She almost didn't hear the key turning in the door. The sound made her stiffen, but she didn't turn around. Damned if she would deign to notice either Artie or Henri.

"My son tells me you're a raving beauty," said a deep voice. "Let me see what has him so smitten. Present yourself, Lady Montieth."

She stood and, very slowly, turned to look at him. Her eyes went wide in shock.

"Uncle James!" *"Regan?"* they cried at once.

She recovered first. "Oh, uncle! You can't mean to kidnap me for another three months of fun aboard the *Maiden Anne?*

Don't you think I'm a bit old for that now?"

Looking as confused as a man ever did, he held out his arms. "Come here, sweet, and give us a hug. My God, you really have turned into a raving beauty."

She hugged him happily. "Well, it's been three years, Uncle James, and I only saw you for an hour that time. It's unfair, you know, having to sneak around to see my own uncle. Isn't it time you made up with your brothers?"

"I might be willing," he said quietly. "But I doubt they are, Regan."

He had always liked being different, even to having his own special name for her. Her uncle, the pirate, had stolen her from under his brothers' noses when they refused to allow him to see her. He'd taken her for a fabulous adventure aboard his ship, determined to have his rightful time with her. She had been twelve, and those incredible three months still lived vividly in her mind.

Of course, they both paid a price for it. James was already in disgrace for being a pirate. When he returned Reggie, all three brothers had thrashed him soundly for putting her in danger. He was disowned by all of them, even Tony, whom he'd always been so close to. James suffered over the rift, and Reggie suffered for being the cause of it. He never blamed her, but that only made her feel worse.

She pushed away from James and looked him over. He hadn't changed very much in three years. He was still big and blond, as handsome as ever — and as outrageous. Look what he had done by bringing her there.

"I shouldn't even speak to you," she said sternly. "You gave me a terrible fright. You might at least have told your men to inform me it was the notorious Captain Hawke who was having me abducted."

James exploded. "I'll have their bloody hides, depend upon it! Damnation!" He threw open the door and bellowed, "Artie! . . . Henri!"

"Uncle, no," Reggie protested.

James' rages weren't like Tony's. Tony could be talked around. Even Jason, a stubborn bull when he was angry, could be talked to. But James Malory was frightening. Though his anger had never been directed at her, she feared it.

"Uncle James," she said, "the men were really very gentle with me, and they saw diligently to my comfort. I wasn't frightened," she lied.

"A mistake has been made, Regan, and I'll accept no excuses for it."

A black brow rose sharply. "You mean I wasn't supposed to be brought here?"

"Of course not. I would have come to see you before I left England again. I wouldn't have brought you to me — certainly not in this fashion."

The two miscreants appeared in the doorway just then, uneasy under James' cold stare. "You wanted us, Cap'n?"

"Do you know who you have brought me?" James asked softly. It was his unpredictable tone.

Henri divined the trouble first. "The wrong lady?"

"May I present gentlemen" — James extended an arm toward Reggie, exploded — *"my niece!"*

"Merde!"

"Yeah," Artie breathed.

Another man appeared in the doorway. "What the devil are you shooting about, Hawke?"

"Connie!" Reggie cried in delight, and rushed into his arms.

This was the man who had taught her to fence, to climb to the crow's nest, even to sail the ship when her uncle wasn't looking. Conrad Sharpe, James' closest friend in childhood, was now first mate on the *Maiden Anne*. A more roguish, though lovable pirate had never lived.

"Is that you, little squirt?" Conrad bellowed. "Damn me, if it isn't!" He hugged her close.

"It's been years and years!"

"Hasn't it though?" Conrad chuckled. Finally he caught sight of James' scowling face and cleared his throat. "I, ah — I don't think you're supposed to be here, Regan."

"So I gather." She turned back to James. "Well, uncle, here are the scoundrels. Will you have them flogged for this dastardly mistake? If so, I want to watch."

"Regan!"

"You're not going to?" She glanced at her abductors. "Well, gentlemen, you are indeed fortunate my uncle is in such a charitable mood. He's letting you off light. I would have taken the skin from your backs, to be sure."

"All right, Regan, you win," James relented, nodding curtly for Artie and Henri to leave.

"She hasn't changed at all, has she, Hawke?" Conrad chuckled when the door closed behind the two kidnappers.

"Cunning little baggage," James grumbled.

Reggie grinned at them both. "But aren't you glad to see me?"

"Let me think about it."

"Uncle James!"

"Of course, sweet." James gave her his open smile, the one reserved for those he loved. "But you really have stirred up a problem here. I was expecting someone else, and now I suppose the watch will be up at Silverley."

"Do you want to tell me what that is all about?" she asked him.

"Nothing that concerns you, Regan."

"Don't put me off, uncle. I'm not a child anymore, you know."

"So I see." He grinned. "Look at her, Connie. She's the very image of my sister, isn't she?"

"And to think she could have been my daughter," Conrad said wistfully.

"Oh, Connie, you too?" Reggie asked softly.

"Everyone loved your mother, squirt, even me," Conrad admitted gruffly.

"Is that why you took me under your wing?"

"Never think it. You wormed your way into my heart all on your own."

"Then maybe you'll tell me what this is all about?"

"No, squirt." Connie shook his head, grinning at James. "This is all his doing. If you mean to ferret out what you want to know, turn those big blues on him."

"Uncle James?"

"It's . . . some unfinished business I have here. Nothing for you to fret about."

"But isn't the Countess a bit old for you?"

"It's not like that, Regan," James protested. "And what the devil do you mean, old?"

"Well, she's not really ancient-old, I suppose," Reggie corrected herself. "She takes very good care of herself, too. But what business can you have with her?"

"Not her. Her husband."

"He's dead."

"Dead? Dead!" James looked at Connie. "Damnation! He can't be dead!"

Reggie looked at Connie, bewildered. "He had a score to settle, squirt," Connie explained. "Now it looks like fate has intervened."

"When did he die?" James asked harshly. "How?"

Reggie was becoming concerned. "Well, I don't actually know how. It's been quite a few years though."

James' look of fury turned to one of surprise. Then both men began to laugh, confounding Reggie further. "Ah, sweet, you had me going there," James chuckled. "But

I don't believe we are thinking about the same man. It's the young Viscount I want."

"Nicholas Eden?" she cried.

"Now you have it. Do you know him?"

"Very well," she said.

"Then perhaps you can tell me where he is. Lord knows no one else can. I've looked everywhere. I swear the lad is hiding from me — and with good reason.

"Good God!" Reggie gasped. "You had me kidnapped as a lure to bring Nicholas to you, didn't you?"

"Not you, sweet," James assured her. "Those idiots thought you were Eden's wife."

Reggie moved closer to Conrad, took a long breath, and then said hesitantly, "Uncle James, your men didn't make a mistake."

"They —"

"— didn't make a mistake," she finished. "I am Nicholas' wife."

The tense silence that followed wracked everyone's nerves. James stiffened. Conrad put a protective arm around Reggie, and together they waited for the explosion. Before it came, the door opened and the young man leaned in. "Henri just told me she's my cousin? Is it true?"

James glowered. "Not now, Jeremy!" The boy flinched.

"No! Don't go, Jeremy." Reggie caught the boy's hand and pulled him into the room. "Uncle James is angry with me, not with you."

"I am not angry with you, Regan." He tightly controlled his voice.

"You were going to yell at me."

"I was not going to yell at you!" he exploded.

"Well, that's a relief," Reggie said.

James opened his mouth, clamped it shut, and sighed with exasperation. His eyes met Conrad's and the message was clearly, *You handle her. I give up.*

Conrad made the introductions. "Jeremy Malory, Lady Regina Mal— ah, Eden, Countess of Montieth."

"Hell's bells!" Jeremy grinned. "So that's why his temper's flown."

"Yes, I don't think he likes . . . well, never mind." She grinned up at the handsome young man whose coloring was exactly the same as hers. "I didn't get a good look at you before. Heavens, you look exactly like your Uncle Tony when he was younger." She turned toward James. "Were you going to keep him a secret forever, uncle?"

"There's no secret," James said gruffly.

"The family doesn't know."

"*I* only found out five years ago. And I

haven't exactly been on speaking terms with my brothers since then."

"You could have told *me* when I last saw you."

"There wasn't time to go into it then, Regan. 'By the way, I have a son.' You would have plagued me with your endless questions, and Jason would have sent the servants out to hunt you down and find me."

"I suppose. But how did you find him? It was five years ago?"

"A little less than that actually," he replied. "And we just bumped into each other in a tavern where he was working."

"You should have seen your uncle's face, squirt, when he saw the boy." Conrad smiled, remembering. "He knew the boy looked familiar, yet he didn't quite know why. And Jeremy couldn't take his eyes off him either."

"I recognized him, you see," Jeremy put in. "I'd never actually seen him before, but my mum described him to me so often I would have known him anywhere. I finally got up the nerve to ask him right out if he was James Malory."

"You can imagine the reaction," Conrad said gleefully. "Everyone on the waterfront knew him only as Captain Hawke, and here was this half-pint lad calling him by his real name. And then, to top it, he says he's his son! Hawke wasn't laughing along with me, though. He took in the boy's coloring, asked him some questions, and damned if he wasn't the proud papa overnight."

"So I have a new cousin, one nearly full grown." Reggie grinned. "Oh, this is famous. Welcome to the family, Jeremy."

He was nearly as tall as his father, which was much taller than Reggie. She leaned up on tiptoes to kiss his cheek, and was surprised by the exuberant hug that squeezed her breathless. The boy wouldn't let go.

"That's enough, Jeremy. Jeremy!"

The lad stepped back. "Can cousins marry?" he asked.

Conrad guffawed. James scowled. Reggie blushed. Now she understood the motive behind that hug.

"Another rake in the family, Uncle James?" she said wryly.

"So it would seem," James sighed. "And learning all the tricks too early."

"He only follows your example," Conrad put in smoothly.

"Well, he's off to bed now."

"Hell's bells," Jeremy protested.

"Do it," James ordered sternly. "You can see more of your cousin in the morning if you can mind your manners and remember she's your cousin, not some tavern wench."

After that set-down the boy might have been expected to leave shamefaced. Not Jeremy. He grinned roguishly at Reggie and winked.

"I'll dream of you, sweet Regan, tonight and every night hereafter."

She nearly laughed. The audacity! She gave him a pert look and said, "Don't be obnoxious, cousin. You held me close enough to tell I'm very much married."

Reggie groaned, damning her heedless tongue. Jeremy cast one look at his father and ran for the door. She steeled herself, sure James had taken her meaning quite clearly.

"Is it true?"

"Yes."

"Damnation take him! How did this come about, Regan? How the devil did you come to marry that — that —"

"You sound as bad as Tony," she cut him short. "You each want a piece of Nicholas. So find him, divide him up between you, cut him into pieces, shoot him, kill him. What do I care? He's only my husband and the father of my child."

"Easy, squirt," Conrad said softly. "Your uncle gave up his plans for the lad the moment he learned you were married to him."

"What plans?" she demanded. "What is this all about, Uncle James?"

"It's a long story, sweet, and —"

"Please don't treat me like a child again, Uncle James."

"Very well," he said. "The short of it is I thrashed him soundly for some insults he had dealt me. For this I ended up in jail."

"And nearly hanged," Conrad added.

"No," Reggie gasped, "I can't believe Nicholas —"

"He gave Hawke's name to the authorities, squirt. The *Maiden Anne* might not fly the Jolly Roger anymore, but England never forgets. Hawke was tried for piracy. He managed to escape, no thanks to Montieth."

"You see why the lads were careful not to mention my name in front of you," James said. "I had to arrange my death; otherwise I would have had to leave England immediately. I'm sorry, Regan," he added gently. "I would have preferred you didn't know what kind of mess your husband has been involved in."

"Don't apologize, uncle," Reggie said tightly. "It only amazes me how often I am reminded of how wrong I was about him. I just don't understand how I could have fooled myself into thinking I loved him."

"Don't you?"

"No. And don't look at me that way. I really don't love him."

"Does she protest too much, Hawke?" Conrad grinned.

"Oh, you think so?" Reggie said heatedly. "Well, would *you* love a wife that deserted you the very day she married you? I will never forgive him, never. Even if he didn't want to marry me, even if he felt justified in leaving, he's hateful for not . . . well, he's simply hateful."

The two men exchanged a glance. "Where is he?" asked her uncle.

"He left England. He couldn't even stand to be in the same country with me."

"He has estates elsewhere?"

She shrugged, lost in her own misery once again. "He once mentioned owning property in the West Indies, but I don't know if he went there. What does it matter? He has no intention of coming back. He made that perfectly —"

She stopped as a commotion started downstairs. James nodded to Conrad to see what it was. The moment Conrad opened the door it was clear the scuffle was going on nearer than the floor below. James followed Conrad out, Reggie right behind the men.

A fight was taking place on the stairs,

between Henri and — *Tony*? Good Lord, it *was* Tony! Artie already lay sprawled at the bottom of the stairs. Henri was about to join him there.

Reggie pushed her way between James and Conrad. "Tony, stop!"

Anthony saw her and let go of Henri, who slumped down onto the steps.

"So I was right!" Tony glared, seeing his brother. "You didn't learn your lesson the last time you ran off with her, did you, James?"

"May I ask how you found us?" James inquired with profound calm.

"You may not!" Anthony retorted.

"Tony, you don't understand —" she began.

"Reggie!"

She gritted her teeth. Tony was so stubborn. This was an opportunity she couldn't pass up. The brothers were together, and it was a chance for them to mend their rift. But if Tony wanted only to drag her straight out of here, how could she get him to calm down and talk to James?

"Ohhhh!" Reggie gripped James' arm with one hand and her belly with the other, doubling over as if in pain. "I feel . . . ohhhh! Too much . . . excitement. A bed, uncle. Get me to a bed."

266

James lifted her gently in his arms. He didn't speak, but he did give her a doubtful look when his eye caught hers. Reggie ignored this and groaned again, quite effectively.

Jeremy came running down the hall toward them, tucking an open shirt into his trousers, both donned hastily. "What happened? What's wrong with Regan?" No one answered him as James and Conrad hurried back to the bedroom with Reggie. "Who are you?" Jeremy demanded as Anthony barged past him to follow the others.

Anthony stopped cold. He'd given the boy only a glance, but it was enough. It was like looking into a mirror of the past. "Who the bloody hell are *you?*"

Conrad laughed and came out of the bedroom. "He's not yours, if that's what you're thinking, Sir Anthony. But he's family, all right. James' boy."

Jeremy covered Anthony's gasp of surprise with his own gasp. "Uncle Tony? Hell's bells! I thought I'd never get to meet any of my father's kin, but here's Regan first, and now you, and all in one night." He grabbed Anthony in a bear hug that damned near knocked the breath out of him. Tony gripped the boy's wide shoulders then and returned the hug, surprising Conrad. "Don't go away, young 'un," he said gruffly before moving on to the bedroom.

Seeing Reggie stretched out on the bed, James beside her, Tony's fury returned. "Confound you, James! Have you no bloody sense a'tall, dragging her around in her condition?"

"He didn't drag me," Reggie protested.

"Don't lie for me, sweet," James admonished her gently. He rose and faced his younger brother. "You are quite correct, Tony. If I had any sense, I'd have found out who Montieth's new wife was before I had her brought here to flush him out."

Tony looked bewildered, then exasperated. "A mistake?"

"A colossal one."

"That's still no excuse," Tony grumbled.

"Agreed."

"Will you stop agreeing with me!"

James chuckled. "You don't need an excuse to have a go at me, if that's what you're itching to do, brother."

"Don't do it, Uncle Tony," Jeremy said as he entered the room. "I would hate to have a row with you when I've only just met you."

"He's very protective of his old man," Conrad put in. "Thinks his father can't manage on his own anymore after the grueling exercise Montieth put him through."

268

"I thought I told you to go to bed, Jeremy." But James' scowl was directed at his first mate.

"I thought you said *you* thrashed Nicholas, Uncle James," Reggie said.

"Oh, he did, squirt." Conrad grinned. "He walked away from the encounter — just barely, mind you — whereas your husband, no doubt, did not."

"No doubt?" she echoed. Conrad shrugged. "We left while he was still out."

"You mean," she demanded furiously, "you abandoned him when he was hurt?"

Conrad and James flinched. "He got help quickly enough, Regan, fast enough to land me in jail within the hour."

"What's this?" Anthony cried.

"Oh, the story should delight you, Tony," Reggie said crossly. "It seems you're not the only one who wants my husband's blood."

Anthony frowned. "I thought you were done defending that blackguard?"

"I am," she replied stiffly. "But he's mine to deal with, *not yours.* I don't need my uncles interfering when I am perfectly capable of making Nicholas Eden regret returning to England, if he ever does."

"That sounds ominous enough," Anthony agreed.

"Doesn't it though?" James smiled. "I

almost wish he would return to her."

"Famous!" Reggie snapped. "I'm so glad you two have something in common again."

"Don't get your hopes up, puss," Anthony warned her. "I don't associate with pirates who abscond with children."

"Oh, bother, Tony," Reggie said irritably. "That was years ago. Let go of it, do."

"Who are you calling a pirate?" Jeremy demanded belligerently.

"Your father is a pirate," Anthony said reasonably.

"He's not! Not anymore!"

Anthony looked to James for clarification, but James stubbornly refused to explain himself. It was Conrad who said, "The *Maiden Anne* retired soon after Jeremy joined the crew. We couldn't very well raise the lad on board a ship, could we? The only voyages she makes now, aside from a few voyages back here to the homeland, are to take our crops to market. We've become planters in the islands."

"Is it true, James?" a quiet voice spoke behind them in the doorway.

"Uncle Jason!" Reggie cried, seeing her oldest uncle. Jason looked distinctly menacing in great-tiered Garrick, and his scowl matched his costume.

"Ah, I'm sorry, James," Anthony offered.

"Forgot to tell you the elders were close behind me."

"Not close enough," Edward puffed breathlessly as he appeared in the doorway next to Jason. "And you didn't have to rush off ahead of us, Anthony. Nice place you found here, James. What's it costing you?"

"Still the businessman first and last, eh, Edward?" James grinned. Then he said, "Would you mind telling me how the devil you found me? Let alone how you knew I was in England."

"Anthony's doing," Edward replied. "Saw a sketch Reggie drew. Stopped by when he got back to London this morning to let me know how she was getting on, and it came to him then where he had seen one of the fellows in the sketch. One of your crew when you first bought the *Maiden Anne*, he remembered. Jason had just come in from Haverston, and he figured out the rest."

"But how did you know to look here?"

"Easy," Edward answered. "This is the nearest port. I thought just maybe you were brazen enough to bring your ship into harbor here."

"Not that brazen," James replied, stung. "She's waiting off the coast."

"Then that's why we couldn't find her. Of course, Anthony isn't one to give up easily.

We spent the rest of the afternoon making inquiries from one end of town to the other. Finally lucked onto a gent who had seen you coming and going from this renter."

"And now what?" James inquired, looking directly at Jason. "Am I to receive a measure from each of you again?"

"Of course not, Uncle James," Reggie answered quickly. "I'm sure they are willing to forget the past if you are. After all, you have given up pirating. You've settled down, and you have a fine son. I know they will want to welcome him into our family."

"A son!"

"Me," Jeremy said proudly, looking at Jason and Edward from across the room.

Reggie continued before her older uncles could recover, "I really don't think I can manage any more excitement today. Why, I could very well lose my baby if —"

"Baby!"

"Why, Tony, didn't you tell them?" Reggie asked in all innocence.

"Very nicely done, puss." Anthony grinned at her. "And I see you have recovered from your earlier upset."

"I just needed to lie down for a few moments."

He shook his head. "Well, I think you can safely leave us alone now to kiss and make up. Run along and find yourself a cup of tea or something. And take my new nephew with you."

"Uncle Jason?" She didn't have to be specific. He nodded. He was wearing his harmless scowl now, so it was all right. "Go on, Reggie. A man can't get a thing said when you're in the room."

Reggie smiled triumphantly and hugged James. "Welcome back to the family, Uncle James."

"Regan, my sweet, don't ever change."

"As if you four would let me change without *your* approval!" She hooked her arm through Jeremy's. "Come along, cousin. Your father will tell them all about you, and you can tell me all about yourself."

"I had best go with them," Conrad said, and did.

As the three left, they heard behind them, "You still have to be different, don't you, James?" This was Jason. "Her name isn't Regan!"

"It isn't Reggie either! And anyway she's outgrown Reggie. Regan is more suitable for a grown woman."

"It sounds to me like you failed to get them to make up," Jeremy said to her.

"Stuff," Reggie giggled. "Tell him, Connie."

"She's right, lad," Conrad said as he escorted the two down the hall. "They wouldn't be happy unless they were arguing about something."

"So just think how happy you've made them, Jeremy," Reggie added sagely. "Now they can disagree over *your* upbringing, too."

CHAPTER 25

The stallion left a trail of dust as it galloped over the plantation road. New spring flowers of the European variety joined with tropical blooms along the roadside to create a profusion of wild color. To the right of the road, less than a mile away, the ocean cast huge waves upon a sandy beach. The hot sun glinted off blue waters as far as the eye could see.

Nicholas noticed none of the beauty around him that sultry early April day. He was returning from the island's small harbor and a meeting with Captain Bowdler, who had reported that his ship would be ready to sail with the morning tide. Nicholas was going home to England, home to Regina.

Six months away had not helped to get her out of his mind. He had tried. He had spent months turning a broken-down plantation house into the showcase of the island, months more in getting the land ready for crops and planting. Nearly every moment had been spent in hard work, but his continuing mood was still dangerously maudlin. A hundred times he had decided to go home. As many times he had talked himself out of it. The situation there would not be changed. Miriam and her threats were still hanging over him and Regina.

But in all this time, Nicholas had overlooked the obvious. Regina probably already knew. Miriam could not live six months with the girl and not try to turn her against him. Yes, she must know by now.

That likelihood had been pointed out to him last week when he got thoroughly foxed with Captain Bowdler and poured out his soul to the man. It took someone objective and just as drunk to make him see that he was sitting on the island brooding like a child because he didn't have the woman he wanted. Well, he'd brooded long enough. It was time to go home and see what was what. If his wife detested him, then that would be the end of that.

But if she didn't? Captain Bowdler asked him that, too. What if she scorned public opinion and judged him on his own merits? Well, the truth was, he had treated her abominably and that was all she *had* to judge him by. Too, she had buckled under one scandal, causing her to want to marry him. He would like to believe that she had married him for reasons other than propriety, but it wasn't likely.

So where did that leave him? Nowhere. Until he got home, he couldn't know how much damage had been done.

A barefoot, chocolate-skinned boy ran out of the large white house to take Nicholas' horse. That was the only thing Nicholas hadn't gotten used to here, owning slaves. It was the one thing about the islands he hated.

"Guests you have, sir, in de study," his housekeeper told him. He thanked her and moved off down the wide, open hall, a little annoyed. Who was calling? He had packing to do yet and another meeting with his estate agent. He didn't have time to chit-chat.

He stepped into the darkened study, where drawn shades kept out the noon heat. He scanned the occupied chairs surrounding his desk. Rather than believe what he saw, he closed his eyes. This was not to be borne.

"Tell me I've imagined you, Hawke."

"You've imagined me."

Nicholas crossed the room and sat down behind his desk. "Then you won't mind if I ignore you?"

"See what I mean, Jeremy? He'd spit in the devil's eye.

"Is he the best you could do for a third?" Nicholas asked dryly, indicating the young man. "I don't go in for hurting children. Can't you and your red-haired cohort manage without help?"

"You don't seem surprised to see me, Montieth," James said evenly.

"Should I be?"

"Why, yes. You left England before the hanging."

"Ah, the hanging." Nicholas leaned back, smiling. "Did it draw a big crowd?"

"You find it amusing?" Jeremy demanded.

"My dear boy, all I find amusing is my own stupidity. If I had known this fellow was going to make it his life's mission to plague me, I'd never have arranged for the guards to turn their backs so he could get away."

"Bloody liar!" Conrad joined in heatedly. "Those guards were unbribable! I offered them enough to know that."

"Connie, isn't it?"

"It's Mr. Sharpe to you!"

Nicholas chuckled. "You should know money isn't always the answer. It also helps to know the right people."

"Why?" James asked softly.

"Oh, never doubt that my reasons were selfish, old man," Nicholas replied. "Since I wasn't going to be around to attend the hanging myself, I decided to deny the rest of the populace that pleasure, too. If I could have arranged a postponement until my return, you can be sure I'd have done it. So don't feel you have to thank me."

"Let me have him, Hawke." Conrad's fury was overtaking him. "She'll never have to know."

"If you mean my housekeeper, the old girl's probably got her ear to the door right now. But don't let that dissuade you, old man."

Conrad came out of his chair like a shot, but James motioned him to stop. The captain stared thoughtfully at Nicholas for several moments, probing those honey-gold eyes, and then he laughed.

"Damn me if I don't believe half of what you've said, Montieth." He was probing Nicholas' eyes with his own riveting gaze. "But I wonder," he went on slowly, "what your real motive was. Did you figure if you got me out of the mess you'd got me into, I would call it quits? I wouldn't have." Nicholas didn't answer and James laughed again. "Don't tell me a man of your nature has a conscience? A sense of fair play?"

"Not bloody likely," Conrad mumbled.

"Ah, don't forget, Connie, I wasn't to hang for what I did to him, yet he was responsible for my arrest."

"Very amusing," Nicholas said coldly. "Now may we dispense with these pointless speculations? Play your hand, Hawke, or get out, I have things to do."

"As do we. You don't suppose I enjoy hunting you down, do you? It seems that's all I ever do anymore," James sighed. "The last six months have been most tiresome."

"You'll understand if I don't sympathize?"

"How much of his lip are you going to take, Hawke?" Conrad growled. "Are you ready to reconsider now?"

"Connie's right," Jeremy put in. "I can't see what Regan ever saw in him."

"Can't you, lad?" Conrad sneered. "Look at that pretty face."

"Ease off, both of you," James warned. "Regan has more sense than to fall for good looks. She had to have seen more in him than that."

"Well, he's certainly not what I imagined," Jeremy grumbled.

James smiled. "You can't judge him by this visit, Jeremy. He's got his defenses up."

Nicholas felt he'd been pushed far

enough. "Hawke, if you have something to say to me, say it. If you want another go at me, get to it. But if you three just want to have an argument over some doxy, you can do that elsewhere."

"You'll take that back, Lord Montieth," Jeremy cried. "She's not a doxy!"

"Who the bloody hell *is* this boy?"

James chuckled. "My son, don't you know. I tried to get him to remain behind on the ship, but he would have none of it. Determined to be here to see how you took our news."

"I doubt you have news that concerns me."

"Your wife is no concern of yours?"

Nicholas stood up slowly, his eyes locked with the captain's. "What about her?"

"She's very lovely, isn't she?"

"How could you — ?" With a growl of rage, Nicholas launched himself forward, flew over the desk, and grabbed James by the throat. It took Conrad and Jeremy together to pull him away from the captain. They held Nicholas, each grabbing an arm.

"If you've laid one hand on her, Hawke, I'll kill you!"

James rubbed his sore throat, but there was a twinkle in his dark eyes. He was satisfied. "What did I tell you, Connie? Is this the reaction of man who doesn't care?" he crowed.

"My wife," Nicholas snarled before Conrad could think what to say, "what have you done with her?"

"Oh, this is famous," James chuckled. Conrad and Jeremy clutched Nicholas tighter. "What sweet revenge it would be, lad, to invent a tale to torment you with. I could tell you I had kidnapped your dear wife, which is quite true, as a matter of fact. I had meant to use her to bring you to me. We didn't know you had left the country, you see. And . . . unfortunately, I didn't know who your wife was."

"Don't tell me the fearless Captain Hawke was intimidated by her family?"

This was greeted by such uproarious laughter from the other three that Nicholas was taken aback. He was able to throw off Jeremy's tight hold, then aim a stunning blow to Conrad's midsection. It gained his release for a moment, but only a moment.

"Easy, lad." James put up a hand to stop Nicholas from any more fighting. "I don't want to hurt you." He grinned. "Especially since it took me weeks to recover from the last time."

"Is that supposed to pacify me? It took me just as long to recover, and it prevented me from discouraging Regina . . . well, that is none of your business."

"Depends on how you look at it, lad. I know you tried to get her to jilt you. A shame she didn't," he sighed, "but that's beside the point."

"Get *to* the point!" Nicholas snapped. "What have you done with Regina?"

"My dear boy, Regan would never come to harm through me. You see, she's my beloved niece."

"Regan? I don't give a damn —"

"Don't you?"

There was so much insinuation in his manner that Nicholas stiffened, searching his mind. Suddenly, what he hadn't noticed before came clear as he stared at Hawke. Hawke and the boy bore a distinctive resemblance to each other and to . . .

"James Malory?"

"The same."

"Bloody everlasting hell."

James laughed. "Don't take it too hard. Imagine how I felt, finding out you had married into my family. That put an end to my plans."

"Why?" Nicholas retorted. "As I recall, your family doesn't acknowledge you."

"That was before our reunion. My brothers and I have patched things up, thanks to

Regan. She does have a way of getting what she wants."

"Doesn't she," Nicholas murmured, his voice heavy with irony. "What are you doing here then? Came to congratulate me, did you?"

"Hardly, dear boy." James smiled. "I've come to take you home."

Nicholas' eyes shot fire. "Not bloody likely."

James' smile turned sharklike. "You will come with us, one way or another."

Nicholas looked from one to the other of them. He saw that they were serious. "Your escort is not necessary." He decided to try the truth. "My own ship is ready. I am sailing on the morning tide. I had already decided to return to England, you see, so you won't be needed, gentlemen."

"If you say so, dear boy," James replied doubtfully.

"I am telling you the truth."

"Sailing out of this port on your own won't guarantee your reaching England. No, I must insist you come with us."

Nicholas' temper was beginning to simmer again. "Why?"

"My brothers don't like it that you have deserted your wife. They want you back where they can keep an eye on you."

"Of all the absurdities! They can't keep me in England if I wish to leave."

"What you do after you get home is of no concern to me." James shrugged. "I'm just following Jason's orders. He said to fetch you home, and so I will."

As they escorted Nicholas out of the room, Jeremy whispered to his father, "Uncle Jason never said you were supposed to bring him back. He only said you were supposed to tell him about the baby if we found him."

"I haven't done my brother's bidding since I came of age, lad," his father whispered back. "I don't want to start now."

"But if he knew, he might not put up a fuss."

James chuckled. "Did I say I wanted him to enjoy the crossing?"

CHAPTER 26

"Nicholas!" Eleanor came quickly to her feet as the three men entered the drawing room of Nicholas' London townhouse.

Reggie stood up more slowly, her eyes narrowing. There were men on either side of her husband. "Uncle James, is this your doing?"

"I just happened to come across him, sweet."

"Well, you can just take him back to wherever you just *happened* to come across him," she said tightly. "He's not welcome here."

"Regina!" Eleanor gasped.

Reggie crossed her arms over her chest, stubbornly refusing to look at Nicholas' aunt. She had become very close to Eleanor in the last months, had even come to love her. But no one, not her relatives or his, was going to make Reggie accept a man who had been forcibly brought back. The humiliation of that was almost as bad as the desertion.

Nicholas studied Regina covertly, pretending he was looking at his aunt. He felt like smashing his fist into something, anything. He also felt like weeping. Look at her! She evidently knew about his parentage, knew and despised him for it. He saw it in the hard set of her lips; the stiff, unyielding line of her posture.

So, Miriam had told her. Well and good. If she hated the thought of being married to a bastard, it was what she deserved for forcing him into the marriage.

Nicholas' being brought home in the hands of her uncle had made him forget that he'd made up his mind to return and had wanted to make amends. He had, in fact, forgotten everything except his fury.

"Not welcome here, madame?" Nicholas said softly. "Am I mistaken, or does this house belong to me?"

Her eyes met his for the first time. Good Lord, she'd forgotten how devastating were those sherry-gold eyes. And he looked wonderful, his skin deeply tanned, his hair brightly sun-streaked. But she couldn't allow him to cast his spell over her.

"You forget, sir, that you refused to share a house with me. To be specific, you *gave* me your home."

"Silverley, not my townhouse. And what the bloody hell have you done to this house?" he demanded, looking around at all the new furniture and floral wallpaper.

Reggie smiled innocently, her voice sweet. "Why, Nicholas, don't you like it? Of course, you weren't here to help me decorate, but I was very frugal with your money. It only cost you four thousand pounds."

James quickly turned around to hide his mirth. Conrad suddenly found the ceiling fascinating. Only Eleanor frowned. The two young people were now glaring at each other.

"Nicholas, is this any way to greet your wife after seven months?"

"What are you doing here, Aunt Ellie?"

"And is that any way to greet me?" His expression did not soften. She sighed. "If you must know, this house is so big I thought Regina could use my company. It wasn't right, your wife living here alone."

"I left her at Silverley!" he thundered.

"Don't you dare shout at Ellie!" Reggie shouted at him. "And *you* go live at Silverley with Miriam. I like it fine right here."

"I think we will both return to Silverley," he said in a cold voice, "now that I have no reason to avoid my *mother* anymore."

"Unacceptable."

"I wasn't asking your permission. A husband doesn't need his wife's permission — for anything," he said harshly.

She gasped at the meaning. "You have relinquished all rights," she said fiercely.

He smiled. "Not relinquished. Just refrained from using . . . until now. After all, your family has gone to *so* much trouble to bring us together again, *I* certainly don't want to disappoint them," he said cruelly.

"Lady Reggie," an older woman servant interrupted from the doorway. "It's time."

"Thank you, Tess." Reggie dismissed the nurse with a nod, then turned to James and Conrad and said, "I know you meant well, but you will understand if I don't thank you for your trouble."

"You did say you could manage very well, Regan," James reminded her.

She smiled for the first time since their arrival. It was her old impish grin, and she gave both men a hug and kiss. "So I did. And so I will. Now if you gentlemen will excuse me, I must see to my son."

James and Conrad burst into great gales of laughter as Reggie left the room. Her husband stood stock-still, rooted to the floor, his mouth open, a look of complete stupefaction on his face.

"What did I tell you, Connie?" James roared. "Is the look on his face worth all the trouble he put us through or is it not?"

CHAPTER 27

Nicholas downed his third brandy in twenty minutes and poured another. James Malory and Conrad Sharpe, his shadows for so long, had just left his house, and he was still stinging from the amusement they had derived at his expense. Even so, he told himself, he had more important matters to simmer over.

He sat in what had so recently been his study, now a small music room. A music room! If that wasn't a piece of malicious spite, he didn't know what was. A man's study was sacred. And she hadn't just changed the study, she'd eliminated it entirely.

Had she expected him never to return? Or had she hoped he would? Damnation take her. His sweet, beautiful wife had turned into a vengeful, hot-tempered woman in the same mold as her two younger uncles. Damnation take them too.

Eleanor paced the room, casting disapproving looks at Nicholas every time he raised the brandy glass to his lips. He was stewing in his resentment.

"What the bloody hell did she do with my papers, my desk, my books?"

Eleanor steeled herself to be calm. "You just learned that you have a son. Is this all you can ask about?"

"Are you saying you don't know where she put my things?"

Eleanor sighed. "In the attic, Nicky. All of it is in the attic."

"You were here when she turned my house upside down?" he accused.

"I was here, yes."

"And you didn't try to stop her?" he asked incredulously.

"For heaven's sake, Nicky, you took a wife. You couldn't expect to keep a bachelor residence after getting married."

"I didn't ask for a wife," he said bitterly. "And I expected her to remain where I put her, not trespass here. If she wanted to redecorate, why the bloody hell couldn't she satisfy herself with remodeling Silverley?"

"Actually, I believe she liked Silverley the way it was."

"Then why didn't she stay there?" he raged.

"Do you really have to ask?"

"What was the problem?" he sneered. "Wouldn't my dear mother turn over the reins?"

"Regina took her rightful place there, if that is what you mean."

"Then they got along famously? Well, why not?" he laughed derisively. "They have so much in common, both despising me as they do."

"That is unfair, Nicky."

"Don't tell me you're going to defend your sister at this late date?"

"No," Eleanor replied sadly.

"I see. You're taking sides with Regina. Well, you wanted me to marry her. Are you pleased with the way it's turned out?"

Eleanor shook her head. "I swear I just don't know you anymore. Why did you do it, Nicky? She's a wonderful girl. She could have made you so happy."

Sudden pain welled up in his chest, choking him. Happiness with Regina could never be his, no matter how much he wanted it. But Eleanor couldn't understand why because Miriam had never told her the truth. The sisters had been estranged for as long as he could remember. And if Miriam or Regina hadn't told her, he certainly wasn't going to. Sweet Ellie would pity him and he

293

wanted none of that. Better she think him the detestable character everyone else thought him.

He stared down at the glass in his hand and mumbled, "I don't like being forced."

"But the deed was done," Eleanor pointed out. "You did marry her. Couldn't you have given her a chance?"

"No."

"All right. I understand. You were bitter. But now, Nicky, can't you try now?"

"And have her laugh in my face? No thank you."

"She was hurt, that's all. What did you expect when you deserted your bride on her wedding day?"

The hand on the glass tightened. "Is that what she told you? She was hurt?"

Eleanor looked away. "Actually . . ."

"So I thought."

"Don't interrupt, Nicky." She frowned sternly. "I was going to say she won't talk about you to me at all. But give me some credit for understanding the girl after living with her for four months."

"She's wise not to tell you what she thinks of me. She knows you have a soft spot for me."

"You're just not going to unbend, are you?" she cried. He refused to answer and she lost her patience. "What about your *son?* Is he to grow up in a household of strife — as you did? Is that what you want for him?"

Nicholas shot out of the chair and hurled his glass against the wall.

Eleanor was too shocked to speak, and after a moment he explained himself by saying in a hoarse voice, "I am no fool, madame. She may have told everyone the child is mine, but what else can she say? Let her try and tell me the baby is mine!"

"Are you saying you and she . . . that you never . . ."

"Once, Aunt Ellie, only once. And that was four months before I married her!"

Eleanor's expression softened. "She gave birth five months after the wedding, Nicky."

He stopped cold, then stated flatly, "The birth was premature."

"It was not!" Eleanor snapped. "How would you know?"

"Because," he said reasonably, "she would have told me about the baby in order to keep me here if she'd been pregnant when I left. You cannot tell me she wouldn't have known if she'd been four months along. Also, she would have shown some sign of it, which she didn't. She could only have been one or two months pregnant when I left and obviously unaware of her condition.

"Nicholas Eden, until you can stop being so perverse, I shall have nothing to say to you!" With that, Eleanor swept angrily from the room.

Nicholas grabbed the brandy decanter, about to send it the way of the glass. He tilted it to his lips instead. Why not?

Yes, she'd have told him if she'd been pregnant when they married. He recalled the times she let other men take her home. He recalled George Fowler in particular and the red-hot rage he had felt over that. Had it been intuition? Had he known the young bastard wouldn't take her straight home?

Nicholas was so furious he could barely think straight. He had tried not to think about the child from the moment he'd learned of his birth. His son, was he? Just let her try and convince him of that.

CHAPTER 28

Reggie smiled absently as the little fist kneaded her breast. Feeding her son had always been such a lovely, satisfying time for her, but tonight her thoughts were downstairs. She didn't even notice when the small mouth stopped sucking.

"He's off to sleep again, Reggie," Tess whispered.

"Oh, so he is. But not for long, eh?"

Reggie gently lifted the infant to her shoulder and patted his back. His head snuggled there, his mouth sucking air for a moment before it went slack. She smiled up at her old nurse, now her son's nurse.

"Perhaps this time he will stay asleep," Reggie whispered to Tess as she put him back to bed. But the moment she laid him down on his belly, his head popped up jerkily, his feet started to wiggle, and those inquisitive eyes opened.

"It's to be expected." Tess grinned. "He

just doesn't need as much sleep now. He's getting older."

"I'll have to start thinking about getting you some help then."

"Bother that," Tess scoffed. "When he's six months old and starting to crawl, then I'll welcome the help."

"If you say so." Reggie laughed. "But you go on and have your dinner now. I'll stay with him until you're through."

"No you won't, my girl. You have company below."

"Yes," Reggie sighed, "my husband. But as I have nothing to say to him, I am not going down. Now go on, Tess. And please have a tray sent up here to me, will you?"

"But —"

"No." Reggie picked up the wide-awake baby again. "This gentleman right here is the only company I want tonight."

Tess gone, Reggie dropped all pretense of ladylike behavior and got down on the floor to play with her son, imitating his sounds and gestures, coaxing him to smile. He wasn't quite up to laughter yet, but that wouldn't be long in coming, for he heard enough laughter around him. His many visitors, from the servants to her uncles, all tried to make him smile with crazy antics that were quite as ridiculous as his mother's.

How she loved this little person. Right before he was born she had fallen into a terrible depression. But after the birth, which had amazed the doctor by being such an easy labor for a first child, Reggie was filled with euphoria. Plainly and simply, her child brightened her life. In fact, in the last two months she had been so busy learning about and enjoying her new motherhood, that she rarely thought of Nicholas, at least not more than a dozen times a day.

"But now he's back, love. What are we going to do?" Reggie sighed.

"You don't expect him to answer that, do you?"

"Oh, Meg, you startled me!"

"D'you want this down there on the floor?" Meg was holding a tray of food. "I caught the maid on the way up here with it."

"Over there on the table, please," Reggie directed. "And now tell me all about your outing with Harris."

Nicholas had left Harris behind, to the valet's endless misery. The poor man had been bereft all these months and especially unhappy after Reggie moved into the townhouse. He was downright hostile, and he and Meg had had a few heated exchanges, defending their territory.

Abruptly, after the baby arrived, all of that changed. Harris warmed to Reggie or, more exactly, to Meg. Meg and Harris astonished themselves by discovering a liking for each other. They had even been going out together lately and got along famously just so long as Meg said nothing derogatory about the Viscount.

Meg put the tray down with a bang. "Never mind about that hardheaded gent I've been passin' time with. I don't think I'll be doin' that anymore. What does he do the moment he hears the Viscount is here? He doesn't give me a by-your-leave, but rushes upstairs to find his lordship! And I could've saved him the trouble. Tess informed me another bottle of brandy was just delivered to the music room."

"The music room? Ah, yes," Reggie giggled suddenly. "The music room. I'd forgotten what I did to his study."

"Tess said he and Lady Ellie were shouting in there," Meg informed her.

"Were they? I'm afraid that doesn't interest me."

"Posh," Meg scoffed. "You'd give your eyeteeth to know what they said about you."

"You assume they were arguing about me."

"If not you, what then?"

"What indeed?" Nicholas asked from the open doorway.

Meg turned in a huff, cursing herself for not closing the door. Reggie, lying on the floor, tilted her head back for an upside-down view of her husband. She was flat on her back, her son stretched out on her chest. She sat up slowly.

Nicholas approached her, seeing a small head on her shoulder, one fist jammed firmly into his mouth. Black tufts of hair and vivid blue eyes were unmistakable. A Malory, through and through.

He came around her and offered her his hand. "Do you do this often, love?"

She wasn't fooled by the mellow tone. There was a hard set to his lips, a heated glow in his eyes. Why, he wasn't pleased about his son at all! How could he stand there looking at him and not be delighted? Her mother's pride came rushing to the fore. She held on to his hand and stood up, but the moment she was on her feet, she turned her back to him.

"If you haven't come here to see Thomas, you can leave," she announced frostily.

"Oh, but I have come to see him." Nicholas smiled grimly. "You named him Thomas, after your father?"

Reggie gently put the baby down in his bed and leaned over to kiss him. She turned and faced her husband. "Thomas Ashton Malory Eden."

"Well, that certainly takes care of *your* side of the family, doesn't it?"

His sarcasm made her boil. "If you wanted him named after your side, you should have been around for his birth."

"Why didn't you tell me?"

Her eyes narrowed. In another moment they would be shouting, and this she would not allow in the nursery.

"Meg, stay with Thomas until Tess returns, will you?" Then she said to Nicholas, "My rooms are across the hall. If you care to finish this conversation, you may visit me there."

Reggie didn't wait for him but stalked across the hall and into her sitting room. Nicholas followed, closing the door loudly. She turned around and glared at him. "If you wish to slam doors, kindly do so in another part of the house."

"If I wish to slam doors, which I did not do just now, I will bloody well do so in *any* part of my house. Now answer me! Why didn't you tell me?"

What to answer? She wasn't going to admit that she hadn't wanted to hold him that way. She wasn't at all certain just then that anything could have held him, not when he had failed to show the slightest inkling of pleasure in either her or his son.

At last she simply asked, "Would it have made any difference?"

"How will we ever know, since you didn't tell me?" A sardonic note entered his manner. "Of course, there is the possibility that you didn't know and therefore couldn't tell me."

"Not know that I was four months pregnant?" She smiled. "I did have very few symptoms, it's true. But four months? Any woman would know by then."

He moved closer until he was standing directly in front of her chair. "Usually at four months everyone else knows as well," he said softly. "For the obvious reason of an increased girth. You were lacking that, love."

Reggie's eyes met his and widened at what she read. "You don't think he's yours!" she whispered incredulously. "No wonder you barely looked at him!" She stood up and he moved back to allow her to pass. She spoke to the room at large. "Oh, this is famous. I didn't once consider this."

She could see the humor in it, though, and under other circumstances she'd have laughed. What a perfect revenge for his treatment of her, presenting him with another man's child on his return. But Reggie was in no condition to feel the humorous side of things. There was the shock of seeing him again, and the nastier shock of his ugly conclusion.

He touched her shoulder, swinging her around to face him. "Is this pretended surprise the best performance you can manage, madame? You have had ample time to invent some excuse to explain why your wedding gown clung to your very tiny waist the day I married you. I am most curious to hear your fabrication."

The gypsy slant of her eyes became more pronounced as they narrowed to furious slits, but she kept her voice calm. "Are you? There is the obvious excuse of a tightly laced corset, so shall I say that's what it was? Would you believe that? No? Just as well, since I never lace my corsets tightly."

"Then you admit it?" he snarled.

"Admit what, Nicholas? I tell you that I had a most unusual pregnancy. It was so unusual, in fact, that I began to worry that something was wrong with my baby when I was seven months pregnant and saw a woman only five months pregnant who was twice my size." She took a deep breath. "Uncle Jason assured me that my grandmother was the same way. People hardly knew she was pregnant until the babies were born. He said he and his brothers were all born just as tiny as Thomas was, and look how they turned out. And he was right. Thomas is growing in leaps and bounds, perfectly formed, perfectly normal. He will probably turn out just as large as his father one day." She finished, out of breath, still furious, but a little relieved. She had told him all of it. What he believed or didn't believe was up to him.

"That was a good, original story, love, certainly better than I expected."

Reggie shook her head. He had formed his opinion and wasn't going to let go of it.

"If you don't want to claim Thomas as yours, then don't. I really don't care what you think," she said simply.

Nicholas exploded. "Tell me he is mine! Tell me in plain words."

"He is yours."

"I don't believe it."

"Fine." She nodded her understanding. "Now if you will excuse me, my dinner is getting cold."

He stared in amazement as she passed him and headed for the door. "You won't try to convince me?"

Reggie glanced back at him and hesitated.

His bewildered, faintly hopeful look almost made her relent. But she had done all she could. The convincing would have to be up to him. "What for?" she answered. "Thomas doesn't need you. He has me. And he certainly won't lack for male attention, not with four great-uncles to dote on him."

"Not bloody likely!" he bellowed. "I won't have those autocratic bastards raising my —" He clamped his mouth shut, glaring at her furiously. "Go eat your dinner!"

As she returned to the nursery Reggie smiled, her humor greatly restored. Well! That certainly gave her something to think about, didn't it?

CHAPTER 29

Nicholas sat up slowly, frowning at the unfamiliar noise that had wakened him. He shook his head and lay down again, but in no more than a moment he was fully awake. The infant was crying. He was hungry, wasn't he?

He had identified the noise, but he remained wide-awake, wondering how often this business of having one's sleep disturbed occurred. But it didn't matter. Tomorrow he would pack them all back to Silverley. And if he stayed there as well, his rooms were farther away from the nursery there than here.

If he stayed? Why shouldn't he stay? Miriam had kept him from Silverley for years, but Miriam had already done her damage in telling Regina about his birth. That done, the rest of the world finding out didn't matter anymore. Miriam couldn't hurt him now. And he certainly wasn't going to let

Regina keep him from Silverley. Silverley was, he reminded himself fiercely, his home. He still had some rights in this world!

The house was quiet now, the infant no doubt being fed by his wet nurse. Had Regina been awakened? He pictured her in the next room, curled up in bed, probably sound asleep. She was probably accustomed to these disturbances and slept right through them.

Having never seen her in bed before, he couldn't get a clear picture of her. Would her hands be clasped under her chin like a child's? Would her dark hair be loose or tucked into a nightcap? How long *was* her hair? He had never seen it other than formally arranged. What did she wear to sleep in? He didn't know anything about her, and she was his wife.

He had every right to walk the few steps to her room, wake her, and make love to her. He wanted to. But he never would. She was no longer the passionate but innocent young woman who gave him her maidenhead on a warm summer night. She would reject him, treat him with contempt and scorn. He wasn't going to let himself in for that.

But . . . she didn't have to know if he tiptoed into her room and looked at her, did she? Nicholas was out of bed and into his robe before the thought was finished. Soon he was in the hall between Regina's sitting room and the nursery. Her door was closed and there was no light beneath it. The nursery door was ajar and soft light spilled out. A woman was softly humming a familiar lullaby.

Nicholas paused with his hand on the closed door, Regina's door. But he felt a strange pull coming from the nursery. The wet nurse wouldn't like being disturbed, yet he suddenly had a powerful urge to enter that room instead of Regina's. He hadn't gotten a good long look at the boy earlier. What better time than now?

Nicholas nudged the nursery door open. The nurse, Tess, was fast asleep in a cot against the wall. A small lamp glowed on a table next to a stuffed armchair. In that chair sat Regina feeding her son.

It brought him up short. Ladies of quality did not suckle their children. It wasn't done. She was in profile to him, her head bent to the child, softly humming. The fashionable short curls of the day framed her face, while the rest of her hair was long and gleaming, spilling over the back of the chair in midnight waves. She wore a long-sleeved sheer white robe, open, revealing a nightgown of the same material, pulled down on one side enough to bare one breast. The infant's mouth was greedily working, and one small hand rested just above the nipple, as if holding the breast in place.

Nicholas was mesmerized. Out of his depth, unfamiliar feelings assailed him, tender feelings, holding him spellbound. Even when she sensed his presence and looked up, he didn't move.

Their eyes met. For a long time, they simply stared at each other. She showed no surprise and no anger. He felt none of the old hostility. They seemed to touch each other without hands, a current passing between them that transcended their differences.

Regina was the first to look away. "I'm sorry if he woke you."

Nicholas shook himself. "No, no, it doesn't matter. I . . . didn't expect you'd be here, though." Then he asked shyly, "Couldn't you locate a wet nurse for him?"

Reggie smiled. "I never looked for one. When Tess told me my mother defied tradition and nursed me herself, I decided to do the same for Thomas. I haven't regretted it for a moment."

"It's rather confining for you, though, isn't it?"

"I have nothing to do, nowhere I want to go that would keep me away from Thomas for any length of time. Naturally I can't make many calls, but that's no hardship for me."

He had nothing to say. But he didn't want to leave. "I've never seen a mother suckling her babe before. Do you mind?" he asked clumsily.

"He's your . . . no, I don't mind," she finished, keeping her eyes on the baby.

He leaned against the door for a moment, studying her. Was the child his? She said he was. And every instinct of his own said he was. Then why was he stubbornly denying the truth? Because leaving a wife who had forced herself on him was one thing. But leaving a pregnant wife was something else again. True, she hadn't told him. But his leaving was still, in view of the pregnancy she'd borne alone, contemptible. Damnation take it. She had put him in this position by keeping silent about her condition. How the devil was he to get out of it?

Reggie turned the boy around to give him her other breast. Nicholas caught his breath as both creamy white globes were revealed to him in the moment before she covered one of them.

He approached her slowly, drawn against

his will, and didn't stop until he stood before her chair. She looked up at him, but he didn't trust himself to meet her eyes. It was all he could do to keep from touching her.

He kept his eyes on the child, but that led his gaze to her breast, and to her open throat, and to her soft lips. What would she do if he kissed her? He bent over to find out.

Nicholas heard her gasp just before his mouth took hers. He kept the kiss short and sweet, the lightest touch, ending it before she had a chance to turn away. He straightened, still without meeting her eyes.

"He's a beautiful baby, Regina."

It was several long moments before she replied, "I like to think so."

He smiled hesitantly. "I envy him at this moment."

"Why?"

He looked directly into those dark, clear blue eyes. "You have to ask?"

"You don't want me, Nicholas. You made that quite clear before you left. Have you changed your mind?"

He stiffened. She'd like him to beg, wouldn't she? That would give her a chance to humiliate him. She had sworn she'd never forgive him and she probably wouldn't. He didn't blame her, but he was not going to make things worse. He turned and walked away without a word.

CHAPTER 30

He was serious! He actually meant for them to pack everything that would go to Silverley and leave within the same day. Nicholas made his high-handed announcement at breakfast, having the unmitigated nerve to use the excuse that he could not remain in a house where he had no study. What could she say, she who had given him that excuse in a long-ago moment of pique? Infuriating man!

Well, she wouldn't go without Eleanor. All she needed was to be stuck in the country with two unfriendly people. No, Eleanor must come along. But she didn't tell Nicholas this, she told Eleanor. Ellie refused at first, but Reggie persisted until she gave in.

And so for the rest of the day they were all kept quite busy — except for Nicholas, who simply stood around looking satisfied with the upheaval he had caused. There was no time for Reggie to say any good-byes to her family. Quickly jotted notes had to suffice for that. But even with everyone pitching in to help — everyone except Nicholas — it was nearly evening before the last trunk was loaded onto the extra wagon that had been procured.

Reggie was no longer speaking to the Viscount, but her annoyance with him ran much deeper than today's nonsense. She was in fact disturbed over her encounter with him last night. Whatever Nicholas had been up to, he'd succeeded in making it nearly impossible for her to get back to sleep. It was not that he had kissed her. If she cared to be honest with herself, it was that he had done nothing beyond kissing.

Therein lay her confusion. How could she still want him after everything he had done to her? But want him she did. She had seen him standing there in the doorway, his silk robe open nearly to the waist, his sun-streaked hair all tousled, an intense look in those honey-gold eyes, and she'd been jolted with a desire so strong it frightened her. Seeing him like that was enough to make her forget all the months of cursing him.

Then what was she to do? It wasn't as if she were going to forgive him. She wasn't.

She had no business thinking of him amorously.

Eleanor and Tess and the baby rode in the larger coach with Reggie and Nicholas, while Meg, Harris, and Eleanor's maid occupied the smaller coach. With three women near him, Thomas did not lack for soft bosoms to sleep against. He was a silent passenger most of the time, and the women conversed quietly now that they could relax. Nicholas made a point of appearing bored with their chatter. They in turn ignored him, Reggie to the extent that she didn't hesitate to lower her dress and nurse her son when he began to fidget. Let him say something. Just let him.

At this point a change came over Nicholas. He had been amused by his wife's haughty air all day, and even his aunt's frigid looks, for sweet-tempered Eleanor had never been able to stay angry with him for long. He was a little surprised that she was going to Silverley, for she hadn't been there since his father's death six years before. He supposed Eleanor felt Regina needed moral support, and this amused him while hurting him at the same time.

Humor was only part of the maelstrom of his emotions, however. He must be depraved to be stirred by the simple act of Regina's feeding the child, but he was stirred. A commiserating voice whispered in the back of his mind that he was being too hard on himself. He was forgetting that Regina had always had this effect on him.

That realization did not help at all. Regina would shun his advances. And he would make a complete ass of himself by trying to woo his own wife, wouldn't he? If they could share the same bedroom, the proximity might help. After all, she was a passionate woman. But the place they had just left and the one they were going to were both so large that they didn't need to share a room.

There was only one way he could ever share a room with her, and that was through necessity, which wasn't likely . . . or was it? By God, yes! There was one way, and he had almost missed the opportunity, for they were more than halfway to Silverley already. He ran the idea through his mind and concluded it just might work.

Without further analyzing the plan, which would only bring to light possible flaws, Nicholas called out to the driver to stop at the next inn.

"Is something wrong?" Eleanor asked.

"Not at all, Aunt Ellie. I just realized I would prefer a hot meal tonight, rather than the cold fare we can expect at Silverley, arriving at this late hour."

"But it isn't that late yet. Aren't we almost there?" Reggie wanted to know.

"Not quite, love. And I find I am absolutely ravenous. I can't wait."

The inn they come to soon was a place where Nicholas was well known. He knew the proprietor well enough to tell the man exactly what he wanted. Now, he thought, if only luck would stick around for the rest of the night. . . .

CHAPTER 31

Reggie giggled as she made her way to the bed. Meg had left after giving her a thorough scolding as she helped her undress. Meg thought she was drunk. Well, of course she wasn't. Eleanor was. That was funny, for Reggie had been obliged to help the older woman up to her room where *her* maid had scolded *her,* too. The cheek of servants these days.

Eleanor had only consumed — what? a half-dozen glasses of that delicious wine the proprietor had been keeping just for them. He had told Nicholas that. Reggie drank just as much, and she was feeling quite wonderful, but she wasn't foxed, no. Her tolerance was just greater than Eleanor's.

She plopped down on the bed, swayed, then righted herself. This wasn't her spacious room at Silverley, but it would do for one night. Halfway through the meal Nicholas had told them to take their time, saying he had been thoughtless in his haste, his excuse being that he wasn't used to traveling with such a large entourage. He'd realized how inconsiderate it would be to arrive at Silverley so late and without notice, for all the servants would have to be roused from their beds to prepare rooms, see to the horses, unload the baggage, and so forth. He had decided they could arrive in the morning, and so he secured rooms for them at the inn.

Dinner was long and enjoyable, Nicholas putting himself out to make amends for the inconvenience he had caused them all. He was quite charming in fact and made his aunt laugh at his humorous anecdotes. Soon Reggie found herself laughing along with them. She hoped Meg and Tess and the other servants were enjoying themselves as much.

Reggie yawned and reached to extinguish the lamp on the bedside table. Her hand went right past it and she giggled. Before she could manage a second attempt, the door opened and Nicholas stepped into the room.

Reggie was more bemused than anything else when she saw him standing there. He didn't apologize for his error. Was it an error? Why was he in her room?

"Did you want something, Nicholas?"

He smiled. A glance around the room showed him that one of her trunks had been brought up, but nothing of his had been unloaded from the coach. Harris had protested at the arrangements, especially when he was told he would be sleeping in the stable with the footmen to give truth to the story that the inn was too full to accommodate them all comfortably.

Reggie frowned when he began to remove his coat. "What — what are you doing?"

"Getting ready for bed," he said casually.

"But —"

"Didn't I tell you?" He frowned. "I was sure I mentioned it."

She seemed confused. "What didn't you mention?"

"Why, that there are only three rooms to be had here. My aunt and her maid have one. Your maid and the nurse have the other, with a safe bed made up there for Thomas. That left only this room."

He sat down on the opposite side of the bed and removed his boots. Reggie's eyes were wide as she stared at his broad back.

"You intend to sleep here?" This came out in a high-pitched voice. "Here?"

"Where else would I sleep?" He tried to sound wounded.

"But —"

She got no further than that, for he swung around to face her, disturbing her by his closeness.

"Is something wrong?" he asked. "We are married, you know. And I assure you, you can be perfectly safe in the same bed with me."

Did he have to remind her that he didn't desire her any longer?

"You don't snore, do you?" she asked, just to be mean.

"Me? Certainly not."

"Then I don't suppose sharing a room for *one* night will matter *too* much. You will leave some clothes on, though, won't you?"

"I cannot abide constriction."

"Then I will turn the light off now, if you don't mind," she said.

"So I don't shock you with my nakedness? By all means."

Was that amusement in his voice? The cad. She would just have to ignore him.

She caught the lamp with both hands this time — she wasn't going to have him accusing her of being foxed — but then she had a terrible time finding the edge of the turned-down covers so she could scoot her feet under them. When that was finally managed, Nicholas had finished undressing and, with no trouble at all, stretched out under the covers at the same time she did. His weight dipped his side of the bed so much, Reggie had to grip the edge of the covers to keep from rolling into him. She lay, stiff as a board, trying not to touch him with any part of her.

"Good night, wife."

Reggie frowned. "Good night, Nicholas."

Less than a minute later he was snoring. Reggie made a disgusted sound. Didn't snore indeed. How was she supposed to sleep with this racket? She waited no more than another minute before shaking his shoulder.

"Nicholas?"

"Have a heart, love," he mumbled. "Once was enough for tonight."

"Once . . . oh!" she gasped, startled to realize what he meant. He thought she was someone else, and that she wanted him to make love to her — again. The idea!

She fell back on her pillow in a huff. A moment later he began to snore again, but she just gritted her teeth. After a few minutes, Nicholas rolled toward her, and his hand landed alarmingly near her breast. One leg fell across her thigh.

It flashed through her mind that the chest pressing against her arm was naked, that the leg lying on top of her was naked that . . . oh, Lord, if she moved she might wake him. Yet this intimacy was bringing back feelings best forgotten, and she couldn't sleep like this.

Very gently she tried to lift his hand. His reaction was to grip her breast. Her eyes flew wide open. Her breathing quickened. And he slept on, blissfully unaware of what he was doing.

Once again she tried to extricate herself, prying his fingers off her one at a time, slowly. When his hand was released, it moved away of its own accord, but not where she had intended. His hand slid slowly down her belly, across the mound between her legs, and all the way back up, stopping at her other breast. Just then, his knee moved enough to rest on her loins. The fingers caressed her breast.

"Very . . . nice." His warm breath blew against her cheek as he murmured in his sleep.

The moan came from deep within her, surprising her and causing a deep blush. This was insane. He was sleeping! How could he make her feel like this when he was sleeping?

It was the wine. It had to be, for she almost wished she were the man and he the woman, so she could turn him on his back, straddle him, and ease her growing ache.

She had to risk waking him. She had to get him on his own side of the bed. "Nicholas?" she whispered. "Nicholas, you have to —"

"Persistent, aren't you, love?" His hand snaked up and around her neck, drawing her face to his. "Come then, if you insist."

Warm lips touched hers, softly at first, then passionately. The hand at her neck began to caress, softly, making her tingle all over.

"Ah, love," he murmured huskily as his lips trailed over her cheek to nibble an earlobe. "You should insist more often."

Reggie was overwhelmed with erotic delight. What did it matter if he wasn't fully awake and didn't know what he was doing? She curled a hand around his neck, exerting enough pressure to keep him close.

Nicholas wished he could shout in triumph. Accepting his kiss had sealed her fate. His lips moved along her neck with tingling heat. Quickly, expertly, he unlaced her gown and, in one swift movement, whisked it over her head and aside.

Reggie's hand, yanked from his neck in the unrobing, fell back onto his shoulder.

His muscles tensed where she touched him. She shivered with her own power. There was no turning back now. He was hers for the night, whether he knew it or not.

Her fingers glided over his back. The skin was soft, warm. She kneaded gently, then harder, then gently again, taking pleasure just in being able to touch him again. It had been so terribly long. And oh, he was making her remember how it was the first time. His lips burned a searing line from her throat to her thighs. Nicholas was becoming intoxicated by the smell and taste of her. Her skin was as firm and as silky smooth as the night he had taken her virginity. Her body had made no change since the baby, except for the fullness of her breasts, and those he was almost afraid to touch, though he yearned to. But they were the territory of her baby now, and he did not want her thinking of the infant just then. He did not want her thinking at all.

Reggie's head moved from side to side, her pulse racing. If Nicholas did not quit the exquisite torture of his exploring fingers, she would soon be begging him.

He must have read her thoughts, for his long body slid over her, the weight so welcome. Her legs raised and wrapped around his hips just as his warm flesh entered her, filled her, thrusting to her depths.

His mouth closed over hers, smothering her cries of pleasure with fevered kisses. She met him thrust for thrust, her arms locked behind his head, fingers gripping his hair.

The climax took them together to shuddering heights, wave after wave washing over them. Pleasure met and savored. Passion spent. The world receded on the same tide, and they slept, wrapped in each other's arms.

Chapter 32

Nicholas woke at a knock at the door, and became aware of two things simultaneously. He was lying with his limbs entwined with Regina's, and the person who had knocked wasn't going to wait to be invited in.

Finding his wife next to him was a lovely surprise, stirring wonderful memories. He turned toward the door and muttered a curse. Regina's maid stood there, a candle in one hand, Thomas pressed to her shoulder with the other hand. A look of ridiculous surprise spread across her face.

"Isn't it customary to wait until you are bid entry?" Nicholas growled.

But Meg wasn't intimidated. "It's not customary at all, your lordship, not when it's my Lady Reggie's room I am enterin'."

"Well, Lady Reggie is not alone, so if you will turn yourself around, I will make myself presentable."

Meg gasped as he stood up without further notice. She swung around quickly, wax spilling onto the floor. What was he doing in Reggie's bed? The poor girl had been heartbroken when he deserted her, and now here he was back without, she guessed, so much as an apology.

"You may turn around now, and state your business."

Meg bristled. She glanced hesitantly over her shoulder just as he came up behind her, blocking her view of the bed.

Suspiciously, she asked, "Does she know you're here?"

Nicholas laughed. "My dear woman, what *are* you accusing me of?"

Meg drew herself up stiffly, trying to think what she should say.

"Is there some problem that brings you here in the middle of the night?" Nicholas asked before she could speak.

"I've brought Lord Thomas for his late-night feeding," she explained, making him wonder how he could have forgotten so soon that the infant required attention in the middle of the night.

Meg continued as if she had read his thoughts. "It's troublesome, true, but it won't be lastin' much longer, these late feedings. A few nights already he's slept right through. It's the travelin' and the strange room that have him fussin' tonight."

"Very well, you may give him to me."

Meg drew back in amazement. "Beggin' your pardon, your lordship, but wouldn't it be better if you just left the room for a while?"

"No, it would not," Nicholas said firmly. "But you may do so. And no, dear woman, I do not imagine I can satisfy his needs, so you needn't look at me like that. I will give him to his mother and see he is returned to you when he is finished."

He reached for Thomas and Meg was forced to comply, though she warned, "Careful. You must support his neck . . . that's right, just so. He's not a rag doll, you know." At the scowl he shot her, she left.

Nicholas sighed. There was nothing for it, he would have to wake her. Blister it, he didn't want to wake her. She had slept long enough to have lost all the effects of the wine. She would be shocked by his presence. Oh, why couldn't the child suckle without her being awake? Her lovely breasts were already bared, and she was lying on her side. Could the child do it on his own?

He gently lifted the boy and placed him close to Regina. Nothing happened. Nicholas sat back and frowned. Why the devil wouldn't it work? Didn't babies possess some kind of instinct? He turned the little face toward her until the baby's cheek brushed against her nipple. But the little head turned away again, and Thomas began making sounds of frustration.

Exasperated, Nicholas lay down behind Thomas and turned him onto his side, guiding the little mouth to the nipple. Nicholas held the boy in place until at last the nipple was found and Thomas began to suck.

Nicholas smiled, pleased with himself and the baby. With his hand covering the back of the baby's head, holding him firmly to his source of food, Nicholas was able to lie there and watch mother and child at his leisure. Every new father ought to be so lucky, he told himself.

He nearly chuckled aloud at his own cleverness. He was feeling damned proud. This was his son — he would bloody well lay low anyone who said otherwise — and *he* had helped to feed him. Well, he had brought the baby to his food, anyway. It was nearly the same thing. He could understand a little of what Regina must feel each time she fed him. It was a marvelous feeling.

Watching them, he was filled again with the warmth and tenderness he had felt the night before, and a wealth of possessiveness, too. His, wife, his child. They belonged to him. Something was going to have to be done to see that they knew it and accepted it.

Nicholas was handling the baby with much more confidence when he walked him down the hall to the room Meg shared with the nurse. He had even managed to turn both mother and child over so that Regina's other breast, quite swollen with milk, could be drained as well. And all without waking her.

Meg opened the door, looking disagreeable. Here, he thought, was a good place to begin gaining acceptance.

"Tell me something, Meg. Is this animosity you have for me personal, or only a reflection of your lady's feelings for me?"

Meg, much older than Nicholas, was bold enough to speak her mind. "Both. You shouldn't have come back. She was doin' just fine without you, and she'll do just fine again once you're gone."

"Gone?" He was truly shocked. "You have me leaving when I've only just returned?"

"Well, won't you?" Meg retorted, working herself into a fine stew. "You didn't want her for your wife. She knows that well enough now."

"And if I don't leave again, Meg? What then?" he asked softly.

Meg held her ground. He was not to be let off easily. "She'll make your life miserable, that's what. No more than you deserve, beggin' your pardon, your lordship. Tess and I didn't raise any insipid miss, I can tell you that. You can't hurt a Malory twice."

Nicholas nodded. He had heard enough. If anyone knew Regina's real feelings, it was Meg, and the maid was outspoken enough to tell him the truth. Was she right? Was there no hope for him and Regina?

CHAPTER 33

It was a quarter past eight and Meg bustled around the room, shaking out the violet dress and short-sleeved spencer Reggie would wear. Reggie sat on the edge of the bed, playing with Thomas. She had fed him already and was waiting for Tess to come back for him.

"I'm surprised Thomas slept through the night, aren't you, Meg? I thought the strange surroundings would have him fretting."

"D'you mean to tell me you don't remember my bringing him in here last night?"

Reggie glanced up, bewildered.

"His lordship brought him back to me all comfy and fed," Meg told her. "I'm sure he'd like to take credit for feedin' the baby, but unless they're makin' men differently these days —"

"Nicholas brought him back to you?"

"He did, and I can see you *don't* remember. I told you too much wine —"

"Oh, hush," Reggie cut her short. "Of course I remember. It just took a moment to . . . oh, never mind. Take him back to Tess, will you? I feel a headache coming on."

"Little wonder, with as much —"

"Meg!"

When the door closed, Reggie lay back on the bed. What was wrong with her? She knew Nicholas had spent the night with her. She remembered him coming into the room and falling right asleep. What happened afterward — yes, she couldn't forget any of that. So why couldn't she recall feeding Thomas in the middle of the night?

She began to wonder if she was sure about anything. Maybe she had fallen asleep soon after Nicholas did, and maybe she dreamed the rest of it. Then she remembered she'd been wearing her nightgown when she woke up. Oh. So it was all a dream, then?

The disappointment hit her like a wave.

As they rode in the coach later that morning, Nicholas' mood was black. He kept to his corner, barely deigning to be civil. What a difference from last night at dinner! What had happened to him?

The three women gave a collective sigh when they finally reached Silverley. They were expected. The doors of the great mansion were thrown open, and a troop of servants waited to unload the baggage. It seemed every servant in the house had turned out to welcome their lord home, and even the Countess was standing poised in the doorway.

Belatedly, Reggie realized that some of the fuss had to do with Thomas, the new lord. One by one people tried to get a peek at him as she crossed from the coach to the great double doors.

Miriam gave Thomas a hard look before her frigid eyes took in Reggie and Nicholas. "So," she said matter-of-factly, "you've brought the bastard home."

Eleanor gasped. Giving her sister a furious look she swept into the house. Poor Tess turned scarlet, thankful that feisty Meg wasn't near enough to hear.

Nicholas, standing behind Reggie, went totally rigid, but otherwise no emotion crossed his face. He was certain the insult was a reference to himself, not the baby. Miriam would never change. Her soul was so full of bitterness that her venom spilled over sometimes. That was Miriam.

Reggie stood still, her face flushed pink with anger, her eyes fixed on the Countess. The woman seemed pleased that she had successfully disturbed everyone within hearing. Her voice low, Reggie said, "My son is not a bastard, Lady Miriam. If you ever call him that again, I shall be moved to violence."

She went on into the house before Miriam could reply. Tess followed her, leaving Nicholas alone to laugh at Miriam's furious expression.

"You should have been more explicit, mother." He called her that only because he knew how much it infuriated her. "After all, there are so many of us bastards around these days."

Miriam didn't deign to respond to that. "Are you planning to stay this time?" she asked coldly.

Nicholas' smile was mocking. "Yes, I mean to stay. Any objections?"

They both knew she wouldn't object. Silverley was his, and she lived there only through his grace.

After Regina had gone upstairs, Nicholas closed himself away in the library, the room he had always favored at Silverley, his sanctuary. He was thankful to see that nothing had changed. His desk was still in its corner, a well-stocked liquor cabinet next to it. He would go over the books today, see if he could understand Miriam's figures. He would also get foxed.

Nicholas didn't actually get drunk. He

couldn't make heads or tails of the books, but that was not surprising. Miriam did it on purpose, he was sure, so that he'd be forced to sit with her for hours while she condescended to explain what she had done with the estate. Her manner always implied that Silverley would fall to ruin without her.

They both knew that she was the reason he'd stayed away from Silverley since his father's death, depending on his agent to keep him informed of conditions. He simply could not stay under the same roof with her for very long. Miriam's threats and barbs made him lose his temper.

She was his father's widow. To the world, she was his mother, so he couldn't very well throw her out. It had always been easier just for him to leave. But now he had his wife and child at Silverley, and Miriam was not going to drive him away anymore.

When he went upstairs to change for dinner, he was in a foul mood. He had not been able to keep from worrying over the problems with Regina, and he was also nagged with guilt for getting her drunk. He had put her nightgown back on so she wouldn't be embarrassed when her maid came in to wake her. But even if she didn't remember their night together, he knew he had tricked her into accepting his ardor.

Three maids were leaving the sitting room that divided the master suites just as Nicholas approached. "Where are you going with all that?" he barked. One was carrying a basket of shoes, and gowns galore were draped over the other two maids' arms.

The servants blanched at his tone, saying nothing. Reggie came up behind them and, after sending them on their way, asked her husband, "What are you snapping at them for?"

"You don't like your rooms?" he asked, wondering why her clothes were being carted out.

"On the contrary, I like them very well. The servants are removing Lady Miriam's belongings, as they did once before. I suppose she moved back in there after I left, thinking I wouldn't return."

That did not appease him. He was too miserable to be appeased. "You wouldn't have returned if I hadn't insisted, would you?"

Reggie shrugged. "I never gave it much thought. I returned to London simply because I wanted to be near my family for Thomas' birth."

"Of course, your dear family," he sneered. "Well, your family is a long way from here, madame, and I thank God for that. You won't be running back to them again."

Reggie stiffened, eyes slanting angrily. "I never *ran* back to them, sir. But if I wanted to do so, I would."

"No, you won't!" Nicholas shouted. "And I'll have you know right now, your bloody uncles are not welcome in this house!"

"You don't mean that," she gasped.

"See if I don't!"

"Oh! Of all the —" She was too enraged to finish the thought. "Oh!"

She swung around and stomped into her bedroom, slamming the door. Nicholas stared at the closed door, his temper past exploding. In two strides he reached it and threw it open.

"Don't you ever walk away from me when I am talking to you!" he bellowed, standing in the doorway.

Reggie swung around, startled, but not at all intimidated by the fury raging through him. She had held back her own fury too long.

"You were not talking!" her voice rose to match his. "You were shouting, and non-sense, too. Do not think you can place such restrictions on me, sir, for I won't have it! I am not your servant!"

"And what, pray tell, are you?"

"Your wife!"

"Exactly! My wife. And if I wish to place restrictions on you, I will bloody well do so!"

"Get out!" she screamed. "Out!"

She shoved the door against him until it closed, with him on the other side. Nicholas scowled, but he didn't try to open the door again. The significance of being banished from her room was too much, symbolizing the rejection he had expected. He looked at the closed door and saw a barrier, solid and unbreakable.

CHAPTER 34

"I suppose I ought to mention that I am expecting guests for the weekend."

Miriam's statement drew all eyes to her. They were dining in the formal dining room, Nicholas at one end of the long table, Reggie at the other. Shouting distance described the length separating the lord and lady of the house. This suited Reggie perfectly. She hadn't said a word to her husband for three days.

Miriam and Eleanor were seated facing each other at the center of the table. It was much easier to talk that way, but the two sisters had nothing to say to each other.

Sir Walter Tyrwhitt was next to Miriam. The friendly neighbor had stopped by earlier and she invited him to join them. As usual, Miriam's manner was very different when the debonair gentleman was present. She was almost warm.

Tyrwhitt was in fact a very likable fellow.

Middle-aged, a few years younger than Miriam actually, he was a fine-looking man with distinguished silver streaks running along the sides of his dark brown hair. His eyes were green. He was a farmer at heart, and never tired of talking about the land, crops, the weather. It was amusing to see how serious he could become when he spoke of these things, because he treated all other topics with casual indifference.

Nicholas put himself out to be agreeable to their guest, a great relief to all after three days of surliness. He humored Sir Walter with a good deal of talk about spring crops. Or *was* he humoring him? Perhaps he really was interested. Reggie was amazed at how involved he became. Was he, too, a farmer at heart? How little she knew about the man she was married to.

But his amiability did not extend to his wife. Everyone else benefitted. Even Miriam received civil answers. But Reggie he ignored. It hurt. She wasn't still angry over their argument, for she rarely stayed angry long. She was hurt because she could not forget that dream. It had seemed so real. She could not forget how it felt in his arms, how it was when he made love to her. Fool that she was, she had accepted him in her heart. Why was she such a pushover, to forgive so easily?

Miriam's statement about guests made Nicholas frown. "The whole weekend? I take it this is not your usual dinner party?"

"No, actually," Miriam replied. "I hope you don't mind. I'm afraid the invitations went out right before you returned. I wasn't expecting you to come home."

"Nor were you expecting me to stay, I'm sure of that," Nicholas said dryly.

Eleanor intervened before an argument began. "I think it's a fine idea. A bit close to the London season, but that won't start for another week or so. How many guests were you counting on, Miriam?"

"Only about twenty. Not all of them will be staying, however."

"This isn't your usual style, madame," Nicholas commented. "May I ask what the occasion is?"

Miriam turned her head directly toward Nicholas so Walter couldn't see her eyes. "Must there be an occasion?" Her eyes shot daggers at him.

"No. If you have started to enjoy large gatherings, however, I suggest you visit London this year and enjoy them to your heart's content. You may even make use of my townhouse, now that my wife has so thoughtfully refurbished it."

"I would not dream of leaving Silverley unattended," Miriam said stiffly.

"I assure you, madame, I will force myself to stay here and look after the estate. I am capable of doing so, though you like to think otherwise."

Miriam did not take the bait. He was beginning to see that she wouldn't fight as long as Sir Walter was present. What a choice situation. What fun! But Aunt Ellie was frowning at him, and poor Tyrwhitt looked embarrassed. Regina, sweet Regina, looked down at her plate, avoiding his gaze. He sighed.

"Forgive me, mother. I did not mean to imply that I wished to be rid of you, or that you lack confidence in your only son." He grinned as she stiffened. Perhaps there *were* a few small pleasures left to him. "By all means have your party. I'm sure Aunt Ellie and my wife will enjoy helping with the arrangements."

"I have everything in hand already," Miriam said quickly.

"Then that completes the discussion, does it not?"

Nicholas resumed eating, and Reggie shook her head. She had considered her little battles with the Countess beneath her, yet she had always been provoked. Miriam had done nothing to provoke Nicholas tonight. Why did he dedicate himself to being disagreeable?

As soon as the ladies left the men to their brandies, Reggie retired to her rooms. But Thomas was sleeping, and Meg was in the servants' wing with Harris, and it was too early to go to sleep. Still, she refused to go downstairs. Being ignored by her husband in front of others was embarrassing.

Nicholas noticed Regina's absence the moment he entered the drawing room, and approached Eleanor.

"Where is she?" he asked abruptly.

"She mentioned retiring."

"This early? Is she sick?"

"My dear Nicky, where was this interest in your wife when she was with you?"

"Don't chastise, Aunt Ellie. I believe I have been run through the mill quite enough."

"And still you go on in your own stubborn way," Eleanor sighed. "Which is only making you miserable — admit it."

"Nonsense," he said irritably. "And you don't know all of the story, Aunt Ellie."

She sighed, seeing the rigid set of his chin. "Perhaps. But the way you have ignored that poor girl is still deplorable. Why, I don't believe I've heard you say two words to her since we arrived here."

"More than two, I assure you."

"Oh, you can be so exasperating, Nicholas!" Eleanor kept her voice down. "You just won't admit that you were wrong, that you have a wonderful wife and no good reason not to cherish her."

"I do admit that. It is my wife who now regrets her choice of husband. I once told her she would. Bitter thing," he added, "to find yourself proved right about the one thing you wanted to be wrong about."

She watched him walk away, her eyes sad. How she wished she could help. This was something he was going to have to solve on his own.

Much later, Nicholas entered the sitting room which divided the master bedrooms and was startled to find Regina curled up on the sofa, reading. She wore a bright aqua satin dressing gown belted at the waist, clinging enticingly to her small frame. Her midnight hair lay about her slim shoulders in sensual disarray. She lowered the book and looked at him.

Her gaze was direct. It had its usual power to jolt him. Bloody hell. Another night he'd have to spend tossing and turning.

"I thought you'd gone to bed." Frustration made his voice sharp.

Reggie slowly lowered the book to her lap. "I wasn't tired."

"Couldn't you read in your own room?"

She managed to appear unperturbed. "I hadn't realized this room was for your exclusive use."

"It isn't, but if you are going to lie about half-dressed, do it in bed," he snapped. He scowled at her for a moment, then went into his room.

Reggie sat up. So much for being available to him. What ever made her think she might be able to entice him? All she managed to arouse in him was anger. She had better remember that, she told herself.

CHAPTER 35

"I just love your house, Nicky," Pamela Ritchie gushed when she found him in the library. "It's — so grand! Your mother was such a dear to show me around."

Nicholas smiled tightly, saying nothing. With anyone else, he'd have been proud to hear his home praised. But he'd learned something about this luscious brunette during their torrid two-week affair of several years past, and that was that she rarely meant anything she said. Oh, she was impressed with Silverley, but she was surely peeved not to be the lady of the manor.

When their affair ended, he heard through the servants' grapevine that she destroyed her bedroom in a fit of temper. He'd seen her occasionally after that. She always had a warm smile for him, but to catch her unawares was to see Pamela fuming.

Women like Pamela and Selena always clashed with his own quick temper eventually. In his wilder days he had known every kind of female temperament, but there was only one he'd been in real danger with, and that was the lovely Caroline Symonds. But fortunately, she was married to the old Duke of Windfield. He had not seen Lady Caroline for three years, and the pain of their separation was long gone.

"We were wondering where you had gone off to, Nicky," Pamela was saying. She perched, uninvited, on the edge of a chair near his desk. "Tea is being served in the drawing room. More people have arrived. Don't know them, some squire or — oh! And your lovely wife finally made an appearance. A charming, sweet girl. Of course, I'd met her before, don't you know, season before last. She was all the rage then. The young bloods were falling all over themselves just for one of her smiles. I was even a little bit envious until it became apparent that something was, well . . . wrong with her, poor thing."

He had known the silly chattering thing was leading up to something, but even so he found himself stiffening. "Am I supposed to guess what you mean by that?"

She laughed, a tittering sound. "I was hoping *you* would tell *me.* Everyone is simply on tenders to know."

"Know?" Nicholas said curtly.

"Why, to know what you found wrong with her."

"I find nothing wrong with my wife, Pamela," he said coldly.

"So you won't fess up? Gallant of you, Nicky, but not very enlightening," she sighed. "You can imagine the stir you've created. It isn't every day one of our most eligible bachelors marries and then leaves his wife practically at the altar. It is rumored that one of Lady Reggie's uncles handed you over to her in chains."

It was not easy for Pamela to be assured that she had scored. Only the tension in his hands showed his anger. She had wanted him to fly into a rage. Pamela harbored more spite for this man than she did for all her other lovers come and gone combined. She had formed serious plans for Nicholas Eden, and he had laid them to ruins. Bloody philandering cur. She was delighted he had ended up with a wife who didn't suit him.

"That particular rumor is an absurdity, Pamela," Nicholas said tightly. "I returned to England in James Malory's company simply because he was kind enough to offer me berth on his ship when he found me stranded in the West Indies. And," he went on quickly before she could say anything, "I hate to disappoint you, but it was business that took me away from my bride. An emergency on an island property that couldn't wait."

"Another man might have taken his bride along, extended honeymoon and all that," she interjected. "Odd you didn't think of it."

"There wasn't time to . . ." he began, but she smiled and rose to leave.

"It will be interesting to watch the two of you, though. Strange that you should be entertaining so soon after your wedding."

"This little gathering was not my idea."

"Yes, your mother sent the invitations, but you were already here, so I assume you wanted a party. Well, they do say the best way to relieve boredom is to have a party. I just hope you weren't thinking of a *personal* party between the two of *us* when you had me included on the guest list. Married men don't attract me, if you know what I mean."

She whirled out of the room before he could reply. Nicholas remained seated, staring at the door. He had been turned down flat, without his even making an offer. The cheek!

A fierce protectiveness rose in him. Something wrong with Reggie, indeed! He left the library with every intention of finding his wife and devoting himself to her fully for as long as a single guest remained in the house. But when he stepped out of the library, glancing toward the entry hall, he saw Selena Eddington alighting from her carriage. Fuming, he went to find Miriam.

"What I find amusing is that you kept such close tabs on me all these years," he told her. "Such devotion. Of course it enabled you to know exactly which people I would *not* wish to see."

"Not at all," she replied with a tight little smile. "There are, in fact, many kind souls who feel a mother should be informed of what her son is doing in wicked London . . . and with whom. You can't imagine how many good intentions I had to sit through, appearing grateful, when I didn't care if my so-called son drowned in the Thames." She gave him a look of pure hatred. "Yet, bits of information do sometimes have uses."

Fury flashed in his eyes. He turned and headed for the stairs, Miriam's delighted laughter following him.

"You can't hide all weekend, Lord Montieth," she called scornfully.

Nicholas didn't look back. What the bloody hell did the conniving, spiteful old bitch hope to accomplish by inviting two of his ex-mistresses to his home? And, good

God, how many more surprises awaited him?

CHAPTER 36

The drawing room was quite crowded, Miriam's twenty people having turned into thirty. The music room was open and sounds of someone tinkering with the harp drifted from it. The dining room was open, the long table set up for a buffet. Guests drifted from room to room.

Selena Eddington had changed little in the year since Reggie had seen her. Dressed in a frilly pink lace creation that made Reggie feel matronly in her dark blue gown, Selena had all the men hanging on her every word. From time to time, she turned toward Reggie with a satisfied smirk.

"Cheer up, my dear. It was bound to happen one day."

Reggie turned to Lady Whately, an acquaintance from years past. She was sitting beside Reggie on the sofa. "What was bound to happen?" Reggie inquired.

"You meeting up with the women from

your husband's past, there being so many of them."

"If you mean Lady Selena —"

"Not just her, my dear. There's the Duchess there, and that Ritchie tart, and Mrs. Henslowe, though Anne Henslowe was just a fling, or so I'm told."

Reggie's eyes flew to each woman the old tabby named, widening when they fell on Caroline Symonds, Duchess of Windfield, a stunningly beautiful blond only a few years older than Reggie. The Duchess sat demurely next to a man in his late seventies. He had to be the Duke of Windfield. How utterly miserable the young woman must be with that old husband, thought Reggie.

Pamela Ritchie, Anne Henslowe, Caroline Symonds, and Selena Eddington. Four of Nicholas' past mistresses in the same room with his wife! This was asking too much. Was she supposed to converse with them? Act the gracious hostess?

Nicholas made an appearance just then, and she wished she could glower at him, but that was out of the question. While she watched, Lady Selena took Nicholas' arm and held on tightly.

"That doesn't upset you, does it, my dear?"

Reggie turned to find Lady Whately gone

and Anne Henslowe in her place. Was she now to be comforted by one of his mistresses? "Why should it upset me?" Reggie answered stiffly.

Mrs. Henslowe smiled. "It shouldn't. After all, she lost him and you have him. She was upset about it."

"And you?"

"Oh, dear. Someone has been whispering in your ear. I was afraid of that."

Reggie simply could not remain vexed. The woman was genuinely sympathetic, her brown eyes compassionate. She wasn't a bad sort. And her affair with Nicholas had happened long before Reggie met him.

"Don't give it another thought." Reggie smiled.

"*I* won't. I just hope *you* don't. Be assured, my dear, that Nicholas never goes back for second helpings."

Reggie giggled, shocked. "Nicely put."

"And true, to the lamentation of the women in his past. Many have tried to get him back, and all without luck."

"Did you?" Reggie asked bluntly.

"Heavens, no. He wasn't for me and I knew it. I was thankful for my one night with him. It occurred soon after I lost my husband, I was close to losing my sanity as well and Nicholas helped me see that my life wasn't over after all. I'll always be grateful to him for that."

Reggie nodded and Anne Henslowe patted her arm. "Don't let it get to you, my dear. He is yours now, forever."

But he wasn't hers, and he hadn't been hers after that one night nearly a year ago.

She thanked Mrs. Henslowe and looked around for Nicholas. He wasn't there, and he wasn't in the dining room or the music room. That left the conservatory, and she retraced her steps back through the dining room and quietly slipped into the glass-walled sun room. It was warm and dark, the only light coming through the far windows of the dining room. It was just light enough to see as far as the fountain, to see the pink lacy gown and short black curls of Selena Eddington, whose arms were wrapped around Nicholas' neck.

"Are you enjoying your tour of the house, Lady Selena?" Reggie called out, approaching them.

Her voice drew them apart. Selena had the grace to look embarrassed. But Nicholas didn't seem at all contrite. In fact, he turned dark with anger. Seeing his anger, Reggie's outrage turned to throat-tightening pain. Ninny! He hadn't wanted to stop holding Selena.

She turned and left as quickly as she could. Nicholas called after her, but she only hurried her step. The philandering libertine! How could she have been so stupid — so foolish — as to hope?

When she reached the antechamber, Reggie stopped short. No, she would not run and hide as if her heart were breaking. Malorys were made of sterner stuff. They did not make the mistake of falling in love with the same person twice. Love wasn't why she had this tight knot in her throat. No, indeed, she was choking on anger, that was all.

She stepped into the drawing room again, the smile she had worn most of the day right back in place. Calmly, she took a seat and plunged into conversation with Faith and Lady Whately.

Nicholas entered the drawing room the moment after Reggie sat down. He took one look at her tranquil expression and his heart sank. What had he expected? Tears? In order to be jealous, a person had to care. The devil take Selena straight to hell for throwing her arms around him and catching him off guard like that. Had she known Reggie was nearby? He hadn't wanted to escort Selena through the house in the first place, but she had challenged him, hinting that he was afraid to be seen with her, whispering that he was no longer his own man. Like a bloody fool, he dragged her from room to room, giving her the tour. Idiot!

She wanted to see what was behind the closed doors of the conservatory, and once inside, a single flower on a twisting vine caught her eye. Nothing would do but she must have it. After two attempts to reach it herself, she had pleaded sweetly for him to get it. He went for the bloody bloom, and no sooner had he plucked it and turned to hand it to her than she had her arms locked behind his neck. Two seconds had passed, and then Regina spoke. It was unbelievable, the worst piece of luck imaginable.

He looked at Regina again and her eyes met his. In that moment before she turned away, her eyes shot blue flames at him.

Nicholas' hopes soared. He grinned. She didn't care? Then why was she so furious with him? Determined now, he approached the three women on the sofa. "May I join you, ladies? What with all the duties of the host, I haven't had a moment to spare for my lovely wife."

"There isn't room, Nicholas," Reggie said flatly.

And there wasn't, not with the ample posterior of Lady Whately taking up half of the sofa. But he was not deterred by that or by Reggie's stiff tone.

He caught her wrist, tugging her up to stand, then sat down and pulled her down onto his lap.

"Nicholas!" she gasped.

"Don't be embarrassed, love." He grinned, holding her firmly in place.

"Scandalous, Lord Montieth!" Lady Whately was even more embarrassed than Regina. "If you are so eager to be near your wife, you may have my seat."

She left, and then Faith moved away as well, pretending a sudden interest in a painting across the room. Reggie slipped off her husband's lap and sat beside him. She wanted to move away from him entirely, but his arm over her shoulder kept her on the sofa.

"That was —"

"Shush," he whispered. "And smile, love. We are being observed." She smiled up at him tightly but her eyes cursed him anyway. He chuckled. "Is that the best you can do?" Then he said softly, "It was nothing, you know."

She didn't have to ask what he meant. "Of course not," she retorted ironically.

"It really wasn't. She made an attempt to seduce me and she failed. It was no more than that."

"Oh, I believe you, my lord," she said flatly, her voice icy. "I believe you because I have twice been told tonight that your ex-mistresses do not interest you once they fall into the ex-category. One of your former ladies assured me that you 'never return for seconds.' So I must believe it even when my eyes tell me differently."

"You're jealous."

"Stuff!"

He grinned devilishly. "Your informant wasn't totally correct, love. Were you the meal, I would return for seconds and thirds and gorge myself to death."

"Oh!" she gasped. "I am in no mood to be quizzed, sir! Good night to you."

She shot to her feet before he could grab her and left the room. He let her go, smiling to himself. He was beginning to think Miriam's gathering was going to be just what was needed to get his wife back. Wouldn't the old bird die to know she had helped him! His grin widened. His mood was becoming positively buoyant.

CHAPTER 37

Warm sunlight spilled into the morning and breakfast rooms, both of which were thrown open to accommodate so many guests. On the long buffet were platters piled high with eggs; kippers; ham and sausage; an assortment of toast, muffins, and rolls; and six kinds of jellies. Hot chocolate was offered, and tea and coffee and clotted cream. Footmen refilled the platters as soon as they emptied.

It was early, and many were still asleep or had availed themselves of the well-stocked stable for a morning ride. Reggie was down because Thomas had awakened at dawn and, after feeding him, she hadn't been able to sleep again. The Whatelys were at breakfast, as well as Pamela Ritchie and the Duke of Windfield. Reggie let their conversation move around her. She wasn't keen to put on a cheerful face again. Brooding thoughts had followed her to bed last night and were still hounding her, Nicholas at the center of those thoughts.

It wasn't as if she hadn't known all along what type of man he was, but, devil take him, couldn't he wait until returning to London before cavorting with another woman? Why was he at Silverley, anyway? She certainly hadn't expected him to be. And that constant scowl of his was so unnerving.

She ought to leave, she knew that. Divorce was out of the question, but she didn't have to live under the same roof with him. She could return to Haverston. Uncle Jason wouldn't mind.

But she had no right to keep Thomas away from his father. And Tess had told her that Nicholas was visiting the nursery at least twice each day, shooing Tess out so he could be alone with his son. He did accept Thomas as his, it was just doubtful he would ever get around to acknowledging that to Reggie.

She sighed deeply. Hadn't she once said it wouldn't matter how her marriage turned out just so long as she didn't have to go on hunting for a husband? How foolishly naive!

"My dear, you have a visitor," Eleanor announced as she came into the room, Lord Dicken Barrett right behind her. "George — ? Oh, dear. I don't remember."

"George Fowler," Lord Barrett supplied.

"Oh, yes, Fowler," Eleanor agreed. "Sayers put him in the waiting room, what with the house so full."

Sayers was standing in the doorway, and Reggie frowned to hide her surprise. She stood up. "The waiting room is no place for George. Put him in the library. It should be empty at this hour. And have tea sent in." She dismissed Sayers with a nod, then turned to Eleanor. "You should have slept later, Ellie, if you're still tired."

"I'm fine, dear. We did have a late night of it, but I enjoyed myself." Her eyes met Lord Barrett's briefly. "I'll be wide-awake once I have my tea. Do you know your caller?"

"Yes," Reggie replied. "But I can't imagine what he's doing here."

"Well, you had best see to him. Dicken and I will just have a little something to eat before going on our ride."

Eleanor, riding? Imagine! "I didn't know you enjoyed riding, Ellie."

"Oh, my, yes. But it's so much nicer when you have someone along for company." She leaned closer, adding, "You and Nicholas must try it."

Reggie answered noncommittally and left the room.

George Fowler stood up the moment she

365

entered the library, coming forward to bow over her hand. She had forgotten what a pleasant-looking young man George was, with his mop of sandy brown curls and neatly trimmed mustache, his dark green eyes and well-cut figure. He was a little on the short side — no, not really. She mustn't compare every man to her husband.

"I fear I've come at an inconvenient time," he apologized. "The fellow who took my horse grumbled that there wasn't room for even one more in your stable."

"It's a bit of a squeeze, but I am in no way inconvenienced."

"But you have guests to attend —"

"Not at all," she assured him. "This is my mother-in-law's gathering, planned before we arrived. Mostly her friends — and my husband's — and only a few are up at this hour. Do sit down, George." They seated themselves facing each other. "You're welcome to stay, too, if you like. You probably know most everyone here, and I'm sure we can find you a place for the night, if you don't mind sharing a room."

He grinned happily. "I would accept, if I hadn't already received a summons from my mum. She's on holiday down in Brighton and I thought I would stop by to see you on the way, see how you're getting on."

Reggie smiled at him. He had gone far out of his way in order to see her. "It has been a long time, hasn't it?" She opened the subject happily, remembering how charming he could be.

"A deuced long time," he emphasized.

Hallie brought in tea, and Reggie poured. "How is your mother, George?"

"As well as can be expected, considering her disposition." He said this with a grimace, as if he expected quite a drubbing when he arrived in Brighton. "The whole family's well. Speaking of family, I saw your Uncle Anthony at the club last week. He seemed in the boughs over something. Nearly came to blows with another fellow just for bumping into him."

Reggie knew what that meant. A week ago would have been the time Anthony learned that Nicholas was back.

"Uncle Tony has his moods, though fortunately he doesn't have them often."

"And do you?" His expression was suddenly serious.

"Have moods, George? Don't we all?"

"You don't mind being buried out here in the country? I would perish within a week."

"I love Silverley. I always did prefer the country."

He seemed disappointed. "I thought

perhaps you . . . weren't happy here. One does hear things." He coughed. Was he embarrassed?

"One should close his ears, then," she chided. "I'm happy, George." But she couldn't look him in the eye.

"You're sure?"

"She has told you so, Fowler," Nicholas stated coldly from the doorway. "And since that is obviously what you came to find out, I shall appreciate your leaving."

Reggie jumped to her feet. "Nicholas!"

"That's quite all right, Reggie," George offered, standing.

"That's *Lady Montieth,* old chap," Nicholas said smoothly, eyes bright. "You will remember that, won't you?"

Reggie was incredulous. "You don't have to go, George, really you don't."

"Oh, but he does, I insist." Nicholas then turned and bellowed into the hall. "Sayers! The gentleman is leaving."

Reggie flushed crimson. "I'm sorry, George. There is no excuse for such rudeness."

"Think nothing of it," George bent over her hand, ignoring for a moment the indomitable man in the doorway. "It was a pleasure seeing you again, however briefly."

Reggie waited only two seconds after

George slipped out of the room before she emitted a cry of rage, her cobalt eyes shooting sparks at Nicholas. "How dare you? Did *I* throw *your whores* out? Did I?" She barely paused for breath. "You are insufferable, sir, utterly!" she raged. "Is this another preposterous rule of yours? First you refuse to allow my family to visit here, and now my friends are not welcome!"

"I would not call an old love a friend," he retorted."

"He was not an old love. And you are a fine one to talk, with four of *your* old loves sleeping in this house last night. Why, you were probably even with one of them — or more than one!"

"If you had shared my bed last night, you would know where I was."

Her mouth dropped open, then angrily snapped shut. Share his bed after she had caught him with another woman? He was annoying her on purpose. Well, he'd succeeded in rousing her fury.

She squared her shoulders. "Your disgraceful behavior has made up my mind for me, sir. I refuse to live another day with such a churlish boor. I am going home."

That brought Nicholas up short. "This *is* your home, Regina."

"It might have been, but you have made it

intolerable."

"You're not leaving," he stated flatly.

"You can't stop me."

"I can indeed do just that. See if I don't!"

Silence followed. They glared at each other, and then Regina stalked out.

Nicholas' shoulders drooped. Why the bloody hell had he lost his head like that? He had intended to coax her back to her old self, then woo her into his bed tonight. Everything could have been right by tomorrow. What the everlasting hell was the matter with him? She was right, his behavior was insufferable, and he didn't even begin to understand it himself.

CHAPTER 38

The door crashed open with a resounding bang. Reggie swung around from the vanity seat, brush still raised to her hair.

"What? No trunks packed yet?" he rasped.

Reggie slowly put her brush down. "You're foxed, Nicholas."

"Not quite, love. Just enough to realize I've been pounding my head against a stone wall for no reason."

"You're spouting gibberish."

He shut the door, leaning against it, his amber eyes on her face. "Consider this. The house is mine. The room is mine. The wife is mine. I need no more license than that to take her to bed."

"I —"

"No arguing, love," he broke in.

She warned frostily, "I think you had better leave before —"

"Will you scream, love? Bring the servants and guests running? They don't dare intrude, you know. You will suffer from acute embarrassment tomorrow."

He was smiling at her, the brute. "You will not have your way, Nicholas Eden."

"But I will," he corrected agreeably. "And let's not have any hysterics."

"When I get hysterical," she said through gritted teeth, "you will know it."

"Good of you to be so reasonable, love. Now, why don't you take off that pretty thing you're wearing?"

"Why don't you go —"

"Madame!" he appeared shocked. "If you cannot be civil —"

"Nicholas!" Reggie shouted in frustration. "I am in no mood for nonsense."

"Well, if you're in a hurry, love, I will oblige you."

He started toward her, and she dashed around the large bed, putting it between them. He kept coming, moving around the bed now.

"Don't come any closer." Her voice rose with each word. But he did.

Reggie jumped onto the bed and rolled across it. She looked up to find him grinning. He was enjoying the chase.

"I want you out of here this second!" Her voice cracked with fury.

He stepped up onto the bed, bending to

avoid being clobbered by the canopy, and she ran for the door. The crashing sound of Nicholas jumping off the bed made her change direction. Behind the Queen Anne chaise longue was safer.

Nicholas went to the door, locked it, then put the key on the ledge over the door, well out of Reggie's reach.

Reggie looked at the ledge she couldn't possibly reach, then back at Nicholas. She grabbed a book from the table next to her and threw it at him. He nimbly sidestepped it, chuckling at her efforts, and removed his coat.

"If you persist, Nicholas, I swear I will scratch your eyes out!"

"You can try, love." He smiled. He moved toward the chaise and pulled her out from behind it, holding her to him firmly.

"Nicho—"

His lips silenced her. A moment later he dropped her on the bed and pressed her against the mattress with his long body. His mouth devoured hers, leaving her no chance to breathe, let alone rail at him. Her fingers gripping his hair could not move his head, nor could her bucking dislodge him. She bit his lip, and he pulled back, grinning down at her.

"You don't want to do that, love. How can

I kiss you properly if you've taken a chunk out of my kisser?" She gave a vicious yank to his hair and he growled, "I should have plied you with wine again. You're much more agreeable when you're foxed."

As he kissed her again, Reggie's eyes widened. Plied her with wine? It hadn't been a dream! He really had made love to her that night at the inn. And he'd planned it! He'd wanted her enough to trick her . . . wanted her enough to give her too much wine . . . wanted her.

Good God, those feelings were sneaking up on her again. How long could she resist?

He looked at her again, his eyes smoldering. "Oh, love," he said huskily, "love me. Love me like you did before," he whispered passionately, and her defenses crumbled. Suddenly she was kissing him back with all the passion she possessed. She wasn't made of stone. She was flesh and blood and her blood was on fire.

Her fingers changed direction, pulling his head toward her. His groans of pleasure were music to her ears. Nicholas wanted her . . . really wanted her. It was her last thought before there was no more time to think.

CHAPTER 39

"Good morning, love." Nicholas' teeth caught at Reggie's lower lip and chewed for a moment. "Did anyone ever tell you what a delightfully rumpled picture you present at sunrise?"

She grinned impishly. "Meg is the only one who sees me at sunrise, and she doesn't say things that go to a girl's head."

Nicholas laughed, pulling her closer. "Your indomitable Meg doesn't like me, you know, and I can't imagine why. I'm such a likable fellow."

"You are an insufferable fellow, and you know it."

"But a *likable* insufferable fellow."

She laughed.

What a marvelous way to be awakened, Reggie thought, snuggling closer to the solid length of her husband. And she wasn't tired, even though she had been loved ardently into the small hours of the night. Not tired.

Feeling wonderful. She would have to insist he force himself on her more often.

Thomas' wail was the only thing that could disturb their idyll, and she heard it in a moment.

"I was wondering when he would get around to that."

Reggie grinned at him. "I'd better see to him."

"You will hurry back, won't you?"

"Most definitely, sir."

When Reggie returned to her bedroom twenty minutes later, it was empty. She checked the sitting room, then went to Nicholas' bedroom. Both rooms were empty. She returned to her own room and waited. He did not appear.

Where had he gone? And why? Would he use her, then treat her with indifference? But she was jumping to conclusions. There had to be a perfectly good explanation for his disappearance.

Reggie rushed Meg with her toilet and then nearly flew out of her room and down the stairs. Voices from the breakfast room drew her in that direction. At the door, she stopped short, suddenly chilled. Nicholas, dressed only in trousers and a short green velvet lounging jacket, stood at the buffet table. His back was to her, as was Selena

Eddington's. Selena stood next to him, so close that her shoulder touched his upper arm. His head was bent toward her and Selena was laughing at whatever he was saying.

Red flashed before Reggie's eyes. "Am I intruding — again?"

They whirled around. No one else was in the room, not even a footman, yet Nicholas didn't look at all abashed.

"You didn't have to come down, love." He smiled. "I was just getting a plate of pastries to bring up to you."

"I'm sure you were," she replied frigidly, her eyes locking with Selena's. "Madame, kindly pack your valises and be gone from my house before noon."

Selena's smug expression turned swiftly to outrage. "You can't do that. Lady Miriam invited me."

"Lady Miriam is not mistress here. I am. And we Edens are positively famous for throwing people out of our home." Having gotten that out of her system, Reggie turned and left.

Nicholas caught up with her in the main hall, grabbing her arm. "What the devil was that all about?"

"Let go of me!" she hissed, yanking her arm away. This time he took hold of her shoulder.

"Come in here." He dragged her into the library and closed the door behind them. "Are you mad?"

"I must be, to have believed you had changed!" she said.

"What do you mean?"

"My bed was still warm when you went looking for another conquest! Well, cavort with all the women you want, sir, but do not toy with me again."

"Can you believe I would want another woman after last night?" he replied, truly incredulous. "What you saw was nothing. Selena just happened to be there when I came in for your pastries. I meant to feed you, mind you, so you would have no excuse to leave your room this morning."

"You have a house full of servants to fetch pastries, sir," she pointed out.

"They are being run ragged by all of our guests. I had time to do it because I was waiting for you to return."

"I don't believe you."

He sighed in exasperation. "This is absurd, Regina. You had no call to fly off the handle, and certainly no call to boot Selena out. I told her so."

"You didn't!"

"If you will just consider how ridiculously

you are behaving —"

The fire glittering in her eyes gave him pause. "Am I? Yes, I suppose I am. I'm a fool, too, and the stupidest ninny. But you, sir, are a bastard, through and through. You can't bear for your lady friend to leave? Then by all means let her stay. Let her move in for good, in fact, for I won't be here to see it. And if you try to stop me from leaving, I will — shoot you!"

His face darkened to a furious expression, but she was so caught up in releasing the months of fury that she didn't know how dangerously angry he was. When he turned around without making a single reply, she ran in front of him and blocked his exit. "Don't you dare walk out when I'm still fighting with you!"

"What more is there to say, madame?" he said bitterly. "You have finally brought it out in the open. I have no defense, you see."

It bowled her over. No lies, and no excuses.

"You . . . admit you still want her?"

"Want who?" he growled. "I speak of my bastardy, of course. I tried to spare you, if you will recall. I did my best to prevent your marrying a bastard."

"You could have changed," she retorted hotly.

"How do you change the circumstances of your birth?"

"Birth?" She frowned. "What is the matter with you, Nicholas? I'm talking about your behavior. You are a bastard."

There was a charged pause, and then he asked, "Miriam never told you? She never revealed my black secret?"

"What *are* you talking about?" Reggie asked him. "Yes, Miriam told me about your birth. She delighted in telling me. What does that have to do with anything? If you ask me, you should be glad she's not your mother."

It hit him like a thunderbolt. "You mean — you don't care?"

"Care? Don't be absurd," she said. "I have two cousins who are bastards. Does that mean I love them any less? Of course it doesn't. Your birth was no fault of yours." She took a breath, then sailed on. "You, sir, have a mountain of faults without adding that one. I am through being only half a wife. I meant what I said. I will not stay here and watch you renew old alliances. If I see you with that woman once more, I swear I will put to good use the lessons Connie taught me and carve the two of you to pieces!"

He wouldn't — or couldn't — stop laughing. It was enough to make Reggie scream. At that moment, Eleanor entered.

"Is there a war going on in here, my dears, or is this just a family squabble?"

"Family?" Reggie cried. "He doesn't know he's part of a family. He would prefer to be a bachelor. He thinks he *is* a bachelor."

Nicholas sobered. "That's not true."

"You explain it to him, Ellie," Reggie said. "Tell him it's one way or another. He's either a husband or he isn't."

Reggie flounced out of the room, slamming the door behind her. She'd gotten no more than halfway up the stairs when his words came back to her, and she nearly stumbled. *I did my best to prevent your marrying a bastard.*

She stood stock-still, staring into space. Could that be the reason for his horrible behavior? Why hadn't she thought of that when Miriam oh-so-casually dropped the information? Did Nicholas believe she couldn't bear being married to a bastard?

Oh, that fool, that idiot! Reggie sat down on the stairs and her own laughter began spilling out.

CHAPTER 40

That evening a cold dinner was served on the back terrace in order to accommodate the croquet matches going on. Reggie brought Thomas down to enjoy the late afternoon sun. With a large blanket spread under him, he delighted in bobbing his head toward sounds that caught his interest. Every guest came by to meet the new Montieth heir.

Only a few of Miriam's guests would be spending another night at Silverley. Most had left that afternoon, including Selena Eddington. Whether Nicholas had spoken to her again or she had thought it prudent to leave, Reggie didn't know.

Pamela Ritchie came over to look at Thomas. An unhappy woman, that. If she weren't careful, those lines of dissatisfaction would become permanent.

Reggie hadn't felt at all distressed when Nicholas and Anne Henslowe played in a croquet match together. They stood side by side waiting their turn and laughing together, but Reggie didn't mind. Her attitude must, she felt, have something to do with all those grins and winks Nicholas had been giving her all afternoon. It was as if they shared a private joke, but they hadn't said a word since coming face to face over lunch. Even so, he had only to look at her to begin chuckling.

He was a happy man. Reggie thought she knew why, and her suspicions made her just as happy as he was.

The sun was beginning to set, and there was a marvelous display of color. Thomas had had enough of the outdoors for one day, and was scooting around on the blanket with extra vigor, a sure sign that he was hungry.

"It's so peaceful out here at this time of day," Eleanor said quietly. "I'm going to miss you and this little fellow."

"You're not thinking of leaving already, are you?" Reggie asked surprised.

"You don't need me here anymore, my dear." They both knew she had stayed only to help Reggie ease into her marriage. "Dicken tells me Rebecca has been nothing short of a harridan since I've been away. Dicken misses me, too. And, truth to tell, this long absence from Cornwall has opened my eyes."

"Why, Eleanor, you and Dicken are . . . ?" Reggie said, delighted.

Eleanor smiled. "He has asked me to marry him many times in the last four years. I think I am finally ready to give it some serious thought."

"Famous! Will you let Nicholas and me do the wedding party, or will Rebecca want to?"

"I'm afraid Rebecca will *insist*," Eleanor laughed. "She has been pushing Dicken at me for ages." Thomas squawked, demanding attention. "Want me to take him up, my dear?"

"Not unless you can manage to feed him, too." Reggie smiled impishly.

"Do hurry back. Nicky has been keeping such a close eye on you all day, I'm sure he'll go hunting for you if you're gone long."

"Not as long as I know where she is," Nicholas said, approaching from behind them. He scooped Thomas up. "So the rascal's hungry, is he? Good God, he's dripping, too!" He quickly held the boy away from him, and the women laughed. Reggie wrapped a smaller blanket around Thomas' bottom. "That's something babies tend to do, and often. Here, let me have him."

"No, I'll carry him up for you." Nicholas leaned closer, whispering for her ears alone. "Perhaps, after you're finished with him, we might have a little time alone?"

"My, what a pretty picture this makes," Miriam's hard voice intruded. "A father doting on his bastard. You Eden men make wonderful fathers, Nicholas. Too bad you're so terribly lacking as husbands."

Nicholas swung around. "I will not take exception, madame. You are, naturally, upset that your well-wrought plot failed to turn out as expected."

"I don't know what you mean," she replied disdainfully.

"Don't you? Let me thank you now, before I forget. If not for your brilliant guest list, my wife and I might still be estranged. We're not. And we have you to thank for our reconciliation, *mother.*"

Miriam's expression mottled with fury she couldn't contain. "I am sick to death of hearing you call me that. And, Nicholas, you don't know just how brilliant my guest list really is," she laughed. "I have a wonderful surprise for you. You see, your real mother is here! Isn't that marvelous? So why don't you make a fool of yourself by spending the rest of the evening asking every lady here if she's the bitch who whelped you?

That would be *such* fun."

Nicholas couldn't move. He was so stunned he couldn't even reach out to stop Miriam from walking away. Reggie's heart twisted when she took Thomas from him, he didn't seem to know she had done so.

"Oh, Nicholas, don't let her upset you," Reggie said gently. "She only said that for spite."

"Did she?" The eyes that met Reggie's were tormented. "Did she? What if she told the truth?"

Desperate for help, Reggie turned toward Eleanor. The older woman was ashen. Reggie understood, but the need had never been greater.

"Tell him," she said quietly, and Ellie gasped.

"Regina!"

"Can't you see? It's time." She grasped Thomas more tightly and waited.

Nicholas looked from Reggie to Eleanor, misery and confusion mixed in his face.

"Oh, Nicky, don't hate me," Eleanor began on a pleading note. "Miriam was being spiteful, but — but she also spoke the truth."

"No!" The word tore out of him. "Not you. You would have told if —"

"I couldn't." Eleanor was crying. "I gave

Miriam my word I would never claim you when *she* gave *me* her word she would raise you as her own."

"Is that what you think she did?" he asked painfully. "She was never a mother to me, Ellie, even when I was a child. You were here then. *You know that.*"

"Yes, and I dried your tears and soothed your hurts and died a little every time. Your father didn't want you labeled a bastard, Nicky, and I didn't either. Miriam kept her word that she would never tell, so I had to keep mine."

"She told my wife. And she put me through hell," he hissed at her.

"She judged Regina correctly. She knew the knowledge would go no further and it hasn't."

"She always threatened to let the fact be known."

"Only threats, Nicky."

"But I lived with her threats. They governed my life. Even so, I would have taken the label gladly if I could have had a real mother. Didn't you see that when I poured out my heart to you all those years? *Why didn't you tell me?*"

The bastardy stigma wasn't as important as this war. Both knew it. Eleanor sobbed, "Forgive me," and ran into the house.

Reggie placed her hand on Nicholas' arm. "She was afraid to tell you, afraid you would hate her. Go after her, Nicholas. Listen to her calmly and let her tell you what she told me. It hasn't been easy for her all these years either."

"You knew?" he asked incredulous.

"Since I gave birth to Thomas," she answered gently. "She was with me during labor, and she wanted me to know the real reason why you weren't there. You see, Nicholas, I'm afraid I didn't believe that anyone could be so foolish as to let his having been birthed on the wrong side of the blanket stop him from marrying." She smiled up at him. "I'm sorry, but I never appreciated how much it meant to you."

"It doesn't mean much anymore," he conceded.

"Then don't judge her so harshly, Nicholas, and hear her out without erupting. Please."

He stood there looking at the house and she went on, "Not every woman has the courage to raise an illegitimate child. Look how *you* dealt with it, after all. You decided never to marry because you didn't want a wife to share your burden. Do you think it's not worse for the mother? And remember how young Eleanor was at the time."

"You would have done it, wouldn't you?"

She shrugged. "Yes, but remember we Malorys are already accustomed to having bastards in the family."

He grunted.

"Go on, Nicholas. Talk to her. You'll find she's still the same woman who has always been your best friend. She's been a mother to you all along. Now it's your turn to listen to her sorrow."

His hand cupped her face tenderly. Thomas was squirming in her arms, and Nicholas said, "Go feed my son, madame."

Reggie smiled as he walked away from her, toward the house. Across the lawn, her eyes met Miriam's and she shook her head as Miriam turned away abruptly. Would Miriam ever change?

She rubbed her cheek against Thomas' head and began walking toward the house. "Don't worry, my angel, you will have so much love you will never miss hers. Just wait until you're old enough to hear about your great-uncles. Why, one was a pirate for a while, and . . ."

CHAPTER 41

Eleanor's bedroom door was closed but Nicholas could hear heartrending sobs from inside. He opened the door soundlessly. She lay across her bed, head buried in her arms, shoulders shaking pathetically. His chest tightened painfully. He closed the door and sat down beside her, gathering her in his arms. "I'm so sorry, Ellie. I wouldn't have made you cry, not for anything, you know that."

She opened golden-brown eyes shimmering with tears. Her eyes were so like his own. Lord, what a fool he was not to have recognized that before.

"You don't hate me, Nicky?"

"Hate you?" he echoed. "You, who have always been my solace, the only person I could count on to love me?" He shook his head. "You can't imagine how many times when I was small I pretended you were my real mother. Why didn't I realize it was true?"

"You weren't supposed to know."

"I should have realized it anyhow, especially when you stopped coming here after Father died. I always wondered why you came here at all. You and Miriam barely spoke to each other. You came because of Father, didn't you?"

"I think you misunderstand, Nicky. Your father and I were together only once. No, I came to Silverley only to be near you. He kept the peace between Miriam and me, making it possible for me to be with you in your home. The reason I didn't come to Silverley after he died was because you were grown. You went to sea for two years, and then you lived in London. You rarely came to Silverley yourself, remember."

"I couldn't stand being with Miriam," he said bitterly. "You saw her all this week. It's never been any different, Ellie."

"You have to understand Miriam, Nicky. She never forgave me for loving Charles, and you were a constant reminder that she'd failed with him."

"Why the bloody hell didn't *you* marry him?"

She smiled hesitantly, a mother's smile for a stubborn child. "Charles was twenty-one when he first came to call on Miriam. She was eighteen, and I, my dear, was only fourteen. I was unnoticeable. He was smitten with her, and I was smitten with him. Fourteen is an impressionable age, you know, and Charles was so very handsome and kind. But they were married the year they met."

"To everyone's misfortune," he said softly, "Everyone's." But she shook her head.

"She loved him, Nicky, those first few years of their marriage. They were very happy. And understand this, Nicky. He never stopped loving her, no matter how difficult she was later on. Miriam was wrong about that. Eden men do make exceptional husbands, for they love only once. But Charles wanted a son, and Miriam had only miscarriages, three of them in as many years. This caused a terrible strain. She was frightened to try for the son he wanted, so she began to resent his attentions. I'm afraid fear turned her against Charles. Her love for him didn't hold up under the strain. But he did love her."

"You lived here then?"

"Yes. You were conceived here." She lowered her eyes, even now guilty over betraying her sister. "I was seventeen years old, and I loved Charles. They had a terrible fight that day because she refused to accept him in her bed. By evening he was drunk and it just . . . happened, Nicky. I'm not even sure he knew what he was doing, though *I* did. We both regretted it afterward and vowed that Miriam was never to know. I went home to my parents house, and Charles devoted himself to his wife." She sighed. "Eventually Miriam might have gotten over her fear of conceiving. They might have been happy again."

"But I came along?"

"Yes," she admitted. "When I realized I was going to have a baby, I was hysterical. One fall from grace and I was pregnant. I even thought of killing myself. I couldn't tell my parents. I made myself sick with worry. Finally, desperate, I visited Silverley to put my dilemma in Charles' hands. Bless him, he was delighted! I couldn't quite believe that at first, but he was. I had been thinking only of myself, of being ruined, but Charles thought first of you. It made me see how selfish I was in wanting to get rid of you. Forgive me, Nicky, but I did think that was the way out. I was young and terrified, and girls of good families did not have children out of wedlock."

He hugged her to him. "Of course, Ellie. I understand."

"Well," she went on, "Charles wanted you.

He was willing to destroy his marriage to have you. He might have done things differently except for Miriam's three miscarriages. He wasn't sure she would ever give him a child. And there I was, three months pregnant."

"So Miriam was told." He knew that much.

"She was shocked, of course. She couldn't believe her own sister would do such a thing. How she hated me from that day on! And she hated Charles, too, never forgiving him. Finally she came to hate you, the only innocent person in the whole mess. She was never the same again, Nicky. Her deepest bitterness was that I'd been able to give Charles the son he wanted. She felt she had failed him, but she blamed him, and me, for interfering before she had a chance to try again. Her bitterness became a monster over the years. Miriam wasn't always the way she is now. I *am* to blame, for I could have stopped Charles the night you were conceived. I could have, but I didn't."

"For God's sake, Ellie, you already said she had stopped loving him by then."

"I know, but she might have gone back to loving him." After a long, thoughtful silence, she resumed. "We were sisters, remember. That did count for something. She even forgot her resentment during those long hours when I was in labor, for it was a difficult labor, and she thought I might die. I was able to get her to swear then that she would never publicly disclaim you. I hoped she would love you, but even then I was afraid she wouldn't. So I made her swear, and she did. But she made me swear that I would never tell you I was your mother. I wanted to tell you so many times, but I'd taken a vow, so I couldn't. And after your father died, Rebecca warned me to leave it alone."

"She knew the whole story?"

Eleanor nodded. "I still don't think I would have told you if Regina hadn't insisted."

"My wife is a gem, isn't she, mother?"

It was the first time he had ever called her that, and Eleanor's face glowed.

"It took you long enough to realize it," she said.

"Oh, I always knew she was wonderful. I've just been ten kinds of a fool about her. How could I blame you for what you did when it was fear of the bastardy stigma that made me almost lose my beautiful Regina? The stigma ruled me as it ruled you."

"You will make it up to her?" she asked him urgently.

"I swear it. And you, love, are moving back to Silverley for good."

"Oh, no Nicky! I mean, well . . . Lord Barrett and I —"

"Bloody hell, you mean I'm losing you to another man when I've only just found you?" he cried, but he was thrilled for her. "Who, may I ask, is Lord Barrett?"

"You know him. He lives near Rebecca, and you've met him there many times. And it's not as if Dicken and I won't visit here often. After all, my first grandchild lives at Silverley."

They looked at each other in complete silence for a long time. He was happy for her. She was happy for him. They had come a long, hard way.

CHAPTER 42

Reggie crossed the sitting room and opened the door to Nicholas' bedroom, quietly slipping inside. To the right was the dressing room, the door leading out into the corridor, and next to it was the master bath, a big square room with walls and floor of blue marble and numerous large mirrors. Huge shelves held all kinds of jars and bottles, towels, shaving apparatus, and other of the lord's necessities. The bath itself was large with cupid spouts for hot and cold water.

Nicholas lay inside, relaxed, eyes closed. Harris was laying out towels and Nicholas' robe and comfortable slippers. It was only nine o'clock, and Miriam's guests were still in the house.

"Good evening, Harris," Reggie greeted him cheerfully. The valet was startled, but he managed to nod and return her greeting. Nicholas gave her a lazy grin.

"Meg has been asking after you, Harris,"

Reggie continued innocently as though she intruded on a man's toilet all the time and wasn't on a romantic errand at all.

Harris perked up. "Has she, madame?"

"Oh, yes. And you know, it's such a beautiful night. There's a lovely summer moon. What a perfect night for a stroll around the grounds, Meg was saying. Why don't you go find her, Harris? I'm sure his lordship won't mind. Will you, Nicholas?"

"Not at all. Run along, Harris. I won't be needing you again tonight."

"Thank you, sir." Harris made a formal bow before, wholly out of character, he turned and dashed from the room.

Nicholas chuckled. "I don't believe it. Harris and sour Meg?"

"Meg is not sour," she retorted. "And they have been very friendly for some time now."

"Is love blooming there, too? You know about Ellie and Lord Barrett, I assume? You know everything before I do."

"I'm so happy for Ellie."

"You don't think she's too old to be contemplating matrimony?"

"You can't be serious, Nicholas," Reggie giggled.

"I suppose not." He grinned, watching as she trailed her hand through the water. He caught it as it neared him, bringing it to his

398

lips for a kiss. "I have you to thank, you know, for my childhood dreams coming true. She would never have told me if not for you. You know, don't you, Reggie, how awful it is to wonder about your mother all the time? Who was she, what was she like? You lost both of your parents when you were only two."

She smiled gently. "I had four wonderful uncles to tell me everything I wanted to know about them — including faults, of which they spared no detail. But you did have your mother all along, you just never knew it."

"One of the things Ellie told me is that we Eden men only love once. That should delight you."

"Should it?"

"Doesn't it?"

"Oh, I don't know," Reggie said evasively. "I'll let you know after we have our talk. Care to have your back scrubbed?"

She scooped the sponge out of the water without waiting for an answer and moved behind him. She was grinning, but he couldn't see her expression.

"I suppose you would like an apology?" he began uncomfortably.

"That would be nice."

"I do apologize, Regina."

"What for?"

"What do you mean what for?" he growled, turning to look at her.

"If you would be a little more specific, Nicholas."

"I'm sorry. I was such a dolt during our engagement."

"No, you weren't very nice at all. But I can forgive you for that. Go on." She began running the sponge along his back, then up around his neck, very slowly.

"Go on?" He sounded bewildered, and Reggie threw the sponge at his head.

"You left me. Or have you forgotten?"

He grabbed hold of the sponge. "Blister it, you know why I did."

Reggie came around to the side of the tub and looked down at him, hands on hips, her eyes glittering. "I beg to differ. I do not know why. It is the only thing I have not been able to figure out."

In a quiet voice, with no fight in him, he said, "I couldn't remain near you without . . ."

She prompted him. "Without?"

"Without making love to you."

There was utter silence. Then she said, "Why couldn't you make love to me?"

"Bloody hell!" he swore. "I was certain you would despise me as soon as you learned of my parentage. I knew I couldn't bear your scorn. I was a bloody fool, I admit it. But I knew Miriam wouldn't keep her mouth shut. I was right about that. I was just wrong about your reaction to my birth."

"Very well. Your explanation will do. You may go on."

He racked his brains. "I told you the truth about Selena. She really did contrive that scene you witnessed in the conservatory."

"I believe you."

This was apparently not what she was waiting to hear. "Oh! Your friend George. I — I suppose I was a bit unreasonable with him, but it wasn't the first time his being with you has rubbed me the wrong way."

"Were you jealous, Nicholas?" Her humor resurfaced.

"I . . . yes, blister it, I was!"

"Duly noted. You may go on," she said, her eyes intent on his face.

"But what else have I done?" he asked, exasperated.

The cobalt eyes sparked. "You are forgetting you had to be returned to me by force."

"No!" His temper exploded. "Now there, you're wrong! I was coming back. My ship was ready to sail. I had decided to tell you everything, explain why I behaved as I did. Your bloody uncle and his thugs arrived the night before I was to sail."

"Oh, dear. I suppose you were too angry over Uncle James' interference to talk to me honestly?"

Nicholas scowled. "I don't like that particular uncle of yours, not at all."

"He'll grow on you."

"I'd rather you grew on me."

"That might be arranged."

"Then you don't mind that I am destined to love only once?" he asked very seriously. But she wasn't ready to declare herself to him, not just then.

"If you could be a little more specific . . ."

"Haven't I told you what you want to hear?"

"You have not," she informed him.

"Then come here."

"Nicholas," she gasped. "I'm not dressed for bathing."

He grabbed her and pulled her into the bath on top of him. "I love you, love you, love you, love you. Is that enough or do you want more?"

"That will do — for tonight." Reggie wrapped her arms around his neck. Their lips met.

After some delightful kissing, he demanded, "Well?"

"Well, what?" she teased. He whacked her

bottom. "Oh. Well, I guess I love you, too."

"You *guess?*"

"Well, I must, mustn't I, if I put up with you? No, no!" she shrieked as he began tickling her. "All right. I love you, you impossible man. I set my cap for you, didn't I? And I never gave up hoping you would return my love. Now aren't you glad I'm such a stubborn fellow?"

"Stubborn fellow, but delightful all the same." He kissed her soundly. "You were right, love, you're not dressed for bathing. Shall we remedy that?"

"I thought you'd never ask."

CHAPTER 43

After bidding farewell to the last guest, Nicholas and Regina stood kissing at the door. "Peace at last," he said with a long sigh.

"Well, not quite," Reggie replied hesitantly, twining a finger in his lapel. "I — I sent a message last night to invite my family out here for the day. Don't be mad, Nicholas. George told me he saw Tony last week and Tony was very upset. I know it was because of us."

"Couldn't you have just written them a letter?" he asked wearily, "and told them you were all right?"

"Letters aren't the same as seeing for themselves how happy I am. They worry about me, Nicholas, and I want them to know everything is finally all right now."

"Then I suppose I will have to bear it for one day." He sighed again.

"You're not angry?"

"I don't dare get angry with you, love." He said this so seriously that she frowned in puzzlement. "You get angry right back."

"Devil!" she retorted.

Nicholas grinned at her. Then, patting her backside, he pushed her gently toward the staircase. "Now run along for a while. You've reminded me that I have some family business of my own to take care of."

He caught Miriam just as she was leaving for her morning ride, delayed until her guests departed. "A word with you, madame, in the library, if you please."

Miriam started to tell him she was too busy, then thought better of it. His manner invited no argument. They walked down the stairs together without a word. "I hope this won't take long," she said curtly as he closed the library door behind them.

"It shouldn't. Do sit down, Miriam."

She frowned. "You have never called me anything but 'mother.'"

Nicholas observed the cold glitter in her brown eyes. It was always there when they were alone. This woman really did hate him. Nothing would change that.

"Imagine," he said, "overnight, two sisters have switched places." Her face went pale, so he said, "I guess you haven't had a chance to talk to Ellie this morning, have you?"

"She told you?"

"Well, you did suggest I ask every lady present if she was my mother." He couldn't resist the barb.

"You didn't!"

"No, Miriam, I didn't. After you opened the wound, my wife healed it. She forced Ellie to confess. I have the whole of it now, finally, and I want to say that I'm sorry for what you've been through, Miriam, now that I understand it all."

"Don't you dare feel sorry for me!" she cried, stunned.

"As you wish," he replied stiffly, no longer uncomfortable over the decision he had come to during the night. "I asked you in here to inform you that, under the circumstance, it is no longer desirable that you live at Silverley. Find yourself a cottage somewhere far from here. I will buy it for you. My father left you a modest income. I will match it. I owe you no more than that."

"Bribery, Nicholas?" she sneered.

"No, Miriam," he said, tired of it all. "If you want to inform the world that it was not you who provided your husband with his heir, by all means do so. My wife knows and doesn't care, and that is all that matters to me."

"You really mean this, don't you?"

"I do."

"You bastard," she said furiously. "You think you have it all, don't you? But wait a few years and your precious wife will hate you — just as I hated your father."

"She's not like you, Miriam." He smiled.

"I always hated it here at Silverley," she said savagely. "I only stayed to keep you away."

"I know that, Miriam," he said quietly.

"I won't stay here a moment longer," she retorted. "And you can be sure it won't be a cottage I'll find, but a mansion!"

She stalked out of the room, and he took a deep breath, grateful to have her gone. It would be worth a fortune to finally have his home back, free of Miriam's bitterness.

A few hours later, a coach rumbled down the driveway with Nicholas' Aunt Miriam in it. The three people on the doorstep breathed a collective sigh as they watched it go. Eleanor went back into the house then, but Nicholas stood there a moment longer, his arms around his wife, holding her close to him, her cheek resting against his chest.

They stayed there too long, for soon two carriages and a coach appeared at the end of the long drive. Nicholas stiffened, then relaxed. What the hell. If Regina loved them, perhaps they weren't all that bad.

"Invaded again," he murmured dryly.

"Don't you dare run away, Nicholas Eden," Reggie scolded.

She held on to him, bubbling with excitement. Jason and Derek and half of Edward's brood alighted from the first carriage. Jason was the first to clasp Nicholas in a hearty embrace.

"Glad to see you came to your senses, my boy. James said you were eager to see your son. Hope your business won't be calling you away too often in the future."

"No, sir, it won't," Nicholas managed to reply cordially, though his hackles rose over what James had told him. Bloody liar.

Derek was next in line, and he got a bear hug. "About time you got around to sending out an invitation, old man."

"Good to see you, Derek."

The cousins were next, and Edward and his wife, all trooping toward the house chattering happily. But then Nicholas caught sight of James and Anthony standing by a carriage glowering at him. He turned to enter the house, muttering about uninvited guests. Reggie heard him and frowned at her younger uncles. "Don't you dare, either of you!" she warned, knowing she didn't need to be explicit. They understood. "I love him and he loves me. And if you two can't make friends with him, I'll — I'll never speak to you again!" She followed her husband into the house, leaving Anthony and James outside.

James looked at his brother and grinned. "I think she means it."

"I know she means it," Anthony replied, clapping James on the back. "Come on then. Let's see what we can do about patching it up with the bounder."

A few minutes later, they cornered Nicholas in the drawing room, dragging him away from the others, one on each side of him. Nicholas sighed in exasperation. Were these Malorys always going to gang up on him? "Yes?"

"Regan wants a truce, lad," James began. "And we're willing if you are."

"Blister it! It's Reggie, not Regan," Anthony snapped at his brother. "When will you ever —"

"What is wrong with Regina?" Nicholas interrupted.

The two men looked at him and began laughing. "Nothing at all, old chap," Anthony conceded. "*You* can call her anything you like. It's this stubborn fellow here who insists on inventing new names all the time."

"And what is 'puss' if not an invention of yours?" James retorted.

"An endearment, that's what."

"And Regan isn't an endearment?"

Nicholas left the brothers to finish the argument on their own. He caught his wife and pulled her down on a sofa beside him.

"You know, love, when I married you, I didn't think I was marrying the Malory brothers, too."

"You're not angry with me for inviting them, are you? I just wanted them to be part of our happiness."

"I know. And I also know you said they were staying only for the day. Your family does take getting used to, especially those two." He nodded toward the corner, and she watched Anthony and James having their heated discussion.

She grinned impishly. "They don't mean half of what they say. And they won't be here that often anyway. Why, Uncle James is sailing next week. He probably won't be back more than once a year from now on."

"And Anthony?"

"Well, Uncle Tony will drop by from time to time to check on me, but you'll get to like him, I promise you will. How can you not when you two have so much in common? Why, the reason I lost my heart to you so quickly was that you reminded me of Tony."

"Bloody hell," he growled.

"Oh, don't sulk," she teased, wrapping her fingers in his. That's not the only reason I love you, you know. Shall I tell you some more reasons?"

"Can we escape for a while?" he asked eagerly.

"I think that can be arranged."

"Then come upstairs with me."

"Nicholas! It's the middle of the afternoon," she hissed, shocked.

"I can't wait any longer, love," he whispered against her ear.

James caught sight of the couple racing out of the room, hand in hand, Reggie holding her other hand against her mouth to stifle her laughter. "Will you look at that?" he cut into Anthony's speech. "Did I tell you he was the man for her?"

"You did not," Anthony retorted hotly. "But of course *I* knew it all along."

ABOUT THE AUTHOR

One of the world's most successful authors of historical romance, every one of **Johanna Lindsey**'s previous novels has been a national bestseller, and several of her titles have reached the #1 spot on the *New York Times* bestseller list. Ms. Lindsey lives in Hawaii with her family.

The employees of Thorndike Press hope you have enjoyed this Large Print book. All our Thorndike, Wheeler, and Kennebec Large Print titles are designed for easy reading, and all our books are made to last. Other Thorndike Press Large Print books are available at your library, through selected bookstores, or directly from us.

For information about titles, please call:
  (800) 223-1244

or visit our Web site at:
  http://gale.cengage.com/thorndike

To share your comments, please write:
  Publisher
  Thorndike Press
  295 Kennedy Memorial Drive
  Waterville, ME 04901